What was it about the man that appealed to her?

Danielle wondered, standing among the throngs of formally attired guests at her parents' posh party. Last night—rather, early this morning—she'd done something she ordinarily wouldn't have: she'd abandoned common sense and twenty-six years of fine breeding to give in to an impulse. All because of a mysterious denim-clad stranger.

I must be out of my mind! Only before Danielle could fret, she felt a mischievous grin curl her lips as she scoped the crowd for *him*.

Right or wrong, she'd extended an invitation to Gabe—she didn't even know his last name— who'd rescued her mere hours ago. His black eyes, jet hair and easy smile had proven disarming, charming—and alarming. Why, in this sea of tuxedos, did she relish the thought of seeing his leather jacket again?

ABOUT THE AUTHOR

Kim got the idea for *Rebel with a Cause* while listening to one of Billy Joel's songs, "Uptown Girl." Music is a constant source of inspiration for her, and her collection of records and CDs covers classical to rock. Kim loves to hear from her readers. Please write to her at: Post Office Box 20827, Greenfield, Wisconsin 53220-0827.

Books by Kim Hansen

HARLEQUIN AMERICAN ROMANCE
548—TIME RAMBLER
604—CLOSE ENCOUNTER

REBEL WITH A CAUSE
Kim Hansen

Harlequin Books

TORONTO • NEW YORK • LONDON
AMSTERDAM • PARIS • SYDNEY • HAMBURG
STOCKHOLM • ATHENS • TOKYO • MILAN
MADRID • WARSAW • BUDAPEST • AUCKLAND

To Elsa with thanks for her invaluable assistance,
and to Aunt Alice with love for her unflagging
loyalty and support.

ISBN 0-373-16634-6

REBEL WITH A CAUSE

Copyright © 1996 by Kim Hansen

This edition published by arrangement with Harlequin Books S.A.

® and TM are trademarks of the publisher. Trademarks indicated with
® are registered in the United States Patent and Trademark Office, the
Canadian Trade Marks Office and in other countries.

Printed in U.S.A.

Chapter One

"Let me out."

"Are you crazy?"

"Stop the car and let me out!" Danielle repeated hotly and yanked on the handle. She had the door open before the silver gray Jaguar skidded to a halt, and was outside a second later.

"You're being childish!" the man inside snapped.

"Really?" She flung the door shut with as much force as she could muster, making the half-open window rattle. "And you're being a pompous—"

The squealing tires drowned out her retort and left her standing in the middle of a deserted street, but she didn't notice her surroundings. Not until the Jaguar had disappeared around the corner at the end of the block. It was only then, muttering under her breath and turning from where the vehicle and its offensive driver had gone, that Danielle swung to look for the nearest phone booth or taxi—and felt her stomach sink.

Caught up in the heat of the argument, she hadn't paid any attention to where she was or what was happening outside the car. But the deed was done. She was out of the car, by herself, and had absolutely no idea where she was.

Her teeth found her lower lip, and she slowly surveyed her surroundings. Wherever she was, it wasn't any place she'd been before, and it was far from her home in San Marino, California.

No tree-lined drives or manicured lawns were in sight. No ornamental lamps lit the walks with a warm, welcoming glow. The street she was standing on had only debris edging its curbs. And the only illumination came from one streetlight posted high above the cement that, she quickly noted, did little to eliminate the eerie shadows cast along the empty porches, hollow doorways and dark alleys flanking the road.

Unconsciously her tongue darted out to lick lips that had suddenly gone dry. Nervously she began edging her way up the street toward the avenue cutting across it at the corner. Surely there she'd find a phone booth or a taxi.... But it was hard to concentrate on what might be ahead when she kept watching out for what lay behind.

Black windows stared at her from scarred buildings, their panes like hollow eyes watching her. The shadows hovering around stairs and alleys seemed to shift constantly, following her with silent intent. Yet the crackling and buzzing streetlight alarmed her the most. It was as if, at any moment, its bulb would blow, plunging her into darkness while surrounded by the menacing unknown. Her heart skipped a beat, and she hurried on.

The last few steps to what she hoped was salvation were taken quickly despite the three-inch heels she wore, but the hope that had been building died when she found the avenue as barren and unwelcoming as the street she'd come from. No telephone booths and no cabs were in sight.

Glancing down at her hands as her fingers wound together in silent consternation, she smothered a groan. Even if she had found a phone booth, using it would have been a problem. She'd left her purse in the car!

Desperate, Danielle turned in a circle once more but found little to reassure—except the fact that she hadn't been followed down the street. She was alone. Nothing and no one stirred.

The sudden clang of metal against metal made her jump. It echoed through the night with a hollow ring and had her whirling in alarm to find its source. But a telephone pole and mailbox blocked her view.

Taking an uneasy step to the side, Danielle held her breath and saw the silhouette of a man bending over a motorcycle. Intent on what he was doing, he hadn't noticed her. Yet.

She darted a quick glance at the diamond-studded watch on her wrist. It was three o'clock on a Saturday morning, and it appeared that she and he were the only ones out on the otherwise silent road.

Looking around again at the street that was a far cry from the smooth pavement and rolling green of Beverly Hills and Pasadena, she suppressed the chill that threatened to shake her and bit her lip once more. She would have felt better if she could have at least seen a phone booth or a taxicab— both signs of escape—but neither was in sight, and it didn't seem likely she'd find either nearby.

She took a deep breath. Her options appeared to be extremely limited. Swallowing any trepidation, she prepared to introduce herself to a complete stranger.

HE SPOTTED HER as soon as she started walking. On a deserted sidewalk in the wee hours of the morning she was hard to miss, but even in a crowd he figured she'd stand out. Especially with those legs.

Long and slim, they seemed to go on forever. Gabe Tyler cocked his head and watched her approach, finding it took some effort to close his mouth and not drool, but he managed—if for no other reason than because he wanted to finish looking her over before she reached him.

The black dress she had on was sleeveless and stopped just above her knees. It clung to the slim lines of her body like a second skin. As she moved, the garment glittered, but the sequins decorating it spoke of glamour not glitz. The matching scarf draped around her neck added a touch of class not flash.

Straightening next to the motorcycle he was working on, Gabe held his breath. In the streetlight she appeared to be a shimmering shadow. And, if he'd been drinking, he probably would have sworn she was a ghost. But he hadn't touched a drop all night, and she wasn't gliding. She was walking—on heels that were at least three inches high, but she didn't wobble once. She just took one step after another with a simple grace that made him want to lick his lips, and the urge grew stronger as she got closer.

Her hair, as black as midnight, was swept back and away from her face. The moonlight danced in her eyes. Green, he realized, and thought the color suited her. Blue would have been too normal, brown, too ordinary. She wasn't either. Her bare, smooth arms were adorned with only the simplest of bracelets. But the ornamentation didn't come cheap. Nor did the earrings glistening in a tasteful waterfall beside her face. The rocks weren't crystal. They were the real thing, and so was she. No hooker on the wrong road, he was looking at a blue-blooded socialite who'd lost her way.

He frowned. She was out and alone on the wrong end of the city. But how? And why?

When Danielle stopped before him, she found little in his appearance or manner that reassured or inspired confidence. His jaw was lined with a scraggly growth of whiskers, his jeans were dirty and the white T-shirt he wore under a battered leather jacket was smeared with grease. His scowl was as black as the night. But, if she found his whole appearance and demeanor dark and dangerous, she couldn't afford to run. He was her only hope. She lifted her chin in defiance of her fear and his steady stare.

"Lost?"

The question was sharp, clipped, and Danielle stiffened, refusing to be intimidated. "Not exactly."

"Out for a walk, then?" the man suggested, a grin slowly cutting through his half-grown beard and brightening his black gaze.

"Just looking for a phone booth," she assured him, crossing her arms in front of her and leveling her most withering glare his way.

"Uh-huh," he said, wiping his hands on the rag he'd been holding. He glanced up and down the street. "Not one around here."

"I noticed." At once she sighed, paced a few steps away and sat on a slab of dirty pavement without giving a second thought to her dress. "This has been the most rotten day of my life."

"Fight with your boyfriend?"

Realizing he must have seen the Jaguar come tearing down the road, she shook her head. "He's not a boyfriend. He's just a friend. A family friend."

"You make that sound like a curse."

"Sometimes it is." She tapped her foot impatiently on the ground. "Have you ever felt that everything you do is for somebody else besides you? That your life is being planned and no matter how much you hate it, there's nothing you can do to stop it from happening?"

His eyes seemed to bore into her, but for the moment Danielle didn't notice. She forgot all about him as she pushed to her feet to stalk away, only to come back again with short, angry steps. Stopping to stare at the night around her, she didn't see the street she was standing on, either. Instead she saw her day.

Her Friday had begun in the office of the family business where she occupied space but where she had little authority and where, too often, her opinion carried no weight. That afternoon she'd lost a secretary due to her own inability to protect the young woman from the predatory advances of one of the company officers, Malcolm Reed, who was her father's "adopted" son and someone who could do no wrong—at least as far as everyone but her was concerned.

Gritting her teeth, she remembered again the condescending tone, the shaking head of her father, who'd dismissed her complaints about Malcolm's behavior as groundless. The blame had all been dumped on her secretary, who was labeled as a troublemaker.

Danielle's eyes narrowed. It infuriated her that she hadn't been able to make her father see he was wrong, that she hadn't been able to better defend an employee who had depended on her. And it aggravated her feelings of frustration overall.

She was tired of being treated as little more than a figurehead, of being accepted as the boss's daughter rather than as a contributing partner. She was fed up with her family's attempts to manipulate her into a marriage that would take her out of the office and into the world of volunteering and charity that consumed her mother's life.

"If someone's punching your buttons, why don't you stop them?"

The unexpected question snapped Danielle back to the present and the man before her. "That's easy for you to say."

"No, it's just easier said than done," he returned. "If you run into a roadblock on the way to the store, what do you do? Go home and wait until it's taken away, or do you find a way around it?''

"I would hardly equate life with shopping."

"Why not? Maybe we don't always pay cash for what we want, but we do pay, don't we?"

With emotion, with time, with commitment. She frowned.

"What were you and your family's 'friend' arguing about?"

She shrugged and watched him bend to pile tools back into one of the leather saddlebags strapped across the back of the bike. "I don't know. Something. Nothing. Everything." She sighed. "I guess I don't care for his attitude. He's just like them. He expects me to be what he wants me to be instead of what I am."

"And what is it that they expect you to be?"

She snorted. "A lady, one who listens and doesn't talk, who has opinions but keeps them to herself. One who has absolutely no ambition."

Gabe looked up from where he stood by the cycle. "At least they got the lady part right."

She laughed and cocked her head as she met his gaze. "How can you be so sure?"

"There are some things I'm never wrong about."

Suddenly breathless, Danielle tensed under his dark gaze and trembled as invisible shock waves washed over her. But he turned away from her, seemingly unaffected by the electric charge that had unexpectedly snapped through the air, and again wiped his hands on a rag.

"You always do what people expect you to?" he asked.

She opened her mouth to deny it. She was stronger than that. Than them. But she wasn't. "Yes." She sighed yet again. "Disgusting, I know, but I guess I'm very easily manipulated."

Gabe's mouth thinned. "So what are you going to do about it?"

It was a demand. A challenge. She didn't walk away from something as simple as a dare. She squared her shoulders as she faced him. "I haven't figured it out yet."

"Yeah, well, you look like you're old enough to have gotten to the point where you can make your own decisions," he told her, and snapped the tool bag on the bike shut. "You have reached the age of majority, unless I miss my guess? You can legally vote and drink?"

"Yes, I'm no longer eighteen." She shrugged. "I'm twenty-seven, actually. An old maid, according to my mother."

"That why you were out with the family friend?" he asked.

"If I answer that, are you going to tell me what you're doing standing in the street fixing your motorcycle at three o'clock in the morning?"

Gabe shrugged. "I just got into town and didn't feel like sleeping."

"So you're out cruising instead?"

"Yup. Want to join me?"

Another dare, and the taunt was clear to see in his eyes. Black eyes that were filled with wisdom and wile and wildness. Again she was struck by his power, his maleness. This was a man's man. He didn't give a damn what others did or said. He did what he wanted to, and he wanted her to do it with him. A thrill of anticipation set her flesh to tingling even as warning bells clanged inside her head. "All right."

He grinned and shrugged out of his jacket. "You're not exactly dressed for the occasion. Put this on."

She accepted and slipped into the leather that was warm from being next to his skin. The heat surprised and made her tremble, as did his scent that lingered in the jacket. Earthy and manly and arousing—she breathed deep and enjoyed as he pointed a finger at her.

"I'd lose the earrings, or they might get blown away."

She pulled them off and handed the diamonds to him as he continued to stare. "No pockets," she offered in explanation, but he didn't look away as he dropped them into one of his.

How he could get anything into the pockets of his jeans, even something as small as her earrings, when the material clung so tightly to hips and buttocks that were lean and trim, she didn't know, and was stopped from wondering when his gaze remained fastened on hers.

She felt he missed nothing, no detail, about her. He saw every movement, understood every reason. It was as if he could see into her soul. The thought was unnerving and made her heart pump, but she kept her blood cool by accepting the helmet he handed her and ignoring the charge that was again sparking between them.

"What about you?" she asked, slipping the headgear on as he swung onto the bike. "Do you have another helmet?"

"Not with me, but don't worry about it." A grin curved his mouth. "My head's probably harder than yours, anyway."

She grinned, too. "I know some who'd argue that point with you."

"Opinions are important things to have," he countered, and gestured to the seat behind him. "Hop on."

She took a step closer to comply, but hesitated. She'd never been on a motorcycle, but she'd dreamed of it, imagined it. Loving to ride horses, she'd always thought it had to be something like experiencing a wild gallop with more speed, more power. The very idea was exciting, liberating, but she'd never had to mount a horse in a short, tight dress or when wearing three-inch heels.

Taking a deep breath, she determined not to let opportunity pass her by, and reached for the bike. It was hard to be graceful or modest getting on, but she managed, thankfully, without him watching. She brought her legs up beside his and instantly felt his sizzling heat on her thighs.

"Grab hold," he yelled and started the engine.

She hastily obeyed, grasping him by the waist as the machine began vibrating beneath her. But she quickly forgot the machine when she felt the man.

His rib cage was hard and strong. No fat lingered around his belt line, and plenty of muscle filled out the width of his shoulders beneath the cotton T-shirt that stretched across his back. Her pulse jumped at the contact. But she was given little chance to enjoy or analyze the strength of the sensation. The motorcycle was quivering like a stallion eager to run, and it abruptly took off with a deafening roar.

The cry she gave was more of elation than fear, and the joy she found in the ride was contagious. It came to Gabe from her touch as she hung on to him with wholehearted abandon, and followed him as he heightened the experience by charging off into the hills above the city.

Both the machine and the woman behind him were responsive to the curves. They clung. The machine to the road, her to him, and his ego loved the strokes. And the long, slim thighs pressing to him were stiff competition for the handlebars he needed to hang on to. He enjoyed the feel of power coming from the engine and the hum of his hormones from being touched by a woman who was as sleek and exciting as the motorcycle he rode.

Slowing, he came to a stop on a road that seemed to overlook the world and heard her gasp.

"That was fabulous!" Danielle laughed and squeezed him hard. She pulled one hand free to wipe at the moisture on her cheeks. The wind had stung her eyes. She'd had to keep them shut and miss most of the view, but the ride itself had been worth it.

"Sorry, I should have given you these." He reached past a long thigh, resisting the urge to touch, and dug in one of the bags hanging on the back of the bike before coming out with a pair of glasses like those he'd put on.

She accepted them with a final wipe at her face and wrinkled her nose. "I must be a mess."

Looking at her running mascara, he couldn't find it in his heart to agree. He liked what he saw. She was a class act, one who had been raised by society proper but who wasn't afraid to let it all go, although she was obviously used to exercising the restraint taught from birth. "Do you realize that you're alone in the middle of nowhere in the dead of night with a man you don't even know?"

"Yes," she agreed, slipping the glasses on. "And if you're going to kill me, please do it quickly so I can die happy." It was amazing that she could be so comfortable with a complete stranger, but she was. And she trusted him. He wouldn't hurt her.

"Do you do this often?" he asked. "Go off with strange men?"

Her eyes dropped from his, and embarrassed heat flooded her cheeks. "Actually, no. I don't often get a chance to give in to impulses." She rolled her eyes. "I'm more likely to exercise decorum."

He grinned. She made it sound like a dirty word, one she preferred to avoid but was forced to use every day.

She took a deep breath of the crisp night air and lifted a hand to tuck some loosened hair back under the helmet while turning to gaze out at the city below her. The twinkling of what seemed to be millions of lights shone against the night that was blanketing the earth. "It's beautiful, isn't it?"

"There's few who'd disagree." But he wasn't talking about the view. He was talking about her, and he was fighting feelings that were contradictory. On one hand he wanted to soothe and protect, keep her safe from those manipulating and causing her pain. On the other, he wanted to drop the bike and pull her into his arms and see if she tasted as good as she felt wrapped around him.

She shifted, and her foot slipped off the bike. "Stupid shoes."

"Get rid of them."

"Okay."

His jaw dropped when she took him literally by yanking them off and hurling them over the hill and into the darkness beyond.

She met his incredulous stare with one of her own. "I don't believe I just did that."

But she laughed, and he did, too.

Sobering, she shrugged in amazed disbelief. "Another impulse."

"It's good to give in to those once in a while," he advised, but her answering smile made his fingers tighten on the handlebars he was desperately gripping.

"It is, isn't it?" She stared into the bushes where the shoes had gone. "I hated them, anyway."

He shook his head. "Then what'd you buy them for?"

"Fashion. Vanity, but I'd buy a motorcycle just for fun."

He watched her stroke it and envied the chrome she touched. "Want one?"

"Absolutely," she breathed. "I never dreamed it was so wonderful."

"First ride?" He wouldn't have believed it, not with the way she'd moved with him and the bike. She'd shown none of the first-time jitters that most initiates did.

"But not the last," she assured him. "Will you help me buy one? Just like this?"

From debutante to biker woman in a flash. The green eyes that met his were earnest, pleading and nearly impossible to resist. He moved his shoulders in a careless gesture. "Maybe not quite like this."

Her pout had the muscles in his stomach clenching. "Why not?"

"You might be a big girl, but I don't think you're big enough to pick this baby up if it falls over."

She scowled down at the still-humming machine beneath her and was forced to see his logic. "I still want one with lots of zip."

"But what will Daddy say?"

The taunt had her eyes narrowing. "Who cares?"

"That's the spirit."

His smile and quick, rich laugh had her wrapping her arms around him once more. "Let's go again."

And they did. Down the hills, into the streets and merging with traffic under the first rays of a rising sun. By the time they were on the streets of San Marino and pulling into the long, curving driveway in front of her home, the black of night had turned to foggy gray. In the growing light she slipped from the bike, and away from him, with a regretful sigh.

"That was wonderful. Thank you."

"My pleasure," he responded, and watched her pull the helmet off and unleash a cap of silky hair. It floated around her face in a cut that was sleek and elegant. Like her.

He reached out to touch the leather jacket she still wore. "Mine, I believe."

"Oh, I'm sorry." But when she shrugged out of and he into it, it was he who was sorry.

Her warmth, her perfume surrounded him like a caress. He breathed deeply, enjoying the sweet torment.

He wanted to see her again, even though he shouldn't. He and she didn't belong together, but he was intrigued nonetheless. By her, by the possibilities.

Meeting his gaze as dawn brightened the sky, she couldn't understand why she'd been afraid to approach him on that dark street. His eyes might be black but they were warm and, suddenly, knowing he was going to leave, that she was going to lose his warmth and his presence, she gestured to the steps and the big white door waiting beyond. "I don't suppose I could offer you breakfast?"

"What would the family say about bringing a strange man home for a meal?"

Her nose wrinkled in joyful contemplation. "Oh, I don't know. Once they find out you rescued me after I was dumped by that family friend..."

"Maybe I could become a family friend?"

"Would you want to be one?" she asked, and wondered immediately why she cared if he did. He wasn't someone who would fit in well in her world. The two of them came from opposite ends of society, and she'd never known the two sides to mix well.

"Would you?"

His question took her by surprise—as did her own response. "Yes." The word came out before she could think and when there were, and had to be, a million reasons for it not to be true, but nevertheless, she realized it *was* true.

He grinned and took the helmet from her. "You better go get some shoes on."

She laughed, suddenly lighthearted, and wiggled her toes on the pavement. Her panty hose were ruined, but it hardly mattered. Not when he was about to ride away. "Will I see you again?"

"I'll be around." He started to push off.

"Wait!"

He stopped and looked up to find her beside him.

"I don't even know your name," she objected with a helpless shrug, but her pulse jumped in alarm when he smiled.

"Gabe. You?"

"Danielle." She nodded back toward the house. "Fitzsimmons."

His eyebrows went up. "As in investments and real estate Fitzsimmons?"

"The same."

"I'm impressed."

"Don't be. It's just a name."

"A rose by any other name?"

"I never liked Shakespeare."

"Oh, I don't know. The old boy had his moments." Gabe grinned. "I kind of liked that balcony scene."

"Yeah?"

"Yeah."

She looked over her shoulder at the house. "We have a balcony."

"Really?" Gabe asked, lifting his gaze from her to the smooth lines of the two-story manor that spread with regal dignity across the front of the drive. "Is it below your window?"

Danielle's heart jumped at the possibility of a night of storm and passion. With him. "Not exactly, but you could come see it. Tonight."

His eyes returned to her. "An invitation?"

"A party."

"Full dress, I suppose."

She bit her lip to stop her smile and wondered if his wardrobe stretched beyond leather. "Tuxedos aren't necessarily required. Just preferred."

He looked from her to the house. "I don't know. Kind of short notice for a Saturday night, and I do have a busy social calendar."

She rolled her eyes.

"What? You don't believe me?"

"I'll believe anything you say as long as you say yes." She didn't know why it was suddenly so important for him to come, for her to see him again, but it was. She didn't want him to just ride away.

"Yes."

He nodded to her as she stood watching him. "Tonight."

"Eight o'clock," she confirmed.

"Only if I don't decide to be stylishly late."

She grinned, liking his sense of humor, his cocky smile and his uniqueness. She'd never met anyone like him. "Just come."

He nodded again.

Gabe turned away, gave the machine beneath him gas while letting out the clutch, and roared away, leaving her behind in the twilight of dawn with the sweet sense of anticipation and his name on her lips.

Chapter Two

Danielle glanced at her watch. It was nine-thirty. She sighed and looked around the room filled with elegantly dressed people who were all smiling, talking or eating their way around the huge room that her mother fondly termed "The Hall."

She nodded politely to another of her parents' guests and moved quietly toward one of the windows overlooking the drive, passing a corporate magnate, an investment whiz, a stock guru and their assorted companions on the way.

The magnate was a longtime business ally of her father's and had a willowy blonde hanging on his arm. She was wearing a clingy silver slip dress, and Danielle had yet to hear the woman speak. She seemed satisfied to only be seen and not heard—something that wasn't true of the whiz's companion.

The whiz was a woman and had an accountant with her. He fit the mousy-with-glasses stereotype and he had a lot to say—to anyone who would listen.

The guru had his hair in a ponytail, as did his date. Each looked to the other for approval every time they spoke. Neither one of them seemed to mind the accountant's domination of the conversation.

Danielle's polite smile faded as she turned her back on them all to stare at the empty driveway. For none of them were as interesting as the man she'd met hours before and who had yet to appear as promised.

She sighed and glanced at the porch that was brightly lit and carefully guarded by uniformed "butlers" whose sole job was to insure no one entered the house who hadn't been invited.

That rarely stopped those determined few who were persuasive enough in speech and manner from gaining admittance. She frowned. Never having crashed a party, she didn't know what it was like to enter where she wasn't wanted, but Gabe probably had. More than once. He wasn't a man who would let much stand in his way—at least, she didn't think he was.

She pursed her lips and considered. It was strange that she could have formed such strong opinions about someone she barely knew, but Gabe had made a lasting impression. And just from their brief time together, he didn't seem to be a man who let opinions or restrictions stop him. He looked at things and people and saw them as they were, and his direct approach to her said he wasn't a man to waffle when making up his mind. She thought he would be quick to act and react, but she doubted she'd ever have the opportunity to be sure that what she believed was true.

Again she scanned the driveway, but she really didn't think he was coming. And she couldn't blame him. And she should be glad, not disappointed.

Gabe didn't belong in a San Marino manor filled to the roof with the rich, the famous and the infamous. And, looking back, she couldn't believe she'd actually asked him to come and meet those who dwelled in the world of money and megapower and who were regularly featured in print or on a movie screen.

Stepping through the ajar floor-to-ceiling windows and out onto the porch set off to the side of the house, she wondered. What was it about him that had appealed to her? Encouraged her to abandon common sense and give in to an impulse that had seen her gallivant through the hills above Los Angeles on a motorcycle with a complete stranger? She must have been out of her mind.

A crooked grin curved her lips. Scared senseless was more like it. On a dark and gloomy street, alone and without a dime, she'd probably been susceptible to suggestion. But with black eyes, black hair and black leather jacket, he'd proven disarming, charming and alarming.

Silently she shook her head in rueful amazement. But, right or wrong, wise or foolish, she really couldn't regret the unexpected night of adventure—even if the evening had proven to be an expensive experience considering Gabe had disappeared with a pocketful of diamonds.

She smothered a soft sigh of disappointment. She didn't want to believe it, but in his position, with nothing but a motorcycle to his name and a nomadic life-style that apparently saw him drift from place to place at will, she couldn't blame him for taking her earrings and running. She bit her lip. Or maybe he wasn't gone.

Gabe had said he'd just gotten into town. Not *back* into town. That would seem to mean he didn't live in Los Angeles but was just arriving, perhaps for the first time, and he was in no hurry to leave. She could hardly call the police because she'd let him carry a pair of her earrings and failed to ask for them back. Yet it was hard to accept the "theft" as purposeful. He hadn't asked her to give him the earrings. He'd only warned her to remove them, rather than taking the chance of losing them during the ride.

She smiled to herself. No, she couldn't think ill of Gabe. If he'd taken her diamonds, it hadn't been intentional, and besides, he had rescued her. If he hadn't given her a ride, she shuddered to think where she might have ended up. Her surroundings had been far from friendly, and the shadows had been wide and deep. But they hadn't bothered him.

The smile on her lips grew. What had he been doing tinkering with a motorcycle in the middle of a deserted street in the dead of night? The idea was crazy, really. Like his lifestyle.

What would it be like to live like him? Riding across the country on a motorcycle? Going where, when and with whom you wanted? Having no one criticizing, expecting more, expressing disappointment, or otherwise dishing out disapproval for acts unbecoming?

Her sigh was long and heavy. No commitments, no restrictions, no expectations. It was a dream she'd never experience, but it was a fantasy she could enjoy. Especially if she could have it fulfilled with him.

Her heartbeat quickened as she remembered the delicious sensations he could encourage with just a look. Piratical in appearance. Taunting in manner, he had asked about her balcony. For a fleeting moment, she had wondered what it would be like to be in his arms, her body pressed against the hard length of his.

Reaching out, she caressed a vine that was climbing the wall beside the porch. Fortunately and unfortunately, Gabe was another fantasy that she would never truly experience, but if he was gone, his inspiration was not.

Danielle had been trying to convince her father to increase her involvement in the business. She'd gone to school. She knew what she was doing, but he continued to resist giving her a chance with more than the less-challenging accounts. Maybe it was time to make her opportunity rather than waiting for it. She could take on her competitor—the man who had her father's ear. Her lips now twisted into a satisfied smile. She'd actually already taken the first step in preparing for battle.

The secretary who'd been so efficient but too pretty to be ignored by Malcolm Reed was coming back. Though she would have to make changes, at least temporarily, and Danielle was helping her....

A distant hum broke through Danielle's determined contemplation, and she listened to the sound that was suddenly very familiar. A motorcycle! But the smile that touched her lips was cautiously disbelieving—until a lone headlight bobbed into the drive. He'd come!

A gleeful laugh followed her as Danielle hurried back inside, through the guests and into the foyer. She was oblivious to the looks, the stares and the frowns of disapproval. Uncharacteristically, she didn't care about anything or anyone but the man who had come when she was sure he wouldn't—and shouldn't.

Reaching the porch in a breathless rush, she was in time to see Gabe hand over his bike to one of the valets, who was obviously uncertain if he should ride or roll the machine into a parking spot, but Gabe was unconcerned with which option the boy chose. He turned toward the porch, straightening the cuffs of his shirt beneath the battered, black leather jacket, and immediately stopped. She was waiting for him.

Gabe wasn't used to having women take his breath away. He'd seen and been with too many pretty women to allow beauty to blind or influence him, but good sense seemed to be overridden by an aching need whenever Danielle Fitzsimmons was anywhere near.

He smiled and started forward, letting his gaze sweep over her in greedy delight. The elegant green gown she wore was simply cut. Its flowing lines accentuated every intriguing curve of a body that would never be termed well-rounded yet was female in each intimate detail. He was sorry to see the dress was floor-length. The lovely legs he'd enjoyed the night before were covered, but the arms were bare. The straps holding the dress in place were fastened behind her neck and left both her arms and shoulders exposed.

He reached the first step and shoved his hands in his pants pockets to resist the urge to touch, and watched her gaze drop from his face to his leather jacket. He stopped before her and shrugged. "Sorry, but my tux was out being pressed."

The careless explanation brought Danielle's eyes to his, but unbelievably, knowing she should be shocked rather than amused, certain she should send him away rather than let him inside, she found herself fighting a smile rather than outrage. "Really?"

"Afraid so."

Danielle pursed her lips in apparent contemplation and stepped forward to circle and inspect him slowly, but if she was looking for imperfections, she could find none. And if she should have been considering what words to use to send him away, instead she found herself wondering why she hadn't noticed the night before that he was handsome. Lost and alone, she'd just accepted him as a whole, an enigmatic man she'd met on the street. Now she noticed the intriguing square chin, the slightly crooked nose and his height.

Stopping in front of him once more and crossing her arms over her breasts, she let her gaze drop in cool appraisal to take in the clean white shirt and tie hidden beneath the leather jacket and shook her head. "That's too bad, but I suppose you'll do. This is California, after all."

His smile made her toes curl in her shoes, and she found herself admiring the face she'd taken too little notice of in the dark the previous evening. The forming beard did give him a piratical look, a derring-do type of appearance, and his presence on her porch said it wasn't just skin-deep. Gabe would dare to do, and his attitude had to be catching for she was feeling the same. She wasn't going to tell him to leave even though, without a doubt in her mind, she knew she should.

"Stylishly late?" she asked.

He shrugged. "Car trouble."

The ironic twist of his lips had her laughing even as one of the attendants held out a disapproving hand for the invitation Gabe was supposed to have. She slipped her arm around Gabe's with a cool look of dismissal and defense. "He's with me."

"Yes," Gabe agreed, liking the ring of possession in her grip and her gaze, and drew her closer to walk with him, hip-to-hip, through the door. The scent of her perfume that had taunted him all the way back to his apartment in the light of dawn reached out to tease his senses anew. "Nice house," he commented, glancing around the foyer that was filled with subtle displays of wealth. A table with a crystal vase backed by an antique mirror, a modestly sized chandelier overhead and a floor that shone to the point of reflection.

"Thank you." She accepted the compliment and watched him study his surroundings. Doubts were forming again about letting him through the door. Not everyone lived in— or regularly visited—mansions, and not everyone knew how to behave in one. She bit her lip. If anyone asked, she didn't even know his last name! Yet, if she expected him to feel or act out of place, to display intimidation or nerves, he didn't. Quite the contrary—he appeared calm, cool and confident. Just as he had on an empty street. Intrigued in spite of herself and the room filled with guests it wouldn't do to annoy, she smothered a smile. She'd been right about him. He would dare anything. "Yes, it's rather small for three people, but we make do."

Gabe's gaze flew to hers at the tone of her voice, but her laugh at his astonished expression took away any doubts. Being rich hadn't made her a complete snob. She was simply poised, polished and deceivingly cool. He grinned and looked up to meet the startled gazes of those who had heard her laugh and turned to find its source. "We've aroused some interest. Shall we go introduce ourselves?"

"By all means," she murmured, keeping her hold on his arm and nodding to a rising movie star who was staring their way. "Where would you like to start?"

"I think the man over there in the corner. I simply have to find out where he got that purple tux."

Only years of practice allowed Danielle to swallow her laughter and get through the introductions without a hitch, but amusement was quickly pushed aside as she determined not to let him out of her sight. Her diamonds were still missing after all. Yet he seemed in no hurry to break away. In fact, he made no effort to leave her side but was happy to follow her lead—or that of the guests who came forward to greet the unshaven, leather-wearing gate-crasher who was holding on to their host's daughter's arm.

Fielding questions and pondering glances, Danielle faced her attackers without batting an eye, but Gabe didn't allow her to go the bouts alone. He swung a few verbal punches that had her gritting her teeth, but none of the guests went into a free-fall. If Gabe rocked them on their heels, he caught them before they went down for the count—and had them laughing before they moved on.

Soon Danielle found she didn't need to defend. The more they circulated, the more Gabe was accepted, and the more he fascinated. She watched with rapt attention as he charmed with a smile, countered with constructive argument or evaded with easy grace. He was amazing, and within the hour she was speculating that he had to be much more than he appeared.

No nomad knew what was happening on Wall Street. Someone who lived on the lam didn't care what stocks were up or down. And anybody who roamed from state to state wouldn't have cared who was running for political office—much less what their positions were on various issues.

Frowning, she watched Gabe go toe-to-toe with the guru's accountant and listened for tips in his words that would give her a clue as to who he really was. A diplomat who'd come to town incognito? A politician in disguise? She didn't know anyone in any other occupation who could field questions or sidestep as well as he did. That kind of expertise only came with practice. But where on earth would he have gotten it?

And she wasn't the only one who was wondering. Personal queries came from others about Gabe and his background, but he managed to never give a direct answer. Somehow he always turned the conversation back to the questioner. And when someone pulled her aside to ask more of the man she was with, Danielle wasn't in a position to fill in the blanks. To any and everyone, Gabe was simply a friend—a word that defined a million different types of relationship, especially in the heart of California.

When a cute redhead stole him away for a dance Gabe went with a wink, and Danielle was finally caught by her father, whom she'd seen circling at a discreet distance, waiting for the perfect opportunity to get her to himself.

"Who is he?"

"His name is Gabe," she returned calmly, sipping the drink in her hand and eyeing the redhead with ungracious animosity. She was petite and cute and had dimples in both cheeks. Watching the woman smile at Gabe, Danielle decided she didn't like her in the least.

"Gabe? Just Gabe? What's he do? Did you invite him?"

Danielle turned to look up at her father, a tall man with a mane of gray hair, a ferocious scowl and intimidating girth. "Yes, Dad, I did invite him, and if you want to know what he does, why don't you ask him?" She glided away, unaffected by the famous Fitzsimmons glare, but didn't get far. Trying to cross the room, she was accosted by more than one person, most of whom were female. They all wanted to know more about Gabe, too. It was disturbing and intriguing that she could tell them little, but she followed Gabe's example and didn't say much in response. Instead she enjoyed hinting at more with coy silence. He *was* a bad influence. And she was having the time of her life!

"I DIDN'T THINK you'd ever rescue me," Gabe accused her a short time later as he took her in his arms. The music was still playing, the redhead was gone and more couples were now dancing.

"You didn't look like you needed rescuing," Danielle returned. "As a matter of fact, you've done quite well on your own."

He cocked an eyebrow at her.

"Everyone wants to know who you are."

"Does that include you?"

"Like everybody else, I'm still deciding."

He grinned. "What are my options so far?"

"At first, opinion was running strong that Lucas Fitzsimmons's only daughter had gone and picked herself up some scruffy, down-on-his-luck outsider to defy her father. But now we have another contingent who's convinced you're a newly arrived candidate for the Hollywood gristmill."

"Ah," he agreed. "A movie star."

"The only problem is that no one can remember seeing you on Broadway."

Gabe shrugged. "Bit parts. That's all they'd give me."

"However, we do have a more conservative membership who believe you may have come in from Chicago. Part of a scouting venture from a new investment corporation." She leaned closer to whisper. "Real estate has been very bad out here, you know."

"The economy," he agreed with appropriate sobriety.

She nodded, and he frowned.

"I'm going to have to work on that midwestern accent."

She smothered a grin. "There is one other group."

"Really? And what do they think I'm here for?"

"They don't care."

His eyebrows went up again. "No opinion?"

"No, they're just interested in your body."

His look of distress had her laughing, but the heat suddenly racing up his neck had him whirling her out the door and onto the porch.

She stepped out of his arms and led him down to the ornamental fountain at the bottom of the steps. "Don't you want their names and numbers?"

"No, I only want to know what you think."

"About what?"

"About me."

Her heart stopped, but she covered momentary confusion by trailing her fingers through the cool water and keeping him opposite her by walking around the fountain. "I'm still making up my mind."

He grinned and put both hands on the smooth marble holding the water-spewing sculptured nymph and watched her. She'd worn her hair loose tonight. It floated around her face in silken wonder. He wished for the opportunity to find out if it was as soft as it looked but regretfully doubted the chance would arise. "What can I do or say to help you decide?"

She was looking at him through the falling water. "When I first met you, I guess I didn't really have a firm opinion. I just wanted a phone and prayed you weren't a lost member of Hell's Angels."

He couldn't help chuckling. "I quit the group before I left Chicago."

"But where are your tattoos?"

"How bad do you want to find out?"

Her pulse fluttered as his black gaze fastened on hers. This was the dangerous Gabe, the one she'd met on the street and been unsure of, the one she wanted in her fantasy but who she couldn't allow in her real life. Round pegs didn't go in square holes, and square was where she lived. Yet she didn't look or back away from his silent suggestion. She met him head-on in what, she told herself, was a perfectly acceptable flirtation. "How hard do you want me to search?"

"Dani," he admonished, enjoying the sparks shooting between them. "I'm surprised at you. You're ready to throw discretion aside—along with my clothes. I thought the upper crust was supposed to hide such primitive urges as lust."

She rolled her eyes. "Being rich doesn't mean we're not human, and if my mother hears you call me that, she'll probably faint."

"Dani?"

Danielle nodded, and he smiled.

"Where is she now?" he asked, watching Danielle slowly make her way back around the fountain to him.

"Probably standing inside desperately hoping no one noticed I went outside alone with you." She stopped next to him. She didn't belong with him, but she wanted to stay with him anyway. He fascinated her. She wasn't sure why. Perhaps it was just the challenge of finding out what it would be like. "It's the image, you know."

"People still worry about that?"

"Some do." She sighed. "I gave it up when I was old enough to realize I wasn't perfect."

"None of us are."

"Thankfully. It'd be awfully hard on the rest of us if anybody was."

Gabe watched her lean back to run immaculately manicured and polished nails through her hair. "You were telling me what you think of me."

She slanted a veiled look at him without turning her head. "Once I realized you weren't going to murder me, I thought you were kind of nice."

"But—?"

"I wasn't sure." She shrugged. "As I told you last night, I'm not used to giving in to impulses."

"Like going for motorcycle rides at night with strange men and throwing away a perfectly good pair of shoes?"

She nodded acquiescence as a blush flooded her cheeks.

"And there was the fact that I disappeared into the sunrise with these."

Danielle smothered a gasp as he pulled her diamond earrings from his jacket pocket. He dangled them in front of her until she reached up to take them from him.

"So what do you think of me now?"

Her fingers closed over the diamonds, and she turned to meet his steady stare. "You surprise me. Constantly."

"Life's too short to be predictable."

"I don't think anyone could ever accuse you of being that."

"And that's bad?"

She smiled. "I'm not sure. I haven't had much practice at doing the unexpected."

"I'm a good teacher."

Suddenly finding it hard to breathe, Danielle backed away to put some distance back between them. She liked Gabe. Perhaps too much. But liking him didn't mean he was good for her, or she for him. They didn't have much in common—except chemistry. It kept bubbling between them.

"You said you'd just gotten into town," Danielle remarked as she turned and walked toward him. All the while his black gaze was riveted to her.

"Last night."

Her fingers tightened around the earrings in her hand. She hadn't expected to get them back, had been prepared to not even ask. "Is there anything you need? I mean, if I could help..."

His smile was bright. "Are you offering me a job?"

"Do you need one?"

His smile faded. "You're serious."

"You helped me. I'd like to help you," Danielle agreed. But her powers were limited. Or were they? An idea started to take shape in her mind. "All right, yes, I am offering you a job."

"Doing what?"

"Working for me."

His eyebrows went up. "For you?"

"With me," she corrected, tilting her chin to a haughty angle. "You needn't sound surprised. I happen to be an officer in the company."

"How high up?"

"High enough."

"Got any pull?"

Her lips twitched. "Not as much as I'd like. Yet." She watched him straighten from where he'd been leaning against the fountain. "Would you like to help me get some more?"

"Can't do it by yourself?"

She shrugged. "It's always easier to have help, especially when you need a hand to get back up after being knocked down."

"Anyone I know?"

"You'll meet him if you come to work with me."

Gabe frowned. "What makes you think you can trust me?"

"What makes you think I'll be a good boss?"

"Are you?"

"You inspired me to be one when I was about to give up." She watched him come slowly toward her, refusing to step back when he stopped before her. "Everyone needs inspiration once in a while, and you *do* read the *Wall Street Journal*."

A grin spread across his mouth. She'd been listening to what he'd been saying while circulating with her guests. "Surprise you?"

"I don't think anything you did would surprise me." She shook her head as he watched. "You have this attitude about you."

He pointed to his shoulder. "Big chip?"

"No, more like, 'I'll do what I want.'"

"'And you better like it'?"

"You said you're a good teacher. Maybe there's some lessons I could learn."

He whistled. "Want to be a tough lady?"

"I want to be taken more seriously, and I think you can help me do it." And she did. He had some business savvy, and she needed an assistant. She could do worse, or at least she thought she could.

He jingled the change in his pockets and considered. "Just what did you have in mind?"

"Associate."

"No fancy title?"

She smiled. "If you want one."

"Typing?"

"I've got a secretary, and I'm not giving her up."

The anger behind the declaration had him staring at her. "There's a story I haven't heard yet."

"I wouldn't want to prejudice you."

"But you do want to use me."

"It could be worse," she said, crossing her arms in front of her. "I could just want your body."

Chapter Three

"That could have its rewards," he suggested.

"I want you in my office, not my bed," Danielle objected coolly, but she felt suddenly breathless and crazy. What was she thinking of? What was there about Gabe that she kept inviting him into her life when it was all too clear that he didn't fit where she belonged? But when she tried to back away, he reached out to take her hand. Her eyes flew to his.

"How much do you pay?" Her pulse beneath his fingers was fluttering. It belied her alleged lack of interest, and he was tempted to try to get her to forget business for pleasure. But he was intrigued. By her, by the situation, even if he did have other commitments. He should say no.

"How much do you think you're worth?" she asked, coolly retrieving her hand from his. The heat of his grip on hers had her flesh tingling. Yet it was his grin that was almost her undoing. It nearly buckled her knees.

"Depends on what I have to do."

"Help me make decisions."

A dark eyebrow arched. "Can't you make them yourself? You did go to school?"

"Yes, and I have passed the age of majority. I vote and drink by myself and I know my own mind, but I like your business sense."

"You don't have any?"

"Show up for work on Monday, and you can find out."

"Sounds like a challenge."

"Can you handle it?"

"Only if I don't have to call you 'boss.'"

Danielle couldn't stop her smile, and she couldn't worry about making a mistake about Gabe. She trusted him. Why, she had no idea. She knew nothing about him except that he owned a motorcycle and had just arrived in California, but as her father was fond of saying: *Sometimes it's best not to question instinct, just accept what your gut tells you.* And Gabe did know business.

He knew stocks, trends. He also kept her on her toes— something that had to be good for a rising young executive. And, if he didn't work out, she could always show him the door.

She shrugged. "You can call me whatever you want as long as you do it respectfully. You also have to watch what you say in front of my father."

"He doesn't like people who talk back?"

"He's not used to it."

"How dull."

Her lips twitched as she smothered a smile of agreement. That's what life had been. Until now. Without him. With him, she doubted it would be anymore, and that was something to look forward to. "Shall we go tell him the news?"

Gabe held out his arm for her to slide hers through and wondered what he was getting into. More than he'd expected. More than he wanted. He liked being independent, but having her as part of his team could have its advantages.

"By the way," he said as they started back up the steps, "where's that balcony?"

"Over there," she said, pointing off to the side.

"By your bedroom?"

"You need to know that?"

"Not yet."

His smile made her heart jump, her breath catch and her mind search out possibilities, but she was saved from comment by the unexpected appearance of her father.

"There you are," Lucas Fitzsimmons grumbled, his scowl dark beneath the unruly gray hair covering his head. "I wanted you to meet—"

"I wanted you to meet," Danielle interrupted, knowing full well it was her mother who'd sent her father out to the porch, "Gabe..."

"Tyler," Gabe finished for her and put out a hand. "Pleased to meet you, Mr. Fitzsimmons. I'm sure we'll enjoy working together."

In bemusement, his fingers already firmly locked in Gabe's, Lucas Fitzsimmons turned baffled brown eyes toward Danielle.

"I just hired him," she explained.

"You... To do what?" Fitzsimmons demanded, ready and willing to fight against a freeloader taking advantage of his daughter—or his company, and not necessarily in that order.

"To help me."

"Do what?"

"Impress you." It was the first time she could recall ever seeing her father speechless. He always had an answer, a comment, a joke. Until now. Smothering a smile, she looked at Gabe and found him grinning.

"We're going to make quite a team," he told her as he led her back inside, and she wondered how good—and if she really wanted their partnership to remain business only.

"GABE, IS THAT YOU?"

"None other," he responded, sitting back on his couch dressed only in the jeans he'd pulled on when he'd crawled out of bed. It was Sunday morning. Early, but he was used to being up with the birds.

"You back in town?"

"You sound half hopeful and half dreadful," Gabe observed, smiling nevertheless as he pictured his friend and partner, Sam Cody, scowling at the phone.

"You've only been gone a week."

"Those were your orders."

"Not that you listen to anyone but yourself."

Gabe grinned. "Sam, are you telling me that I'm hard to get along with?"

"Depends on what mood you're in."

Gabe sighed regretfully. "You were right about the vacation."

Sam heaved a sigh of relief. "I hate to say I told you so."

"But I needed it."

"You did."

"Matter of fact, I need some more."

"You're kidding."

Gabe ran a hand over his almost full beard, trying to decide if he liked it or not. He'd never been much for facial hair, but after a week of avoiding a razor, the change in image was growing on him. Literally. "I never kid, you know that."

"Uh-huh."

"Seriously, I want to take some more time. Any problem?"

"How long you talking?"

"Why do you suddenly sound relieved?" Gabe asked, and pictured Sam smiling from ear to ear.

"Maybe I like being in charge."

"Maybe I could get used to liking letting you be. How about a month?"

Sam whistled. "You must be having some picnic."

"Picnics aren't any fun alone." Gabe immediately had to pull the phone from his ear as Sam's hoot of laughter echoed over the line.

"A woman! You've met a woman!" Sam's voice lowered. "What's she like?"

"Interesting."

"The best kind. Do I know her?"

"Not yet."

"Sounds serious."

"Don't call the church yet, okay?"

"Just looking out for your best interests."

"Uh-huh. Her name's Fitzsimmons."

"Fitzsimmons? As in *the* Fitzsimmons?"

Gabe recognized the disbelief. He felt it himself, along with the irony. "Small world."

"You know—" Sam warned.

"I know," Gabe interrupted, very well aware of what his friend was going to say. "Keep me apprised."

"How do I reach you?"

"Leave a message on the answering machine. Otherwise, I'll call in when I can."

"Stay in touch—and try to have some fun."

Gabe didn't bother answering. He hung up and prowled to the bathroom where he stared in the mirror. He was tempted to shave the beard off. It wasn't really his style, but it had suddenly become a necessity. He frowned. Deceiving

Danielle wasn't something he was going to enjoy, but staying close to her was.

He turned from the mirror and stepped out of the jeans and into the shower. Actually, he didn't think she really needed him. Not from listening to her talk. She was intelligent, knew what she wanted and could go after it. What he suspected she needed was some support. Something she apparently wasn't getting from her family who, without her coming right out and saying so, appeared to be more interested in marrying her off into the proper family and getting her out of the business than allowing her to stay in it and contribute what she had to offer.

Gabe turned on the water full blast and sighed as the bathroom started to steam. He'd quit when he'd gotten into a similar dilemma with his family. It'd made for a lot of bad feelings, anger and hurt, but in the end, the move had been the best for him. Yet he didn't know if Danielle could make a break. He didn't know how strong she was or how badly she wanted to prove herself. She might fold at the first sign of opposition from her father, or anyone else in the company.

He reached for the soap. Maybe he only wanted to believe she wouldn't, but she was already trying to forge her own path by not only staying in the business but by rebelling against the family "friend" when she'd jumped out of the car. A smile twisted Gabe's lips. Then she'd not only invited a complete stranger to her home but brought him into it when his attire had been anything but correct. Gabe's mouth twitched. She'd surprised him by taking him at face value the night before. He'd half expected her to find some diplomatic way to send him away and out of her life. But his surprise had been nothing compared to her father's when she'd hired someone without consulting him first. Gabe's grin broadened. He didn't imagine Lucas Fitzsimmons had liked that all too much.

Gabe stuck his head under the water. Danielle's feelers were out. Her frustration was growing. She'd said he'd inspired her. In reality all he'd done was give her a kick in the pants—made her do what she wanted to instead of doing the expected, the traditional and exercising that decorum he suspected she secretly loathed.

His smile abruptly turned into a frown. Yet if Danielle was more than she appeared, he wasn't at all what or who she thought he was, either. Whether that was disappointing or not, in the end, would be up to him, but before he stepped into the lion's den and assumed his role, he had to do some research. About her and about Lucas Fitzsimmons and company. It was something he'd been expecting to do anyway. He'd just have to do it a little sooner than anticipated.

But reading about Danielle Fitzsimmons on paper wasn't enough. Or at least it didn't seem to be, because before the day was half gone, Gabe found himself steering his motorcycle up her drive and past a half dozen Mercedes, Porsches and BMWs to her door. He knew he shouldn't go. It could complicate things and a situation that was already more complicated than it should be, but he couldn't resist the temptation, or the unexpected need to see her again. And he was a man who enjoyed giving in to impulses.

Cutting the motor, he kicked the stand on the bike into place and slid from the seat to approach the porch, shrugging away the vague sense of uneasiness that was plaguing him as he went. Some part of him was warning that this was one impulse he could regret. But, stubbornly, he refused to listen to his intuition—something he usually trusted. Danielle Fitzsimmons was no threat to him. He knew what he was doing with her. He was in control, and no harm could come from spending more time with her. At least, he reminded himself, not as long as he kept his hands in his pockets.

He reached for the doorbell.

Inside Danielle looked up at the ring and away from the cup of tea she was pretending to sip and enjoy. She yearned to use the fading echo of the bell as an excuse to escape from the meeting her mother had insisted she attend, but it was impossible for her to avoid the planning of yet another one of Helen Fitzsimmons's "benefit bouts." Not when the session had been planned for a Sunday afternoon just to accommodate, as her mother put it, "my daughter's work schedule."

Danielle smothered a sigh and glanced covertly around the circle of women in the airy den with her. Her mother's friends, all unemployed except for charity, didn't have a clue as to why she would want to go to an office every day any more than her own mother did. And Danielle was helpless to explain to those not motivated as she was that earning a salary made her feel good about earning her way, about doing something with her life that she hoped made a difference.

Granted her job wasn't as fulfilling as it could or should be. She had to fight for every opportunity and had yet to gain her father's complete confidence and acceptance, but she'd done well so far, earned praise, had successes. But she wanted, needed, more. And she was making headway toward getting it. Slowly.

Leaning forward to put her cup down on the long coffee table in front of the couch, Danielle pushed thoughts of the office aside and tried to focus on the conversation humming around her and accept her fate. She was trapped for the duration. Or at least she thought she was until the butler unexpectedly appeared to whisper discreetly in her ear that she had a visitor.

Surprised but immediately thankful for the interruption, Danielle murmured a polite excuse, gave her mother an apologetic smile and gratefully made her way toward the foyer. She had no idea who could be calling for her. Certainly she wasn't expecting anybody, but she wasn't about to question good fortune, especially when the distraction would give her the chance she needed to get to the medicine cabinet. A headache was beginning to throb in her skull. After she saw to whoever was at the door, she'd go get the aspirin she desperately needed if she was going to make it through the rest of her mother's "meeting."

Straightening her shoulders and putting on a polite smile of greeting, Danielle reached the foyer and was shocked to find it empty. No one was waiting, at least not inside. A shadow through the curtains on the floor-to-ceiling windows bordering the entrance told her that her visitor was outside. On the porch. Frowning and wondering what had possessed the butler to break protocol and lock a caller out rather than in, she reached for the door. Wonder vanished when she saw who had come to call.

"Gabe!"

He turned from the contemplation of her massive front yard and the sprinklers fighting the summer sun with jets of water to meet her startled stare. He'd been reconsidering his decision to come, contemplating leaving, but watching her eyes light up made him realize that he'd made the right choice. For her and for him.

Quickly his gaze dropped to skim over her. Dressed for the heat of summer in a sleeveless sundress, she looked cool and classy. It made him want to mess her up by smearing her lipstick with a kiss and tangle her hair with his fingers, but he resisted the urge by hooking his thumbs in the belt loops of his jeans. "Hi."

"Hi, yourself," she greeted.

The spontaneity of her smile made his stomach flip, but her gaze quickly darkened in concern under his.

"You haven't changed your mind, have you? About the job?"

Her distress was real enough to make him want to sweep her into his arms. He settled on leaning against one of the porch pillars instead. "Actually, no."

Puzzled, she stepped forward to stand beside him next to the pillar.

"I came to see if you wanted to go looking for that motorcycle."

"Really?" The light was back in her eyes instantly, and the reserve she seemed to take on and off like a cloak dropped as she danced across the porch in enthusiastic anticipation. But she quickly slipped it back on again when her steps stopped and she found herself facing the cars parked in the drive.

"Unless I'm interrupting something?"

She turned back to him with a tight shrug. "Just another of my mother's benefit bouts."

His lips slowly curved into a grin. "Benefit bout?"

"What some would call a brainstorming session," Danielle explained, moving back to the pillar and him. "She and her friends get together to think up new ways to raise money."

"And what's the plan this time?"

"This time, the plan has some interesting possibilities."

He liked the way her lips curved in sly appreciation. "Let me guess. A bake sale?"

"Nothing so ordinary," she denied with a haughty toss of her head that set her black hair to swinging around her face.

He frowned. "Crafts, then?"

"Nope, but it is a sale." She leaned closer, her eyes sparkling with unspoken delight. "Of men."

His eyebrows shot up.

"An auction. Attendees get to bid on a various assortment of gentlemen." Danielle smiled as Gabe's shock dissolved into disbelieving amusement. "All money goes to the charity, and the women get to spend the evening with the man they 'buy.'"

"And whose idea was this, I wonder?"

She shrugged innocently. "It was just a suggestion, and there is a catch."

"What's that?"

"Each of us on the planning committee has to enlist the aid of a minimum of six available men." She leaned closer once more. "Interested?"

"What's in it for me?"

"A titillating evening with a woman eager to donate time and money to a worthwhile cause."

Gabe grunted. "What if she's eighty and deaf? It could make for a long evening."

"I wouldn't let that happen."

"You'd rescue me?"

"I'd deplete my savings account just for you."

"Yeah?"

"Yeah."

Somehow, while talking, they'd gotten closer and closer, and suddenly, her mouth was just inches from his. She held her breath.

"About that motorcycle," Gabe murmured, restraining himself and his need to touch and curbing the desire to see if she tasted good as she smelled.

"Motorcycle," she repeated, and hastily backed up a step, telling herself it was just as well he hadn't kissed her. They had to work together starting tomorrow. And she really wasn't attracted to him. They had nothing in common, nothing to share, or at least she didn't think they did. "I..." She looked over her shoulder to the door.

"Have to stay?"

Resentment burned. Just because she was living in her parents' house didn't mean she had to be at their beck and call. She had a life of her own, and it was time she made them realize it. "They can decide what color tablecloths to use without me."

"I wouldn't want to deprive them of your company," Gabe objected mildly, but he liked the fight in her eye and the set to her jaw. He hadn't been wrong. She was straining against the bit, and unless she was given some room to move, the reins were going to snap.

"I would." She swung toward the door. "Give me ten minutes."

"Gladly," he told her, but she was already gone with a stiff back and a determined stride—but she didn't let the door slam. Gabe frowned. He'd have to work on getting her to release that restraint.

Ten minutes later she was back on the porch, skipping out the door wearing a bright red T-shirt, form-fitting designer jeans and carrying a dungaree jacket. Leaning against his bike, Gabe watched her come down the stairs while pulling her hair up into a silky ponytail and enjoyed the surge of blood that had his pulse rate accelerating. She was going to be the best-looking boss he'd ever had.

"I love a woman who doesn't take an hour to change."

"You just have to provide the right motivation," Danielle told him saucily, propping sunglasses on the tip of her nose before shrugging into her jacket.

"I'm flattered."

"Don't be," she told him, and patted the bike. "It's the motorcycle, not the driver."

"Maybe I should let you walk."

"Maybe you should let me buy," she countered, and slipped behind him on the seat as he reached for the key. "I know this great hamburger stand that has the best custard in the whole world."

"Hungry?" He grinned over his shoulder.

"Starved. I missed lunch."

"Overslept again?"

Her eyes narrowed. "What salary did you say you wanted?"

"Blackmail doesn't become you."

"And you'd look funny showing up for your first day of work with a black eye."

He whistled. "I don't think you're going to need me to take on the company board to get what you're after, but I am going to enjoy being there to watch the fireworks."

She wrapped her arms around him as the bike came to life. And as Gabe roared out of the drive with enough power to make the windows of the house rattle, it was easy to convince herself that the need to hold on tight was necessary to spare life and limb. Pressing against him had nothing to do with the fact that she liked the feel of muscle and heat and man. Safety was the only reason she had to sit close, breathe deeply and relax.

Unfortunately, she soon had to let go. The custard stand wasn't far. She directed him to it and, after ordering, led him to a bench set beside a rippling, artificial waterfall. Around them other people sat, eating hamburgers, drinking malts or devouring a cone filled with the flavor of the day, but she barely noticed any of them. Her attention was totally absorbed by the man she was with and the debate he started about stocks and bonds.

The conversation veered from finance into current events, market trends and the summer weather that had baked California dry, and she forgot who he was or who she was.

She didn't think of him as belonging to one part of society and she another. It didn't matter that she was rich and he, apparently, without many means. Sitting with him in the sun, he was just a man with a quick mind, acute business sense and a smile that could make her knees knock—and any other female's in sight.

When he left her briefly to get them both another scoop of custard, she noticed a long-legged blonde giving him the eye, and following the woman's intent stare as Gabe returned, Danielle could hardly fault the blonde for her taste. In a black T-shirt that clung to the hard lines of his chest and hip-hugging jeans, Gabe Tyler was devastating. She doubted any warm-blooded female who wandered into his dark gaze would fail to be affected. But he was with her.

Not stopping to examine the need to establish a proprietary claim or the drive to keep his attention centered only on her, she abruptly stood and dragged him away from the other admiring glances and back with her to the bike and the road.

She let him do the steering once they were on the street again, but doubt and anticipation curled in her stomach as she thought of actually buying a bike such as the one she was riding. For herself it was a reach beyond the normal into the fantasy—a realm she seldom dwelled in. For her family it would be a shock—one she wasn't sure they could withstand. And none of her friends rode motorcycles. None of her friends even owned a motorcycle.

She began to question the wisdom of investing in a bike, but when Gabe stopped and parked, Danielle found he wasn't taking her where they could shop for one. Instead he held out a hand to lead her down the streets of Old Towne Pasadena.

Delighted by his choice, she took his fingers without question and turned with him to be greeted by a group of mimes, who amused and entertained until a gentle tug moved Danielle on with Gabe to a street magician. Her hand stayed in his as they stood side by side watching trick after trick, and she didn't pull away from his touch when they left the magic behind to browse through the shops lining the streets.

Danielle couldn't say why she didn't untangle her fingers from his. Public demonstrations of affection were something she'd been brought up to avoid. It didn't make sense that she allowed the show of intimacy to continue with this nearly complete stranger. But she couldn't find the strength or need to break the contact.

The warmth of his palm against hers was comfortable, comforting, and she didn't want it to stop. And she didn't want to question why. That might come later, but for once, she was happy to forget the watch on her wrist, to ignore the inbred habit of accounting for every moment that passed and gladly neglected the need to get home for dinner.

Instead time ceased to have any relevance as she enjoyed a day that ended up on one of the many beaches lining the California coast and the company of the enigmatic man who took her there.

Standing beside Gabe on a boardwalk, she looked out over the sand that the soaring summer temperature had crowded with people and smiled. Men, women and children were everywhere, their blankets, umbrellas and swimsuits creating a kaleidoscope of color against the sunbaked grains and lapping ocean that stretched for as far as the eye could see.

"A mass of humanity," Gabe observed from behind the dark lenses of his sunglasses as the sun dipped toward the western horizon behind him.

"Reminds me of rush hour without the cars."

His smile flashed as identical twins raced by with their mother in hot pursuit. "Speaking of rushing."

Danielle smiled, too, but was glad she wasn't the one doing the chasing. The heat of the day didn't encourage rapid movement, and the clear blue sky above said no relief would come soon.

The months of June and July and now August had been warm and dry, and it didn't appear the conditions would change before the Santa Anas were due in September. But it was difficult to dread the coming of the annual barrage of the so-called "devil winds" and the fires and fear they usually brought when other challenges lay directly ahead—such as the man beside her.

"Tell me more about the company," he unexpectedly asked.

She squinted against the dying day's light, her own sunglasses forgotten as they sat propped on top of her head, and reluctantly looked up at him. The turn in conversation served to remind her that the day was temporary, as was the pleasure it had brought. "What do you want to know?"

"Who the officers of Coastal Marketing Sales and Management, Inc. are," Gabe answered. "I'd like to know a little about the people in charge."

"Do you want me to include those who have officer status for ego and salary's sake or just those who are officers because they actually make corporate decisions?"

He looked at her over the top of his sunglasses. "Just those whose toes I have to avoid stepping on."

She laughed and followed him back to the bike, filling him in on the company's background before they rode back to her house. She hated to leave the beach and the day behind, but knew she had to. Duty and reality called. Fantasy could only be indulged in for short periods, if at all.

In moments she was back on the highway with the wind whipping through her hair and the sun fading from the sky. By the time they reached San Marino, Gabe had the motorcycle's headlight on, and the beam cut through the darkness that led up her drive and to the front steps of the Fitzsimmons home.

She slid from the seat and away from him, telling herself it was only the warmth of his friendship she hated to be parted from. "Back to work tomorrow."

"The start to work for me."

She put out a hand in an automatic gesture of reassurance. "Nervous?"

He caught her fingers. "Are you?"

"Absolutely. You're my first associate. I want you to be able to make a good impression, start off on the right foot, blend in..." she stammered, suddenly trying to find a way to broach the subject that had been bothering her since he'd accepted the job. "You're okay with tomorrow? I mean, you just got to the city and you must have a place to stay, but do you need...time or..." She cleared her throat, and he grinned as she avoided his gaze.

"Dani, are you asking me if I need money?"

She retrieved her hand from his. "It's just that with your only arriving, I didn't know if you—"

"Have more in my wardrobe than T-shirts and jeans?" He shook his head as the bike continued to idle smoothly beneath him. "I won't embarrass you."

"I didn't think you would," she denied quickly, raising her eyes to his. "And it wasn't me that I was worried about."

He reached out to clip her chin, touched by her concern and the sweetness behind it. "Thank you. I'm fine."

She nodded, swallowed and tried to stop the heat from flooding her cheeks. "I'll see you tomorrow, then."

"Yes, boss."

Her smile followed him out the drive and back onto the road. It haunted him as he headed for the house that wasn't that far—at least in value—from hers.

Danielle's and his wasn't an honest relationship, and that bothered him, especially considering he'd given in to an errant impulse he should have avoided. Going to see her had been a bad idea. He'd considered it an act of idle curiosity, but he'd been lying to himself.

He was attracted to Danielle Fitzsimmons. Under normal circumstances, they could have enjoyed something other than a business association—and he could have enjoyed defrosting that cool exterior with which she faced the world. But the circumstances he now found himself in were far from normal.

Letting himself into his dark house, he didn't bother to turn on the lights but moved by memory around the clutter of furniture to the windows overlooking the city. He'd gotten involved with Danielle by accident, prolonged the association out of curiosity and maybe even some sympathy. He'd been where she was. He didn't want to go back, and he didn't want her to stay. She deserved and wanted better, but simple motivations were getting complicated.

She intrigued him. Her looks, her class, the rebellion bubbling beneath the cool exterior. The situation appealed, too. It was a different type of challenge than he was used to, but he wasn't remaining objective. He was getting personally involved. He was starting to care for Danielle, to see her as more than an exercise of wits and a problem to be solved, and that wasn't good. Not if he was going to help her. Especially considering that the deal he was already working on could make them mortal enemies.

Chapter Four

Monday morning Danielle was in her office working, or at least pretending to work, by seven o'clock. She was having doubts about Gabe, about herself, about what she wanted to do, and she hated herself for it.

Throwing down her pencil, she stared at her desk without seeing anything on it. Her family had instilled confidence in her. That she had used that confidence to go to school and was now trying to be part of the family business was not what they had wanted or expected. Only she couldn't make them see that, not even her father, who should understand her need for the challenge of thinking and trying, failing and winning. She sighed and focused on her desk. The only reason there was anything on it was that she constantly forced her father to give her something to do.

It hurt that he didn't trust her. Not that she was particularly close to her father, or her mother, for that matter. Sent away to the best schools when young, her relationship with both of them always seemed to be at a distance, though they loved her in their way. A very limited way, and she'd tried to nurture and expand those limits without much success and without daring to stretch too far the tenuous bonds that bound them together. She didn't want to disappoint them, but they were smothering her....

A knock had her spinning to the door and watching as a young woman slipped inside. For a moment all Danielle could do was stare at her, but after the shock wore off, she burst out laughing.

"Kelly, you look...different."

Indeed, the Kelly Sanders who had worked for Danielle the week before was gone. No more the sleek secretary in cool, tailored suits and loosened hair. The colorless skirt and jacket perfectly matched the old-maid image of the bun holding her blond hair in place at the base of her neck and the awkward pumps on her feet. Kelly shoved the huge glasses she'd purchased to replace the ones she usually wore back up her nose.

"Do I look awful enough?"

Danielle hurried around her desk to confront her secretary. "I don't think Malcolm will give you a second glance." Kelly's eyes fell, and Danielle reached out to take her hands. "Kelly, I'm so sorry. I wish I'd known earlier. If I hadn't been so wrapped up in my own problems—"

Kelly shook her head. "It's not your fault. I could have said something. Probably should have, but I just kept hoping he'd give up when I ignored him. And you had enough to worry about." Kelly raised her eyes to Danielle's. "I just appreciate your giving me another chance. All the money you brought me Saturday to buy all of this," she said, gesturing to the clothes and shoes. "I'll try not to let you down."

Danielle squeezed the fingers in hers. "You've never let me down." But she grinned as she looked over her secretary again. The disguise was a wild idea. Maybe one that wouldn't even work, but no one was going to lose their job because of her. Not if she could help it. All that aside, Kelly was a good secretary and an excellent mind reader, a combination necessary to keep an executive on top of things.

Danielle shrugged. "It was time for me to return the favor. You've been here with me more times than I can count burning the midnight oil making out reports and adding figures."

"That were all ignored until Malcolm took and represented them as his ideas."

Danielle's mouth thinned. "You leave Malcolm to me. He's stolen his last proposal. We're going to show everyone what he really is, and if he bothers you in any way, you have my official permission to deck him—or come get me and I will." Her smile was predatory. "Matter of fact, the possibility of knocking him flat is something I could learn to look forward to."

"I get first dibs."

Danielle nodded. "Agreed, but we may not have to fight alone. I've hired an associate." She grimaced. "It's about time we filled that empty office next to mine."

"Does that mean your father, I mean, Mr. Fitzsimmons is going to let you—"

"I don't think he's going to let me anything, but I'm going to make him see me, once and for all, as more than his daughter." Danielle turned with her toward the door. "And once we become a power to be reckoned with, you can get back in your own clothes and we can get on with business."

"Human Resources—"

"Will think you're Karen Sanderson. No one will notice you and Kelly Sanders have the same social security number." Danielle opened the door. "I have to call them first thing about Gabe, too," she told Kelly, and when she opened the door, suddenly, he was standing in front of her.

Gone was the leather jacket. Gone was the biker in sunglasses and ragged blue jeans. Instead she was facing a man dressed in suit and tie—both of which, to her trained eye, had come from a posh men's store.

She'd secretly been worried about him, coming to an office where ridicule could be quick and cruel for someone who didn't appear to fit in, but the tailored outfit he wore was perfect. Cut in lines that caressed the width of his shoulders, the dark blue weave carefully blended with the light blue of his shirt and set off his dark looks in a way that stole her breath—and her tongue.

Yet, he was anything but speechless and not at all shocked by the crisp business jacket, skirt and blouse that she had on. He'd already made up his mind that no matter what she wore, she looked fantastic, but the idea that he had surprised her once again gave him a great deal of pleasure. "Ms. Fitzsimmons," he greeted with a polite nod, and immediately turned toward the woman beside her. "And you are?"

"She is," Danielle managed, "Kelly...Karen Sanderson."

Gabe put out his hand. "Pleased to meet you, Karen. Gabe Tyler. Ms. Fitzsimmons's new associate. I'm looking forward to working with you."

"You're...we're..." Kelly stammered. "I better get to work. I'll call personnel—"

"In a moment," Danielle objected quickly, finding she needed a moment—or several moments—to recover her composure. At least she hadn't been the only one to gawk. Kelly had been staring, too. "Please won't you come in, Gabe?"

He followed her gesture inside but stopped almost immediately upon entering her office. It was neat, clean, businesslike. No feminine frills, just light touches. A single flower in a vase, plants on the windowsill and her perfume in the air. It was intoxicating in and of itself, but she'd obviously carefully avoided anything that detracted or distracted in order that she and anyone else who entered the room could concentrate on business.

"Nice."

Aware of her closing the door behind him, he walked to her desk and then to the window behind it.

"Good view, too."

"You're punctual," she observed, finally finding her voice and licking lips that had suddenly gone dry on seeing him.

"First day," he told her, and turned to watch her join him by the panes overlooking downtown L.A. The cloak of reserve was back on with the cool front she used to keep people in their place. Unfortunately for him, her hands-off attitude served more as a dare for him to put his hands on. He resisted temptation by lifting his hands to straighten his already perfectly knotted and centered tie. "I wanted to make a good impression."

"You made one on Kelly...Karen, I mean."

"Can't remember the name of your own secretary?"

Danielle's eyes narrowed on him. "There's a story there you don't know about, remember?"

"I'm intrigued even if she is trying to be a mousy little thing."

"Oh, no, only trying? You don't think she's unattractive?" Danielle questioned in alarm. "I mean, would she catch your eye if you liked women?"

"I do like women."

"No, no, it's just..." Danielle sighed. "I'm not making any sense."

"You don't want her to be attractive?"

"I don't want her to be noticed, at least for a while."

Gabe ran a hand over his beard and discovered he was getting used to stroking it. "I think what you're trying to ask me is if I'd take a second look at her?"

"Yes."

"Then, no. I'd rather look at you."

Danielle's office suddenly got smaller, and she took refuge by quickly sitting in her chair before her knees gave out. Standing close to him wasn't a good idea. It made it hard for her to remember that he was an employee and she his employer. She'd have to be sure to keep the desk between them. "Speaking of appearances, you look . . . nice."

"The suit?" he asked with a raised brow. "I wasn't sure it would do, and it did cost . . . well, the motorcycle . . ."

She was up and out of her chair in a flash. "You didn't sell it?"

Gabe merely smiled, satisfied that he'd found who he was looking for. The warm woman with emotions surging just below the surface, not the cool socialite in executive wear. "Not without consulting you first."

She glared at his subterfuge and sank back into the chair again. "I'm glad you came."

"Still nervous about throwing down the gauntlet?"

"Nervous about failing again."

"Not the first charge?"

"No, and there are . . . complications," she told him with a frown. "Being the daughter of the man in charge has its advantages and disadvantages. Some people are willing to let you succeed because of who you are. There are others who are determined to see you fail for the same reasons."

Gabe nodded understanding. "You have a competitor."

"Yes," she agreed slowly. "One who was firmly entrenched before I came on board."

"It pays to know your enemy."

"It sometimes pays not to antagonize them, too."

"Negotiation rather than confrontation?"

"My father respects his opinion."

Gabe grunted.

"And we're part of the same company, the same team. We should work together." Her gaze lifted to his. "Besides, men hate aggressive women."

He grinned. "Oh, I don't know. Aggression has its place."

The look he gave her made her glad she was sitting, but he didn't linger on the subject. Instead he shrugged and walked away to the other side of the desk.

"Some women act as if they have something to make up for when competing with men. It can alienate people." He fingered the flower in the vase sitting by her calendar. "But business is war, and there's a difference between being aggressive and defending an idea you feel is right."

"Coming from a woman, some think it's the same thing."

"The insecure do." He watched her frown. "When do I meet this paragon of virtue who's afraid of a smart woman?"

She couldn't stop her smile. "Soon enough." Standing, she led him to a small conference room table in the corner of the room where papers were neatly stacked. "You said business is war. We're going into battle."

He watched her pat a pile of folders.

"This is my attack plan. I need you to go over some figures for me and give me your thoughts." She picked up the mass of papers and turned to him. "We're thinking of acquiring some property in Malibu. There's a meeting this afternoon to go over any proposals. I want mine to be the one they choose."

Gabe accepted the load she plopped in his arms with a raised eyebrow. "I thought hired help was supposed to be broken in easy."

"No one said this job was going to be easy," Danielle reminded him, and took his arm to escort him to the door. "Your office is right next to mine. Karen can get you whatever you need and will take you to Human Resources when they're ready to process you both in. The meeting's at three o'clock. You have an hour lunch break, and the coffeepot's down the hall in the copy room. I'll see you at two for a complete briefing.''

Left stranded beside what was to be his office door, Gabe watched her stride away. He liked the confidence in her step, especially the way it made her hips sway against the material of her skirt, and he liked her faith in him. He wasn't prepared to let her down, but if he was going to teach her anything, it was that she could release the control she kept on herself.

Upbringing no doubt had taught her to always appear calm and cool, to not get visibly rattled. But in doing business, letting go was okay on a regular basis. During negotiations—during corporate battle—raising your voice and your temper could serve its purpose. It made an opponent know you meant what you said. He sighed. Unfortunately, those personal lessons would have to wait. At least for a little while.

Nodding at Karen, whose real name he'd already figured was Kelly, he went inside the room and took a seat at the desk and began to read. It didn't take more than a couple of pages to catch his interest, and an hour later he barely noticed when Kelly quietly put a cup of black coffee beside him. He just kept reading.

The real estate involved was some of the best. Development had endless possibilities, and even in a depressed real estate market could be sold again in pieces or as a whole for a healthy profit. The consideration was, once bought, what way was best to proceed? Break up the whole into parts, slate it for business or residential use? What would bring the best recovery? The quickest capital turnaround?

Options popped into his head as he sipped the hot brew Kelly had brought him, but if he thought he was one step ahead of Danielle in his analysis, that was all he was. She lined up with his opinion every time, drawing clear and concise pictures of ventures and opportunities. And her figures were good. She knew what she was talking about and missed only a few drawbacks that were due more to inexperience than oversight. His research had told him that she'd been on the job for less than two years. She had a lot to learn yet, but she already knew enough to recognize a sweet deal when she saw it.

At lunch, Gabe convinced a stammering Kelly to go out to a corner deli with him. He wanted some insight into the operation of the office and its people. If she was hesitant to give it at first, by the end of the hour she was opening up and telling him what he wanted, and needed, to know.

Who she really was and why she was in disguise remained a mystery when they returned, but it wasn't one he needed to solve immediately. He was willing to wait for answers, and instead of wasting time wondering, he closed out possibilities and went back to the report that he'd locked in his new desk and quickly finished it.

BEHIND CLOSED DOORS but not far away from Gabe, Danielle started watching the clock the moment she walked away from him. Anxious for his thoughts, for his approval of her ideas. She knew her logic was sound, but she needed to hear someone else say it. For once, she needed someone to be on her side, in her corner and fighting for rather than against her.

When first moving into her office, she'd run all of her ideas through Malcolm. She'd wanted to ease into the operation smoothly, not ruffle feathers, and make friends with the other officers. It seemed the thing to do, but all too soon she'd learned that her trust had been misplaced. Malcolm had listened well enough. He'd also taken her thoughts and ideas and presented them as his own to the board or to her father behind her back.

She'd been silently fighting Malcolm ever since. Malcolm hadn't gotten where he was without learning a few tricks. While outwardly supportive, he always found a way to delay a decision or refute her facts on a project until he could represent her proposals as his own. Danielle's mouth thinned. But that wasn't going to happen this time. Everything was going to be solid this round. Irrefutable. She wasn't going to be relegated to the background anymore, to the projects Malcolm thought were too inconsequential. She was moving into the big leagues. Whether he wanted her there or not.

Abruptly the pencil she'd been holding snapped between her fingers. Danielle started at the sound, but the intensity of her feelings wasn't a surprise. She'd been patient. The projects she'd handled, she'd handled successfully and well, but still she was stymied from moving into other areas, bigger problems, more complicated transactions because Malcolm kept telling her father she wasn't ready.

Why she believed Gabe could help her change that, help her break Malcolm's influence on her father and the other officers, she couldn't say. He was just a man. One she knew next to nothing about. For all his seeming expertise, he might really be an ex-Hell's Angel, but she didn't think so. Didn't want to believe it. She wanted, needed, to trust him, and he'd done and said nothing to make her believe that she couldn't, and everything to believe she could.

Still, she had a lot of unanswered questions about Gabe Tyler. Throwing the broken pencil into the trash, she scowled at the paper she'd been trying to read for the past hour and determined to get hold of his résumé from the

Human Resources people as soon as she could. Background was important, and while she should have asked, she'd simply gone on instinct in asking him to work for her. And she didn't know if it was good to depend on instinct. Not with him.

He made her feel unbalanced. While mentally he could reassure, physically he set off all the alarms. Never had she met a man like him. She couldn't ignore his masculinity. It was too strong. But she would have to deal with it. After all, he was hardly her type, didn't come from her neighborhood. Unconsciously she squared her shoulders while gripping the paper in her fingers with determined intensity. The only type of relationship available to the two of them was professional. She was his boss, he her employee. Nothing more.

The electrical charges that kept jumping between them would just have to be ignored. She'd told him that she wanted him in her office, not her bed, and she'd meant it. The trouble was she kept remembering the heat of his body against hers, the strength of the muscles under her hands when she rode behind him on the motorcycle. She nearly sighed aloud. How easy it had been to touch and hang on. How tempting it was to do it again—on or off a bike.

With a murmur of angst, Danielle shook her head and looked at her wristwatch. One-thirty. She'd tried to stay inside the office, making Kelly come to her rather than going out to the desk when she needed something, but it had been hard. Especially when she'd finally gone out for lunch and seen her secretary getting into the elevator with Gabe.

Danielle sighed. She'd felt betrayed and angry, and why? How could she be so possessed—obsessed—by a man she barely knew?

A knock on the door provided welcome distraction, and she jumped at the interruption. "Come in." But it wasn't relief on the other side of the wooden barrier. It was Gabe.

He held up the heavy folders she'd given him hours before. "Am I too early?"

"What did you think?" she countered, knowing the response was too quick but finding it impossible to hide her anxiety as he stepped inside and kicked the door shut behind him.

"It looks like a good investment."

Wounded by his flat observation, she stiffened, ready to defend. "But?"

He dropped the folders on the table she'd taken them from earlier, but didn't look away from her as she remained behind her desk. "How badly do you want approval on this?"

Her eyes gleamed with determination. "Very."

He grinned. "Good, then come over here and sit down so we can make sure you get what you're after."

Danielle quickly joined him at the table and spent the next hour seated beside him with papers spread in organized chaos between them. Finally, slapping the folder shut, she frowned down at the tablet she'd been jotting notes on. "I think that does it."

"You did a good job."

"You did better."

He shrugged indifferently, unwilling to take the credit when she deserved it. "I just offered suggestions. You did the work."

Propping her elbow on the table, she rested her chin on her hand to study him as he sat back in the chair beside hers. Cool, confident, knowledgeable. Who was he? Surely not a man who simply rode a motorcycle from town to town. "We make a good team."

"Glad you hired me?"

"You bet," she assured him, and felt her toes curl as a slow smile spread across his mouth. It wouldn't do for her to start wondering what his lips tasted like, but as she licked her own in unconscious anticipation, both he and she leaned toward each other—until the door behind them suddenly burst open.

"Ms. Fitzsimmons, it's Mr.—" Kelly never got a chance to finish her sentence.

"Never mind, darling," a tall, blond man interrupted. Dressed in a smartly tailored suit that was accented by a splashy tie, he sent her a wink. "Ms. Fitzsimmons knows who I am."

"It's all right," Danielle said, standing with a cool nod of understanding and dismissal, but her stomach flipped in alarm as she watched the man in the door eye Kelly as she left to return to her desk. Had he recognized Kelly despite the disguise?

"You know, Danielle, your taste in secretaries has taken a decided dip for the worse."

The cool observation had Danielle gritting her teeth, but it was mixed with relief. The ruse had worked. "Malcolm..."

"Oh, and this must be your new boy." Malcolm Reed grinned, spotting Gabe and quickly noting the close proximity between him and Danielle. "I hope I wasn't interrupting anything."

Having followed Danielle to her feet, the unsubtly veiled insinuation had Gabe's fingers curling into fists. Without introduction, he was ready to plant his knuckles against the newcomer's teeth that were big and bright enough for any mouthwash commercial. Yet he had to remember his place and Danielle. He was in the office to help not hurt her, but as he watched her stiffen with regal fury and stalk up to the man, Gabe wondered if she was going to slug him for herself.

"Gabe Tyler, this is Malcolm Reed, my father's vice president in charge of operations," Danielle announced coolly. "Malcolm, this is Gabe Tyler."

Malcolm turned to give Gabe a condescending smile, but Danielle stepped between them to make sure his focus stayed on her.

"Gabe is not my boy. He is my associate, and as such, you will address him with the same respect you do me or, for that matter, anyone else who works for me."

Malcolm's eyebrows came together, and his smile faded.

"What you were interrupting was a final review of the report I'm about to give at the meeting, which is, I'll assume, why you came to fetch me. You really are too considerate."

Listening, Gabe relaxed his fingers. He liked Danielle's sarcasm. It dripped from every word with a deflating effect that had Malcolm Reed's bright blue eyes darkening, but if Danielle noticed Reed's reaction, she gave no indication. She continued on.

"And as far as my secretary goes, maybe you should remember that secretaries are here to work, not to be groped." Giving Malcolm one final, withering glare, she turned to Gabe. "Gabe, you're with me."

As she headed for the door, leaving Malcolm Reed in her wake, Gabe couldn't help grinning. And he couldn't help rethinking his plans of teaching her how to lose her temper. Ice worked as well as heat. She'd frozen Malcolm Reed where he stood without raising her voice. Maybe she didn't need to learn how to yell or slam doors. Maybe she could teach him something.

Hastily hurrying after her and past Malcolm, Gabe grabbed a stack of folders from Kelly, who'd already photocopied the proposal for presentation to the board, and headed for the hall. He was aware Malcolm Reed was following him, but Gabe was more aware of Danielle, who was a few steps ahead.

The anger was still running high. He could see it in her stiff shoulders, hear it in the decisive click of her heels on the tiled floor before she hit the carpet leading to the conference room. While it might not be the first time Malcolm Reed had gotten under her skin, Gabe had to believe it was the first time she'd come at the man swinging. Otherwise, Reed never would have made such vocal, intimate suggestions, or looked so surprised when she'd confronted him.

One step behind Danielle as she entered the conference room that was bordered by floor-to-ceiling windows on one side and computers, slide machines and screens on either end, Gabe figured he also knew why Kelly was masquerading as Karen, but if Malcolm Reed had a thing for the ladies, at least he wasn't dumb.

Gabe watched Reed smile and shake hands with an older man in a gray suit. If Reed had been stupid, he'd have made a play for Danielle. Or, maybe he had and been turned down. The thought had Gabe's blood boiling, but seeing Danielle smoothly meet and greet the other company officers entering the room, he doubted it. She had too much class for a man like Reed even though Reed surely would have contemplated the benefits of wooing the boss's daughter. The trouble was that such a relationship could cause problems, too, especially if Reed couldn't keep his attention on one woman at a time.

Gabe smiled satisfaction, sat back and watched the meeting begin.

Danielle was the only woman seated at the conference room table, but that didn't surprise Gabe. Lucas Fitzsimmons had a reputation for being old-fashioned, for run-

ning a traditional company with conservative standards, and
it showed in the decisions he made and the people he used
to help make them. Men. That meant Danielle was fighting
prejudice as well as the image of the boss's daughter, but
during the meeting she made intelligent comments, got approving responses and otherwise appeared respected. Still,
her father was apparently holding her back.

It seemed impossible to Gabe that Lucas Fitzsimmons
couldn't get past his own bigotry for the sake of his daughter, but he wasn't ready to believe that yet and had no more
time to think about it. Danielle was starting her presentation.

Holding his breath, he knew it could be the beginning she
needed to force the attention and responsibility she deserved. The project was big in scope, in value, in possible
profit. Bigger, said Kelly, than anything Danielle had ever
handled. All she had to do was not fumble after the kick-
off.

"I've investigated the property owned by Bob Anderson
and think you'll find we have some interesting options if we
choose to proceed with the purchase," Danielle announced, and nodded to Gabe to pass out the copies he'd
been holding.

The room got quiet as she spoke, but no one appeared
inattentive. Gabe watched for those who were ready to dis-
miss her before she began, but no one seemed so inclined.
When she was finished, not a person at the table was unaware of the benefits to be reaped from making a deal.

"I believe our best option when planning resale," Danielle concluded, "would be residential not commercial."

Several heads nodded agreement, but one officer sighed
in loud disapproval. "I believe I have figures that would
contradict that recommendation," Malcolm announced

with an expressive shrug. "But in any event, this entire project is unlikely to become reality."

Gabe stiffened, as did Danielle.

"Why not?" she demanded.

"Because Bob Anderson just isn't willing to sign on the dotted line," Malcolm said, turning away from her to address her father instead. "I've spoken with him several times, and again today, but he isn't willing to enter into a contract."

"The money?" Lucas Fitzsimmons asked.

"No," Malcolm denied. "He wants conditions on the sale. He wants to dictate terms in the contract that would limit what we could or couldn't do with the property after purchase."

"Such as?" Danielle asked.

"It hardly matters, Danielle." Malcolm smiled and dismissed in the same breath. "We simply can't have our hands tied."

Irritated, Danielle opened her mouth to speak again, but her father put up a hand to silence her.

"Do we have competition?" Lucas Fitzsimmons asked. "Is someone else bidding for rights?"

"I'm sure others are making inquiries," Malcolm responded with a nod. "I can try to find out what terms they're seeking—and their price."

"Do that," Fitzsimmons ordered and, rising, dismissed the meeting, but Danielle wasn't willing to give up that easily. She followed Malcolm out of the room and down the hall.

"I'd like to know more about Anderson's conditions," she insisted, keeping pace with Malcolm's longer strides.

"Danielle, I appreciate your concern," he assured her, not slowing his pace to accommodate her, "but I'm on top of this." He finally slowed as they approached her office door and Kelly's desk. "Nice report, by the way."

"Thank you, but if you'll let me work with you, maybe we can find a way around Anderson's objections." Danielle tried again. "This is too good an opportunity to let pass. The profit margin—"

"Yes, I know, and I appreciate your enthusiasm—as does your father." Malcolm smiled. "But—"

"I want to talk to him."

Malcolm blinked. "To whom?"

"Bob Anderson."

Malcolm laughed. "You'll have to wait for your own project, Danielle. This one's mine, and besides, if I can't convince him to sign, who can?"

The frustration and anger ran so deep, she couldn't speak as he walked away. She could only clench her teeth to stop from swearing—or crying. The project was right, her figures were good, the board approved, but . . .

"So, are you going to call Mr. Anderson, or should I?"

Danielle blinked and swung to look at Gabe. She'd forgotten him, forgotten everything except losing her goal, but the gleam in his eyes had her flagging spirits rising again. "I will." She turned to Kelly. "Kelly—"

"I've got his number right here," Kelly told her, flipping through a Rolodex. "I'll put him through as soon as I reach him."

"You do that," Danielle declared, and marched away, but this time Gabe didn't follow. He stayed where he was and returned Kelly's wink instead.

Chapter Five

Danielle knew she was late. The meeting always started at nine o'clock sharp every Tuesday morning, but her delay was understandable. Justifiable. Everyone would accept her tardiness, she was sure, if she could just get to the room!

Finally the conference room doors loomed ahead, and she spun to nearly collide with Gabe, who was following on her heels. He was in gray today with a white shirt. She didn't know how he could have gotten better looking in twenty-four hours, but he had. Or, maybe she was only tired, and her blurred vision from being up all night with him and Kelly, typing and sharpening the contract, was making him more attractive. But she doubted the lack of sleep had anything to do with it. "How do I look?"

Gabe retreated a step to let his gaze drop to go over her from head to toe and found little he could object to. Her black hair had been pulled back for the day, leaving her face clear to view and her eyes incredibly green. The business suit was a variant of the one she'd worn the day before. It was white instead of pearl gray and did little to hide her femininity but everything to present a businesslike air. He figured it'd put off most men, but not him. "Good enough to eat."

Her mouth fell open, her eyes widened in surprise and she nearly swayed on her feet.

Unrepentant, he grinned. "Sorry, you needed to have your mind taken off what's in your hand. You're too excited."

She managed to close her mouth and swallow the excitement that suddenly had nothing to do with the documents she was carrying. "Better?"

He reached out to take hold of her lapels in an apparent attempt to straighten them, but it was really an excuse to step closer, to breathe in her perfume and to watch the pulse in her throat jump in alarm. "Perfect."

Unexpectedly unable to get any air in her lungs, Danielle gasped.

He smiled, liking the way her eyes had dilated, and released her. "How about dinner tonight?"

"Dinner?" Eating was the farthest thing from her mind with him standing next to her.

"You'll want to celebrate."

"Celebrate?"

His grin widened, and he nodded to the door behind her. "Your victory."

"Yes, of course," she stammered, and fumbled for the handle. "You're coming?"

"Blow in my ear, and I'll follow you anywhere."

Flushing to the roots of her hair, she stepped inside the room and felt a chill hit her as a dozen pairs of eyes stabbed her where she stood. It was sobering enough to get her attention back where it belonged. "Gentlemen, please excuse my late arrival, but I believe you'll understand why when I show you this."

Her father scowled at her from the head of the table, his brown eyes brooding and filled with disapproval. "Really, Danielle, we were in the middle of discussing—"

"Bob Anderson, I hope," she interjected with a disarming smile. "Because I have his signed contract right here."

"Signed...!" Malcolm nearly jumped out of his seat, and murmurs erupted up and down the table as Gabe swiftly passed out a copy of the contract to everyone present.

"I visited with him last night, and we took a drive together out to the site in Malibu, where we discussed his concerns about the sale," Danielle explained, immediately silencing the whispers of speculation as she stood by her chair at the table. "It's a lovely area, and his worry in signing a contract with us is the possibility of seeing the land's natural beauty ruined."

"But..." One word was all Malcolm was allowed. A glare from Lucas Fitzsimmons stopped him.

"He doesn't want it torn up and made into a tower of condominiums or a shopping mall, and I believe he's right. It would be in our best interests to preserve the environment of the area. It would silence those who, in the past, have objected that our real estate dealings often neglect such concerns," Danielle continued, sparing a brief glance to Gabe, who was standing to the side smiling. Her heart skipped a beat, and she had to take a quick breath to regain her ability to speak. "And, in doing so, we won't lose a dime, as the figures I presented yesterday show. Dividing the parcel into residential lots—"

"I disagree," Malcolm objected. "My figures say otherwise, and your entering into a contract without the full board's approval endangers our position."

"Our position is not endangered," Danielle shot back. "The contract is exactly as you initially wrote it with very minor alterations, but if you have figures that would disprove mine, please present them. I'd like to see them—as would we all." The sweep of her hand took in everyone who was sitting at the table.

Malcolm followed her gesture to the others, who were all looking at him in silent expectation. He stammered. "I—I don't have them with me."

"We'll wait." Danielle smiled, and behind her Gabe coughed to smother the bark of laughter that was threatening to erupt from his throat. She had Reed on the hook and wasn't about to let him off.

Malcolm shrugged and straightened his tie. "They're only preliminary..."

"Thankfully, mine aren't," Danielle concluded and flipped a page on her copy of the contract to draw attention back to the matter at hand. "Gentlemen, you'll see the change on page two specifying the condition regarding residential sale, and if you'll also turn to the last page, you can read the only other change of great significance. It's a clause Mr. Anderson insisted on inserting regarding his future dealings with our company."

Lucas Fitzsimmons scowled as he read. "He wants no contact from anyone but you?"

"Apparently, he liked my style," Danielle responded, and took her seat without so much as a blink.

"You're good, lady," Gabe murmured in her ear half an hour later as he followed her from the conference room.

His praise meant more than she could say, but she had no chance to tell him. Not when Malcolm Reed touched her arm.

"Danielle."

She glanced at him over her shoulder but didn't stop. She made him hurry after her as he had forced her to do the day before. "Yes, Malcolm?"

"You really should have consulted me about this."

"Why?"

"The legal issues . . ."

"There were no legal issues. I have full authority to sign a contract for the company."

"You were lucky."

"I was right." She stopped to confront him. "You're just angry because you didn't get his name on the dotted line."

Malcolm's lips curled. "Maybe he just liked dealing with a skirt."

Danielle's glare was glacial. "I'll forget you said that, Malcolm. Just like I'll forget to mention to my father that you never contacted Mr. Anderson yesterday like you said you did."

Malcolm blinked but stopped her when she swung away. "It's just one victory, Danielle. Don't let it go to your head."

Having seen the first glare while standing off to the side, Gabe was glad he wasn't the one receiving the second, and it gave him great satisfaction to see Danielle force Reed to take a step backward.

"It's one of many to come," she promised with cool certainty. "Remember that, Malcolm, and stay out of my way." She started to turn but abruptly stopped. "And one more thing." She went toe-to-toe with him. "If you ever try to steal one of my ideas again, I'll ram it down your throat in front of the entire board."

Malcolm's eyes darkened in unspoken menace, but the gleam of animosity was quickly covered by a sigh, a shrug and an apologetic smile. "Danielle, we're a team. We're not going to war here."

"Oh, yes, we are," she denied. "You declared it as soon as I walked through the door and took an office, and by default, you won the first few skirmishes. But I just took the first battle. Let me know when you want to sound the retreat."

Malcolm never got the chance to respond. She whirled away, and Gabe quickly fell into step behind her as she stormed down the hall. He was proud of her. As a student, she was a quick study. He figured she was as close to losing her temper as she ever had been, and if a door had been handy, he guessed that she might just have been tempted to slam it. That kind of behavior deserved a reward. He touched her arm and asked, "How's that celebration sound now?"

Her steps slowed as she met his grin. "I could use a drink."

"Is an early lunch an option?"

Her laughter followed them down the hall to her office door.

"TO YOUR VICTORY."

Laughing, Danielle touched the rim of her glass to Gabe's. "We already drank to that." They were at a restaurant by the ocean, sitting at one of the tables on a patio overlooking the rolling sea. The early lunch hadn't happened. They'd had to wait for the chance to eat and celebrate, had to leave the office separately before meeting again at night, after the sun had set, to savor "the win" the two of them had achieved together.

She hadn't had enough champagne to make her feel as warm and silly and wonderful as she did. She supposed it might be Gabe making her feel all those things.

"We need to do it again because I keep seeing Malcolm Reed's face when you announced you had a signed contract." He was encouraging her because he liked to hear her laugh, see her smile, watch her eyes shine with humor and then darken with the unspoken emotion that was rippling between them. He touched the rim of his glass to hers. The cool socialite was gone. Sitting with him was the woman behind the mask, and he wanted to know her better. "Do you know that your eyes turn from green to gray?"

She hid her smile behind her glass. "Yours are dark and mysterious—like you."

A grin came to curve his lips. "You make me sound like the villain in a horror movie."

"No," she quickly objected, her hand reaching across the table so that her fingers linked with his. "The hero."

"Do you see me charging to some damsel's aid?"

"You came to mine."

"You didn't need my help. What you did, you did on your own. I only gave you a little push to make sure you did what you wanted and knew you had to."

"Maybe." She stared into his eyes. "You are dark and mysterious, you know. I don't know anything about you except that you ride a motorcycle and look wonderful in a business suit."

"Wonderful?"

"Gorgeous."

"Stop. You're making me blush."

His eyes dropped from hers as he pushed his glass aside, but there was no heat in his cheeks under the beard that was growing thicker every day. She wanted to touch it to see how it felt, stiff and hard or smooth and soft, but somehow she managed to keep her fingers wrapped around her drink. "Tell me about you."

"I'd rather hear about you."

She rolled her eyes. "You're very good at that."

"What?"

"Turning the conversation back on the person asking the question." She frowned. "I think you're really a politician or maybe a diplomat who's traveling incognito."

He reached for the bottle of champagne to refill their glasses. "Maybe I'm an industrial spy, a modern-day pirate, sent from another country to steal American technology."

"That would match your beard."

Her quick retort had him laughing, and she pulled her hand away from the glass with a scowl.

"I'm serious. How many politicians do you know who have beards? And you did remind me of a pirate the first time I saw you."

"I thought it was a Hell's Angel?"

"That, too," she agreed as a smile crept across her mouth.

"I love a woman who can make up her mind."

"Well, I can't. Not about you."

"Back to that again." He signaled to the waiter that they were finally ready to order and successfully diverted her attention from him, at least for a few minutes.

"I think you used to own a business," she announced as soon as the waiter was gone.

Gabe sat back in his chair, stretching his legs out beneath the table and watching her as he swirled the champagne in his glass. "Why do you say that?"

"Because of all you know about running one." She shrugged. "Those figures you went over, the suggestions you made. You understood everything about it."

"Maybe I just ran a good bluff." Her eyes narrowed on him, and he grinned. "Okay, so I understand real estate transactions and can read a contract."

"You wrote one, too."

"A law student could do that."

She glowered at him. "What about the way you dress?"

"What about it?"

"Your suits," she said, admiring the white sports coat he wore over a blue shirt in rakish style. The shirt was open at the neck, revealing an expanse of tan skin. It made her wonder how his flesh would feel, too. "You didn't get them at a bargain basement."

"And that proves I owned my own business?"

"It proves you were, maybe are, successful. That you're more affluent than I thought."

"Maybe I spent my life savings to impress you. Tomorrow I could come in wearing my leather jacket and jeans."

Her eyes narrowed again, but the glitter in them was due more to frustration than fury. "You're not going to tell me."

"It's more fun making you guess."

She looked away from him and into her champagne. "I read the application they had you fill out in Human Resources."

"That was underhanded," he told her, but he was smiling as he watched her nonetheless.

"It didn't tell me a thing."

When her eyes collided with his, they were accusing and reflected disappointment, but he was more interested in their color that was set off perfectly by the soft mint green of the shell she was wearing over a white, split skirt. She wasn't wearing stockings. He'd already looked. Just sandals. He tipped his head to the side with what appeared to be a sincere frown. "Nothing?"

She pouted. "Just that you're three and a half years older than me—if you told the truth."

"Would I lie?"

"Would you?"

He leaned forward to set his glass on the table. "Why do you care?"

"Because you interest me."

His grin returned. "We have something in common. You interest me, too." Sparks erupted between them with silent promise and heat, but he sat back again to study her and broke the intimacy warming between them. "I keep won-

dering how it is that with old-fashioned parents and surrounded by stuffed shirts at work day after day—except for
Reed, who should be in toothpaste commercials instead of
investments—you turned out the way you did.''

Danielle collapsed with laughter. "He does have a lot of
teeth.''

"Absolutely. All of them pearly white. I think they're
capped.''

The soup came. French onion with cheese melted across
the top. She breathed in the aroma and reached for a spoon.
"Do you think I'm a snob?''

"You try to be.''

"Only try?''

Gabe sipped his soup. "A snob wouldn't go off for a
motorcycle ride in the dead of night with a stranger, much
less give him a job in her office.''

She grinned. "I'm glad I'm different from them.''

His eyebrows shot up in surprise. "Want to explain
that?''

She shrugged. "It was just, growing up, I tried to act and
be like they were, but the more I was away from home, the
less I seemed to be able to do it.''

"They sent you to school?''

"The very best,'' she said with a sigh. "I think it must
have been seeing the other girls in the school with me that
made me turn out the way I did. They were supposed to be
examples for me to follow, by paying attention to how they
acted.'' She grimaced. "Too much of what they did and said
convinced me that I *didn't* want to be like them.''

"College?''

She smiled. "That was the best. Complete freedom.'' She
sent him a conspiratorial grin. "I told my parents I was going to Radcliffe, but I didn't. They were furious when they
found out.''

"But you enjoyed it?"

"I liked being treated like a normal person, whatever that is." She shrugged. "The young women I went to school with weren't like me. They didn't have money to burn."

"You didn't tell them?"

She flushed. "No. I wanted to belong, and they accepted me. Trusted me without question." Her color deepened. "I used to leave twenty-dollar bills lying where my friends would find them when I knew they were broke. That was wrong, I suppose."

"Honesty isn't always the best policy." He finished his soup and put the bowl aside. "So they taught you the true meaning of a buck."

"I learned to appreciate doing without." She groaned. "I never ate so many hot dogs in my life."

He grinned. "Cheap food." The waiter came back with two shrimp appetizers, and she sat forward.

"This is much better."

He watched her slip the first shrimp into her mouth to savor it and for the first time in his life felt envy for a piece of food. "Did they ever find out?"

"I only stayed in touch with one. Linda." Danielle smiled. "We still write."

"And she forgave you for the deception?"

Danielle nodded. "I told her it was the best time of my life, and it was. Somehow, she understood that."

Gabe watched her push her dish aside. "What's your friend do?"

"Linda's a journalist. A good one." Danielle grinned. "I told her if she ever wants to come work for a Hollywood tabloid, I could get her plenty of interviews."

"Where's she live?"

"Boston. She likes snow."

He grimaced. "I don't think she'll move here, then."

"Have you ever lived where there's snow?"

"When I was young," he conceded, and she grinned.

"That wasn't so hard, was it?"

"Not all men like to talk about themselves."

"A myth?"

"For some."

The rest of the meal came and the playful talk subsided to less personal subjects, but Danielle was far from finished in trying to understand him better. Gabe Tyler had depths she wanted to explore, but it was too hard to concentrate on the search with champagne humming through her veins and him gazing into her eyes. She liked the attention. She liked him. Why simply didn't matter, and neither did who he was.

"Can we walk on the beach?" she asked as they left the restaurant to go to his motorcycle.

"You'll get your feet wet."

"So, I'll take my shoes off." And she did, in the middle of the parking lot, before sending him a taunting grin and dancing off toward the sand.

Watching her go, he hesitated, focusing on the enticing sway of her hips and the buzzing in his head. Yet it wasn't champagne making his head light. It was her. He hadn't had enough of the bubbly for it to have affected him, but he wanted, needed more of her. And if the saner part of him was warning that going out on a moonlit beach with her probably wasn't wise, the temptation was too much to resist. He followed her and watched her spin across the beach, but quickly found she didn't want to enjoy the surf alone. She held out her hand to him.

"Come walk with me."

He didn't have to be asked twice. Stepping forward, he caught her fingers with his. She swayed closer, but he avoided the kiss he wanted to take. He frowned as she wound her arm around his. Perhaps it was the taking that bothered him. She wasn't really ready to give it. Yet. Not to him. Just to whom she thought he was.

"I love the sea. When you listen, it seems to be whispering, but it never tells you its secrets." She looked up at him. "Just like you."

Guilt gave him an unfriendly stab, but he refused to give in to it. He wasn't hurting her. Didn't want to. Wouldn't. If he could help it. "You don't have any secrets?"

She bit her lip as she considered and breathed in deeply the scent of sand and sea. "I don't think so." She linked her fingers with his as sand squeezed between her toes. "You have to be interesting to have secrets."

He grinned. "And you're not?"

"Nope." She abruptly let go and raced off into the surf, wading in and lifting her skirt until the water lapping around her was almost knee-deep. "It's warm and wonderful! Come in with me!"

Left behind, he shook his head and refused to obey the nearly overwhelming urge to join her. "I can't. Somebody has to save you if you fall in."

"You don't trust me."

But she trusted him. He clenched his jaw and reminded himself that he hadn't lied to her.

"Won't you come in?"

Her plea had him weakening, but he shook his head. "I can't. I don't want to scare you."

She looked at him in question, a vision in the moonlight with her hair blowing in a quiet breeze, the water whispering at her feet and her eyes pools a man could drown in.

He swallowed against the growing want and pointed toward his shoes. "Ugly feet." He held out his hand. "Come on. It's late. We have to go to work tomorrow."

She groaned but couldn't refuse the need to go to his outstretched hand. A satisfied sigh escaped her as they fell into step together, fingers entwined. "It's a good thing you don't have a car."

"Why's that?"

"I'd get sand all over it."

He handed her a pair of glasses as they reached the motorcycle and she wobbled back into her sandals. "We'll blow it off."

"Good." Eagerly she followed him onto the machine, slipping on the glasses and wrapping her arms tightly around him. She didn't have to maintain such a determined grip. Not to stay on the bike. But she needed it to stay next to him, and her clinging touch suddenly made Gabe regret that he hadn't driven them in a car.

The way she was hanging on, with hands that stroked as they linked, a cheek that nuzzled between his shoulder blades and breasts that yielded to the hard width of his back, was making it difficult not to turn around to return the embrace. He cleared his throat, put his key in the ignition and tried to remember who she was and why he was with her. "Maybe I should let you drive."

"Would you?"

Gabe nearly groaned aloud when she let him go. "I think we should wait until it's daylight for your first lesson."

She moaned in disappointment, and he gritted his teeth as she made him suffer through the sweet agony of her relaxing against him again. "Soon."

"This weekend?"

"Promise?"

"Try to keep me away." But he should stay away. He should run like hell. She was driving him crazy, pushing his limits of sanity and willpower, but he wasn't willing to quit.

Not yet. She still needed him, wanted him, and he wanted to enjoy that as long as it lasted.

The night air was cool, the sky clear, the roads free of most traffic, but in no time it seemed Gabe was steering the bike up the driveway to her front porch. He grinned when he saw the door to the main entrance was well lit, and he looked over his shoulder to her.

"Why is it that parents always leave the lights on when they know one of their children is out on a date?"

"It's an unwritten law," she told him, reluctantly slipping from the bike and letting him go. "But they'll tell you it's because they want you to be able to see when you put your key in the lock."

"Think they're up now, watching us from behind a curtain?"

She followed his gaze to the seemingly dark and deserted panes of glass overlooking the drive. "If they are, they'll be waiting to see if you walk me to the door like a proper gentleman."

"Then let's not disappoint them." He kicked the stand into place and swung off the bike to solicitously take her arm.

"They were quite shocked when you appeared on a motorcycle," she told him as she turned to walk with him up the steps toward the door.

"I thought they would be."

"Actually, I think my mother thought it was incredibly romantic and would have loved to go in my place."

"And your father?" Gabe asked as they crossed the porch.

"Doesn't believe in fraternizing," she said with a dignified sniff. "You are only an employee after all."

Gabe laughed. "And you? What did you think?"

But he didn't have to hear her answer. Not when he could see it in her eyes, eyes that darkened in wonder and anticipation.

Suddenly he was aware of how quiet it was, how alone they were, and of how it might feel to have his arms around her instead of the other way around as it was on the bike. And she seemed to understand his want even as he tried to deny the need. She leaned closer, and he lost hold of common sense and made his second mistake of the night.

He reached out to touch her.

Chapter Six

When Gabe's hands dove into her hair, Danielle gasped and stumbled forward to plant her hands against his chest.

"I've wanted to do this since I first saw you," he told her, his voice rough and grating as his fingers combed through the black mass of thick strands. He tugged gently to make her lift her head. "And this, too."

His mouth covered hers, the strength went out of her knees and she collapsed against him in a trembling heap. But if she expected his embrace to be tender, tentative, she was wrong. His kiss wasn't soft. Not like a first date's usually was. He offered no tenuous touch or inquisitive grasp. He took what he wanted, and the greed and want his mouth possessed set off alarms. But they were easy to ignore. She closed her eyes and stepped head-on into the storm, leaving it for him to find a way to struggle back to sanity.

"I probably shouldn't have done that."

"Probably," she agreed, the vibrant timbre of his words sending a delicious shiver through her body, but she didn't care about shoulds and shouldn'ts. Not when the heat of his skin was warming hers and not when keeping him at arm's length was something she knew was impossible. Gabe Tyler wasn't a man to be contained or held at bay. She'd recognized that in him from the start. Had wondered at it, been intrigued by and fought against it. She gave up the fight and released the stranglehold she had on his shirt to reach up to bring him back down to her.

It was an action that forced him to swallow her sigh. Yet it was a sweet reward, and he was ready for another taste. The first nibble had been overwhelming, her flavor so all-consuming that he'd nearly devoured her whole. But he wanted to savor the next taste. He wanted to enjoy every nuance of her mouth as she pressed it to his.

Coaxing her lips open, his exploration deepened until the blending was such that he didn't know where he ended and she began. It was a startling realization, and it made it easy for him to abruptly break away from her.

"I'll see you in the morning."

Not waiting for her to agree, disagree or respond, Gabe just strode away, jumped on the bike and thundered out the drive, but he couldn't escape the desire burning in his blood. He could only curse himself for being drawn in, for forgetting that he was with her only because the challenge had appealed and the game she'd offered had compelled him. But he didn't want to play anymore. At least, not by the original rules, because the stakes had changed.

He didn't want just what he'd set out to accomplish. He wanted more—which would be acceptable if he didn't keep forgetting what it was he had originally set out to achieve.

Cursing himself again, he roared down the freeway toward his own exit ramp.

Losing track of a goal was unheard of. At least for him. He was known for his single-mindedness, his unerring aim, his unrelenting drive in going after—and getting—whatever it was he wanted. That quality was what made people either love or hate him, depending on what side of the negotiating table they were sitting on.

But Danielle Fitzsimmons had managed to distract him. She was the first and only person to do that in years—since his inexperience had given way to hard-line decision making that allowed him to ignore sentiment and go straight for the jugular. It made him wonder about getting involved with her, staying involved, and it made him doubt himself. And he didn't like that.

Pulling into his driveway, Gabe coasted into the garage where he parked the bike before going up the short flight of stairs into his house and the living room to impatiently click on a light.

It annoyed him that he'd lost sight of what he was doing, especially when all it took was the stimulation of his libido. Danielle Fitzsimmons was more than he'd expected. The whole situation was. He stalked to one end of the room only to pace back again. And that was the problem. He'd made an error in judgment.

The challenge Danielle had offered wasn't like those he was used to taking on. This venture had emotional issues, something he could usually ignore in the coldhearted world of business. But that wouldn't work this time, because instead of dealing with hard facts and buildings and figures, he was contending with a woman who had wants and needs that were triggering wants and needs of his own. It was an unexpected complication.

A smile spread across his mouth; he was used to dealing with complications. And, as complications went, he'd suffered through worse than Danielle. Still, she was a problem he'd have to deal with. The pull of attraction that erupted so easily between them would have to be ignored, set aside, until he was free to deal with it. And her. And until she knew who he really was.

Gabe grabbed the phone and punched out a number, mindless to the time and the groggy mumble that came across the line. "Sam, it's Gabe. What did you find out about that property in Malibu? Why didn't we know about it?"

A long groan was his first reply, rapidly followed by a resentful, "Do you know what time it is?"

"That wasn't the answer I was hoping for." But Gabe's lips twitched nonetheless.

"You're heartless."

"That's why I'm so good at what I do."

"Tell that to someone who doesn't know you," Sam grumbled. Gabe could tell that he was searching for the light and consciousness on his end of the phone connection. "Why are you up so late?"

"Celebration."

"Same lady?"

Gabe grunted.

"It doesn't sound as if it went very well."

"It went well enough under the circumstances," Gabe responded, his blood heating again as he remembered the embrace on Danielle's porch. The truth was going to have to come out soon. "But I'm starting to feel like a spy inside the enemy camp."

"She does know who you are, doesn't she?"

"She knows my name."

Silence filled the phone line.

"The property?" Gabe prompted, unwilling and not in the mood for lectures or philosophical comment from his friend.

"It was a private sale. That's why we—and everybody else—knew nothing about it. It went through a Realtor who's an old friend of Lucas Fitzsimmons, but Fitzsimmons never got it directly. It went through one of his officers, Malcolm Reed."

Gabe frowned. But Malcolm had led Fitzsimmons to believe there were other bidders, probably to make it look as if he was working harder than he was to close the deal when he'd actually just been waiting for the seller to cave in—an act that could have lost the sale completely if the seller had gone elsewhere. "I've met him."

"Sounds like you liked him, too."

"Let's just say he reminds me of a particular piece of anatomy on a horse."

"Front end or back?"

Gabe grinned. "What's the story on the takeover?"

"The bidding is hot and heavy."

"Fitzsimmons still in it?"

"With Malcolm Reed leading the charge."

Gabe felt relief lessen the weight of guilt. At least Danielle wasn't standing directly in his path. That left possibilities for the two of them even if there was a bloody battle. "You're—"

"Following your instructions to the letter, boss."

"Deadlines?"

"None have been set. They're either holding out and trying to shake everyone off, or they're waiting for the numbers to go higher."

"Up the ante."

"Any suggestions?"

"Use your imagination. I'll be in touch." Gabe hung up and shoved his hands in his pants pockets as he wandered restlessly to the patio doors.

Half of him wanted to back out of his job with Danielle. It would leave him free to pursue her on a different level—if she'd still have him when she found out who he really was—but he didn't like leaving jobs half done. And she was still vulnerable.

With her victory in Malibu, she'd shown her father, Malcolm Reed and the rest of the board that she was a power to be reckoned with, but her battles were far from over even if she had finally realized nice guys finish last and that teamwork didn't always mean being a team player. Malcolm Reed would be out for revenge, and he was bound to play dirty. Given the chance, he'd undercut her with her father, and Gabe didn't want that to happen. It would hurt her—not that, save for an attraction he was sure would pass once the heat of passion had been unleashed to burn itself out, he was overly concerned with what happened to her.

She was a big girl and could take care of herself. Otherwise she wouldn't be where she was in her father's firm. It was just that he didn't like anyone tearing down what he'd built up, and he had only just started turning Danielle into the fire-breathing business exec she needed to be to play in the major leagues of corporate combat. Problem was, could he keep his hands to himself during the transformation? When the ice she tried to keep herself encased in started to melt, he couldn't imagine standing idly by.

Gabe smothered a sigh. But keeping her at arm's length was only a small part of his worries. He had a job to do, a decision to make, and when it came time to look out for himself, he didn't know if he could protect her, too. Or keep intact the feelings of mutual attraction that were pulling them closer together.

DANIELLE HURRIED BACK down the corridor toward her office, excitement making her steps quick, but her speed and the rhythm of her step faltered when she rounded the corner and saw Gabe waiting at the desk outside her door.

Immediately her heart thudded off beat, her pulse accelerated and she desperately tried to remember all of the excuses she'd thought up, after he'd left her on the porch, to justify her behavior of the previous night.

The champagne had been a contributing factor. She'd had too much of it. That was why she'd lost control and ended up in his arms. It wasn't that it had been inevitable, that the pull of him as a man appealed to her as a woman. Or, even if that was it, she had better sense.

He wasn't for her. She wasn't for him.

They were too different. They came from different worlds. Oil didn't mix with water. But it'd felt like a flood when he'd kissed her. She'd nearly drowned in the waves of sensation she'd felt while in his arms.

Danielle gave herself a mental shake and continued to walk. She'd have to explain, make him understand that there was a line that couldn't be crossed. She wasn't willing to cross it. Not really. Sex appeal was great and satisfaction sweet, but it was also short-lived. And, in this case, with them being who they were, it was ill-advised. But how did she tell him to stay away when her body was already humming because he was near?

Gabe looked up as she stopped by him, his dark eyes giving away nothing, and she took a breath. Maybe he would be a gentleman. The evening embrace wouldn't have to be discussed, but with him, she never knew. That was part of the mystery, part of what made her keep moving closer to him when she should be moving away. Was he really who she thought he was? "Gabe, can I see you in my office?"

He followed silently, closing the door behind him and remaining quiet as she paced restlessly back and forth behind her desk. "Problem?"

The quiet prompt had her clenching and unclenching her hands together and her stomach somersaulting. She turned to face him. "Actually, yes—and no." But looking into his eyes, she found herself unable—or unwilling—to bring up a personal side to a conversation when there was business to discuss. She lifted her chin. It was why she'd hired him after all. "The Malibu project? My father's agreed to let me handle the development."

A slow smile spread across his mouth. "Great. So what do you want me to do?"

"I don't know."

His eyebrows went up as she gestured helplessly.

"I mean, I've never done anything like this before, and suddenly I don't know what to do!"

Gabe moved closer. "Take a deep breath."

She did as he said.

"Now, tell me, what's the first thing you need before you can plan any project?"

"Financing."

He shrugged. "See, you know what to do. You just can't let emotion blind you."

Relief had her sighing. "Okay. So I call the bank, but what about a contractor? Bids?"

"The bank can give you some recommendations. Banks, after all, are very particular about to whom and how they lend money."

"Or, Malcolm could have some suggestions." Danielle considered with a frown. "He's done this more times than I can count."

"Do you really think Malcolm wants you to succeed?"

The frank statement brought Danielle up short, and she sank down into the chair behind her desk to bite her lip. "You have a point," she finally admitted. "But won't the bank recommend the same people he would?"

"Not necessarily, and only if you use the same bank he does. Why not choose a different one?"

"But we've always—"

"Rules were meant to be broken," Gabe interrupted. "Besides, competition is good for the soul. A new bank's going to want to impress you because they're going to want more of your business."

She smiled slowly and sat back to admire the way his beard was filling out to line the square strength of his jaw. "You've done this before."

"I've been involved in putting up a building or two."

His shrug was nonchalant, but her curiosity was piqued. Again. "For yourself?"

"Why do you ask?"

"Why won't you answer the question?"

He grinned, recognizing her frustration but unwilling to satisfy it. The time wasn't right. "I told you, it's more fun making you guess."

Resentment sparked anger, but the heat that ignited between them had little to do with fury as her eyes locked with his in silent combat. More, it was desire that stirred her blood, and suddenly she was drowning again. Finding it difficult to break away from the warmth of his gaze, she managed by sitting up straight and wheeling her chair tightly next to her desk to use it as a shield against him. Somehow, though, it seemed a feeble defense. "Gabe, about last night..."

"Our celebrating got out of hand."

Danielle's eyes flew to his in surprise and quickly darkened with disappointment at his ready and easy dismissal of their heated embrace.

"I didn't say I was sorry," Gabe told her, recognizing the emotions too easily read in her eyes and coming forward to put his hands on the desk so that he could lean toward her.

Unconsciously, drawn like a magnet, she leaned forward, too.

"I just prefer we wait a while before testing that balcony."

"Balcony," she repeated numbly, wondering how his mouth had so quickly gotten to within mere inches of hers and if his lips would be as firm, as coaxing, as devastatingly sapping as she remembered if he kissed her again.

"I'll go call the bank."

She almost hit her chin on the desk when he abruptly swung away. "Bank?"

"You'll want to set up a meeting."

"Meeting," she murmured in bemused agreement, struggling to catch up with him, get her mind back on the conversation and business at hand, and act like the professional she was pretending to be.

"As soon as possible?"

Seeing him stop at the door to look back at her, the hunger in his eyes said he could have cared less about the bank or the meeting. And neither could she. She licked her lips and watched his gaze focus on the action. "Absolutely."

His hand hesitated on the knob, and she held her breath. Would he come back to her? But suddenly the door was opening of its own accord, and Malcolm Reed was striding inside.

"Danielle, your father tells me that you'll be handling the development of the Malibu property."

"Yes," she agreed, her guard snapping up, her back stiffening and her gaze sharpening on her unwelcome intruder. "Gabe and I were just discussing calling the bank about financing."

Malcolm smiled, the flash of teeth bright in his deeply tanned face, and ignored Gabe who stood not two feet from him. "Moving quickly, aren't we?"

Danielle merely smiled, trying but unable to see any malice in his eyes or his words.

"I'll be happy to help," Malcolm offered agreeably. "I can give you the names of some contractors, or if you need advice..."

"I appreciate the offer, Malcolm. Any assistance you can give would be appreciated, wouldn't it, Gabe?"

"Of course," he rapidly agreed.

But watching him, Danielle realized that, like Malcolm, she could read nothing in Gabe's eyes. She nodded to him. "Why don't you go set up that meeting? I'll chat with Malcolm for a while."

Gabe hesitated, unwilling to leave her alone for fear she'd be talked into something that would put her behind rather than ahead of the game. But when his eyes locked with hers again, he recognized the steel in her green gaze. She wasn't ready to be duped, misled or patronized, but she was going to let Malcolm think she was. For a little while, anyway.

Gabe swallowed his words, smothered a smile and went out the door to set up the meeting. Maintaining his silence when he would have liked to speak was something he found himself doing a lot of over the next few days as he followed Danielle through one business meeting after another.

It was difficult to sit back and let someone else do the work when he was used to taking charge himself. But if his patience was tried while he sat with Danielle through endless sessions with bankers and contractors, at least he was never bored. And she remained open to his input. She didn't always agree with his suggestions, but she never dismissed them without thought or being able to give a logical argument, either. He found it exasperating when she followed her own line of reasoning to a decision, especially when he felt he could get the same result faster if she followed his, but it was exhilarating, too. She had a sharp mind, and he liked watching it, and her, work.

"What do you think, Gabe?"

He turned his head to look at her. It was Friday afternoon. Standing with her in the setting sun, he'd been listening to the contractor they were considering hiring as the
three of them stood on the Malibu hillside overlooking
ocean, beach and sloping shore. Gabe nodded. "I think it
sounds good."

"I do, too."

Her smile was enough to make his heart skip, his stomach flip and his mouth water for another taste. And when
she directed her attention to the contractor, the man was
equally bowed by the brilliance of her acceptance, the shine
of her eyes and the femininity that couldn't be disguised by
a business suit or agenda. "You'll get us the bid by Monday?" Gabe asked, rescuing the man as he tried to stammer
out a sentence.

"I'll hand deliver it."

"We'll see you Monday, then," Danielle said, offering her
hand and continuing to smile as her fingers disappeared in
a grip that was twice the size of hers. Grady Thompson was
big and rough, but he knew his business. It showed in his
suggestions, his enthusiasm and his experience. He'd
worked out in Malibu before, and he'd proudly taken her
and Gabe on a tour of some of the homes he'd erected along
the California coast before laying out his ideas for the new
project. "I like him," she said, looking away from the contractor's departing figure to Gabe.

"Not a requirement when doing business, but it makes
things easier," Gabe agreed. "He'll do good work."

She sighed in satisfaction, feeling confident and secure
that the project was proceeding at a good pace. "The bank
was right about him, and you were right about the bank."
She watched Gabe shrug and look away to gaze out at the
waves rolling in to pound the shore in a soothing rhythm.
Like her, his suit jacket was being held not worn. It was a

concession to the temperature. The summer was rapidly dying away, but its heat was continuing on the back of the Santa Ana winds that had already started the first seasonal fire.

She let her eyes wander over him. The suit he had on was another in a series of well-cut, expensive business wear that he'd worn throughout the week. This one was light tan and clashed not at all with the arrogantly striped tie that was still knotted, if askew, at his throat. But she'd ceased to wonder, over the long hours of negotiations and meetings, about his attire or his business sense. She just accepted and expected both from him, just as she had stopped believing he was simply a motorcycle groupie who owned nothing but his bike and leather jacket.

Why he'd wanted her to believe he was penniless and broke she had no idea, nor could she understand why he'd needed the job she'd offered him. His application hadn't set forth much in experience, but that, she was sure, had been by purpose not lack of expertise. Gabe was hiding something. He was hiding his true identity—or running away from it.

A small frown touched her mouth. She wanted to determine which but didn't know how hard—or if—she should try to find out.

The mystery of him intrigued, enticed, puzzled, but some mysteries were better left unsolved. Except she wanted to know more about him. Very badly...

"Are you coming to the party tonight?" she asked, interrupting his thoughts and wondering what they were, but all wonder vanished when he turned to level his dark gaze on her.

"I thought your father frowned on fraternizing."

"This is different. This party is for all company officers, their families and their staff. Besides," she said, cocking an eyebrow at him in question. "I thought you didn't care what my father thought." But she didn't wait for his answer. She turned to start down the hill toward her car. He rapidly followed.

"I never said that."

"You didn't have to," she told him over her shoulder. Breathing the sea-salted air was like an elixir. She loved the ocean. Her dream was to some day live in a house right beside it.

"Still think I have an attitude?"

"Don't think. Know."

"How's that?" he asked, reaching her side and falling into step beside her.

"It shows in your eyes."

He grinned. "What does?"

"Your attitude." She glanced at him. "Like when I decided not to go with that other contractor. You thought you were right."

His grin grew. It had been one of their more lively debates. "Everyone has an opinion."

"You like making decisions. Makes me wonder if that's why you were without a job when I met you."

His eyebrows arched.

"If I'd been a man, I think you would have punched my lights out." She stopped to face him in front of her car. "Maybe you did punch your last boss."

Gabe shook his head as he thought of his father. "Nope. I just disagreed with him—all the time."

"Thankfully that hasn't happened to us," she said, turning toward the driver's door.

"Yet."

She stopped to look at him again and was suddenly struck once more by the pirate in him. His dark hair was blowing in the breeze, his legs were set wide apart as if he were balancing on a tilting deck, and his suit coat was carelessly tossed and held over one shoulder as he confronted her. All he needed was a sword and an eye patch to make the illusion complete. Even incomplete, seeing him so took her breath away. "You're expecting us to disagree?"

He smiled slowly, and the heat in his gaze reached out to make her blood begin to boil. "At first, but I think we'll come to an amicable agreement."

"Really?" she responded, crossing her arms in front of her in a vain attempt to ward him off. "That sure of your persuasive skills?"

"Sure you'll want to be persuaded."

This time it was her eyebrows that arched. "Cocky, aren't we?"

He stepped around the bumper to stop before her, and the temperature on the beach seemed to go up another fifty degrees. "Just confident." He lifted a finger to run it down her arm, bare below the sleeveless shell she wore. Her skin was as soft as he remembered. "We work well together."

"We think alike," she agreed, refusing to step back even though her flesh was burning from his touch.

"Sometimes." He pushed his free hand into his pocket and away from the temptation to touch her again. "But I think you don't like fraternizing, either."

"What do you mean?"

He put his head next to hers to breathe in her perfume and whisper in her ear. "You're trying to keep me at arm's length." He leaned back to put his face directly in front of hers and watched her eyes darken and her pulse leap erratically in her throat. "It won't work."

It was more a promise than a threat, and she was more thrilled than afraid. And she was beginning to believe he was right. Shallow or not, proper or not, socially acceptable or not, she was ready to set aside right and wrong if he would just take her in his arms again. But she wasn't willing to be conquered too easily. She wasn't going to surrender, yet. "Maybe."

His smile was unworried as she turned away to unlock the door.

"Can I drop you somewhere?"

He waited until she was seated and closed the door for her before going to the passenger side and responding. "The office. I need to pick up my bike."

She started the engine. "I could drive you home. Even pick you up to take you to work tomorrow."

He didn't answer, and she was forced to turn her head to meet his gaze as the air conditioner began to hum.

"What?" she asked innocently, refusing to acknowledge the light of humor in his eyes. "I'm just trying to be helpful."

"You're just being curious."

Scowling, she reached for the gear lever. "You *are* cocky."

"No, it's just that I know that the only address I put on my application was a post office box."

She gritted her teeth. He was also a mind reader. Putting the car in Drive but leaving her foot on the brake, she turned her head again to glare at him. "I *am* going to find out more about you whether you want me to or not."

His smile had her heart accelerating before the car did. "I'm willing to let you find out all you want."

Suddenly finding it hard to get air into her lungs, she hastily returned her attention to the windshield and the gas pedal and away from the man sitting beside her. Only it was impossible to escape thoughts of him, or of all the possibilities that lay between and before them, when his cologne, his sweat, his very presence demanded she give him every consideration. And when she couldn't wait for the discovery to really begin.

Chapter Seven

Gabe wandered around the backyard of the Fitzsimmons manor, mingling with the other guests, admiring the swimming pool, strolling in the garden and looking for Danielle. He'd been at the party for nearly an hour already, and he hadn't seen her yet.

He raised his glass of champagne while looking over the multitude of people around him. Perhaps she was avoiding him. He sipped at the mellow but soothing liquid. But he didn't really think so. That wasn't her style. She didn't run from challenges. That was part of her appeal—as was the fact that she was willing to throw convention, society and all the rules away to let him make insane and passionate love to her.

He skimmed the faces surrounding him, most of which he recognized from the office, but unconsciously searched on for the one he wanted. It wasn't arrogance telling him that Danielle was as willing as he was for the passion to begin. It was human nature. He was a man, she was a woman, and when the two of them were together, the sparks flew. She might be trying to ignore it, he might be temporarily resisting it, but it was there. Undeniably. Unavoidably.

He began walking again. It was odd, but he couldn't remember pursuing or wanting to pursue another woman more than Danielle.

The chase was something he enjoyed. It was a subtle game of intrigue and suspense that he liked to play, and his prey were always beautiful and intelligent. Danielle wasn't any different in that respect, but in other ways, somehow, she was. He couldn't quite pinpoint why or what made her unlike the other women he'd come to be involved with. She was, simply, unique....

"Donald, there really isn't anything more to say."

The words stopped Gabe as he strolled beside the house. They'd come from Danielle. But he couldn't see her. He was alone in the shadows as far as he could tell.

"Look, if it's about the other night..."

The male voice led Gabe to look up, and a grin burst across his mouth. The balcony.

"It's not," Danielle interrupted. "It's more than that, and you know it." She sighed and studied the scowling man before her. Donald Riley was tall and blond and handsome in the tuxedo he was wearing. He was also rich and had a bright future. But even if he was, or at least should be, everything Danielle wanted in the man who wanted to marry her, she wasn't interested.

"Donald, you're a nice man."

"But not nice enough for you."

Danielle reached out to stop him when he would have swung away. "Nice has nothing to do with it. We just don't see things the same way."

"Would you like to?"

Danielle smiled into the brown eyes searching hers and wondered briefly why the shade didn't seem as dark as it should be. "We can't change who we are even if we want to."

"Meaning you won't change your mind? You won't reconsider?"

"I won't marry you, Donald. I'm flattered, but..."

"We could make it a long engagement. It would give you some time." Donald took his hands from his pockets to grasp her by the arms. "It's a big step, I know. For both of us, but it will work out if we let it. Let's just take things slowly and see what happens, okay?"

Danielle opened her mouth to disagree, but it was already too late. Donald Riley was walking away, leaving the balcony and her, and as usual, he hadn't heard a thing she'd said.

"I'll meet you downstairs," he called over his shoulder with a wave and promptly disappeared out the door.

Sighing heavily, she lifted a hand to push her hair back from her face. She'd left it loose for the night, preferring a casual style and a more conservative cocktail dress for the evening that was to be spent with co-workers. She wasn't out to impress. Just to blend in, but before she'd had the chance to try, Donald had arrived.

Her mouth thinned. She suspected her mother was behind Donald's visit, because engagements had been the subject of conversation at the dinner table just prior to the party. It was really getting to be too much. Her mother—

"Hark, hark, what light through yonder window breaks?"

Danielle froze where she stood, shock holding her speechless until recognition bubbled in her throat on a gurgle of laughter. Straightening, she moved to the corner of the balcony. "Oh, Romeo, Romeo, wherefore art thou, Romeo?"

"I thought you didn't like Shakespeare."

She leaned over the railing to look down at Gabe. "It depends on who's playing Romeo."

"What's your preference?" he demanded.

"Someone tall, dark and handsome."

"Then I'm your man."

She laughed as he threw open his arms in immodest acceptance. "I see that no one in your family has any humility. You have it all."

He grinned and tossed his glass into the bushes. "Move aside. I'm coming up."

"Are you crazy?"

"No," he said, grabbing hold of a vine. "I've just always wanted to play knight-errant." And he did, especially when it would put him together with the woman he wanted to be with and opposite the man he wanted his fist to meet.

Gabe reached for another vine, ignoring the ominous snap of twigs and the precarious sway of his footing.

Standing under the balcony listening to some other man try to make love to the woman he wanted had not been the highlight of his evening. But at least she'd said no. She wasn't marrying the jerk. Whoever he was. And Gabe didn't think she'd kissed the guy. At least he hoped she hadn't, but he wasn't willing to stay on the ground any longer waiting for the man named Donald to get a second chance.

Above him Danielle squealed as another branch snapped, but the vines held.

"Never fear, my lady. Nothing will keep me from you."

She bit her lip, caught between fear and amusement. "I think that line's from another play."

"That or a bad movie," Gabe grunted, and abruptly wondered what the hell had gotten into him. Why was he risking life and limb to climb a bunch of dirty vines to get to a woman who was considering marriage to another man? What did it matter if Danielle Fitzsimmons was altar bound? She was nothing to him. He just wanted her to be. At least until he could find out if all of her skin was as soft as the small part he'd touched. That was hardly worth breaking his neck for, though, was it?

Heaving himself upward, he grabbed hold of the cement balustrade and found Danielle looking down at him. "I must be out of my mind," he told her.

"I believe that's what I said." She smiled. "But I like the effort. Very theatrical."

He got the other arm around the railing and tried to catch his breath, but it was being taken away again. By her. In a simple black dress with a square neckline and a length that just brushed her knees, she was slimly elegant, delicately alluring and delicious enough to eat. "Does that mean you're pleased to see me?"

She laughed. "You're pushy as well as cocky."

"No, just jealous." And it surprised him to realize he was telling the truth, but the smile curving her lips vanished at his confession.

"You heard Donald."

"I heard you say no."

"Then you heard just about everything."

He heard her sigh and watched her lift a hand to brush at her hair that was floating softly around her face. "Donald is the family friend?"

Her smile returned as she remembered the deserted street Donald had left her on. It was where she'd met Gabe, and Gabe was part of the reason she'd said no. It was Gabe's dark gaze she'd been thinking of when looking into Donald's eyes. That was why Donald had paled—by unconscious comparison. "He drives a Jaguar."

"I noticed."

"And my mother likes him."

"Double whammy."

"She wants grandchildren."

"Doesn't sound like a love match to me."

"It's not, but she keeps pressing."

"Ignore her."

"Impossible while I'm living here."

"Then move out."

Danielle frowned.

"Why are you living here, anyway?" Gabe asked. "After college..."

"And being independent I had other ideas," she admitted. "I wanted to come home, work in the firm and have my own place. I was looking forward to it." She chewed at her lip. "But my mother was sick, my father was worried and I..."

"Was available."

Her smile was feeble. "I thought she needed me."

"Does she still?"

"All parents need their children."

"All parents have to let go some time." He studied her in the shadows flickering across the balcony. "I bet I could find you a place."

Her eyes lit up under his.

"Or you could move in with me."

Her mouth opened in surprise, but before she could register the shock, he had her laughing instead.

"That way you could find out where I live."

Her laughter washed over him as he remained clinging to the balcony railing. "You are outrageous!"

"But are you interested?"

Murmured voices suddenly came from below.

"Wait..." she interrupted.

Danielle's eyes widened as she recognized her father's voice, and she grabbed for Gabe. "Get up here!"

Her whisper was harsh, and he hastened to comply but the vine stopped him. "I can't! I'm stuck!"

Unable to imagine what her father would say if he caught Gabe climbing into the house by going over the balcony and not knowing whether to laugh or cry at the possibility, she hurried back to Gabe and the railing and bent over both to reach the pants leg that was hooked on a determined branch. "There!"

She pulled, he pushed, and together they rolled backward to collapse onto the balcony floor and out of sight to anyone below.

Danielle immediately pressed her hand over his mouth. "Shh!"

"Maybe it was a rabbit or a stray cat in the bushes," someone suggested from beneath the balcony.

"I suppose," Lucas Fitzsimmons murmured in dubious response.

"Come on. Whatever it was is gone. Let's go back to the party. You *are* the host."

Footsteps rustled away, and Danielle took her hand away from Gabe's lips to find him grinning. "What if he'd seen you!"

"Who cares?"

She should have been ready for the kiss. It shouldn't have taken her by surprise, not when they were lying on top of one another with their limbs tangled and their breath mingling, but it did. He did. He never did the expected, but she didn't resist when he changed his ways. And he didn't want her to.

When she melted in his arms, it was as if she blended right into him. He and she were no longer separate. They were one. Together, and this time the discovery didn't scare him. It made him want more, and he took it.

Searing kisses across her face and down her neck, he found she tasted as sweet and her skin was as soft as he remembered. He rolled, taking her with him—and yowled when his elbow cracked into hard cement.

Laughing, she sat up to look down at him as he rubbed the bruised limb. "Poor baby. It's just a bump."

"Easy for you to say," he told her, but the pain was forgotten quickly enough as she stood and he was faced with the long legs that had captivated him on a deserted street. "I like the view from down here."

She rolled her eyes and grabbed his arm to try to hurry him from outside into the room beyond the balcony doors. "Get up and get in here."

"Why, is this your bedroom?"

"No, it's not."

"Ouch!"

"Be quiet!" she admonished. "Everyone will hear you."

"How can I be quiet when I can't see where I'm going and I keep running into things?" he demanded. On entering the darkened room, he'd walked straight into a table. "Why are the lights off? Didn't your father pay the electric bill?"

"No. I just didn't turn them on."

Gabe blinked as the flick of a switch unexpectedly lit the room, and his eyes quickly narrowed in suspicion. "A quiet rendezvous with Donald in the dark?"

She crossed her arms over her breasts. "A quiet evening of watching *you* weave through the crowd."

"You were watching me?"

His grin was annoying. And arousing. "Don't look so delighted."

He reached for her. "I am, but I'm better up close."

She stiffened when he pulled her against him, but resistance was futile. He was too big, too strong, and she didn't want to fight, anyway. Her arms lifted to circle his neck, but all too soon he was pulling away.

"Does this mean you're ready to acknowledge ours isn't the normal business relationship?"

She slipped out of his arms. "Our relationship, as you put it, doesn't seem to be normal, business or otherwise. Not from the start to..."

"The finish?" he asked, and cocked his head to study her. "We're not finished yet, are we?"

"I'm not sure what we are." She sighed, and her heart jumped as a satisfied smile curved his mouth and he took a step closer. She hastily sidestepped to avoid an all-out retreat.

He followed her. "Show me your bedroom, and maybe I can help you make up your mind."

"Wherever we are, we're not there yet," she protested, holding a hand out to prevent his approach in a desperate gesture of self-defense.

He obeyed her signal to stop. Reluctantly. "Let me know when."

"You're very sure of yourself," she said, using her fingers to brush her hair back into proper order after his had been tangled in the strands.

"It pays to know what you want."

More laughter floated into the room through the balcony doors. "It also pays to know when to wait." She dropped her hand from her hair to her dress and grimaced when she came away with a leaf. "And how to look!" She groaned and began brushing at the other leaves and twigs that had transferred themselves from him to her.

His jaw clenched as he watched her, and he was abruptly reminded of what he was sure she saw as their class differences. Her rejection was caused by more than bad timing. "Sorry, we peasants do get dirty."

She looked up to watch him toss a twig aside. "You're not a peasant. I'm not sure what or who you really are, but it doesn't matter. Not to me."

And her eyes told him it didn't. He started toward her again.

"But," she said, holding him off with a warning glare, "I think we need to take one step at a time no matter what our relationship is." She indicated the window through which the echo of talk and laughter could be heard. "We'll be missed."

"Appearances," he acknowledged, and shoved his hands in his pockets.

"We are in my parents' house," she reminded him.

He grinned. "I can find you an apartment tomorrow."

"*We'll* find me an apartment tomorrow."

"Deal." He held out his arm for her to take. "What do you prefer? Beachfront or canyon?"

"You know some place in Canyon Country?"

"I do."

"I like the ocean, too."

He sighed and reached for the door. "I can see this decision may take a while."

She wrinkled her nose at him. "Making the right choice isn't always something that can be done quickly. After all, I'm still trying to make up my mind about you."

"A little mystery adds some spice to life," he suggested as he led her out of the room, and immediately began imagining what seasoning he'd try with her first. But before he could make a selection, she was pulling away. The staircase lay a few steps away, and by the time they reached it, she'd slipped the cool mask of social convention back into place. He didn't like the transformation. "I don't think I care for worrying about appearances."

Surprised, she turned to look at him as he walked beside her down the carpeted steps. "Why?"

"It's too restricting. It's strangling you."

Her eyes widened, but he gave her no chance to respond. He moved past her instead to descend the last few stairs before disappearing into the crowd, but while he left her behind, he didn't go far.

Keeping her in sight as the evening wore on, he remained at a discreet distance until, following the ebb and flow of people as individuals traveled the busy circuit from group to group, he eventually managed to draw close enough to maneuver himself into one of her conversations—with her mother.

"I'm glad you didn't mind that I invited Donald," he heard Helen Fitzsimmons tell her daughter, and followed her gesture to where a man stood beside Malcolm Reed by the pool. "I know this is a company party with the anniversary and all, but I thought you'd be pleased to see him—especially since you've been so busy lately."

"Yes, well, you certainly surprised me," Danielle managed, also following the gesture to where Donald was standing, but when she looked back, her heart skipped in surprise because it wasn't her mother's eyes she found herself staring into. "Gabe."

He smiled, her knees shook and she quickly stammered out an introduction.

"Mother, I don't believe you've met Gabe Tyler. He's—"

"The one who owns the motorcycle," Gabe cut in smoothly. "Perhaps I can talk you into taking a ride with me some day."

Helen Fitzsimmons flushed as he took and held her hand in his while mesmerizing her with a roguishly appealing grin. "I'm a bit old...."

"Nonsense," Gabe assured her, and leaned closer. "Actually, I almost mistook you for Danielle. I can see where she got her looks."

Danielle bit her lip to stop from commenting or smiling as her mother's poise was demolished by pure male charm. While it was true she and her mother were similar in build and shared the same green eyes, the hair that had once been midnight black for Helen Fitzsimmons was now peppered with gray, but the flattery had the desired effect. Her mother was stammering and eating out of his hand and in no time was maneuvered away and into a group of people standing nearby. The move left Danielle alone with Gabe, something she didn't mind at all.

"Nice lady," he said, turning to face her.

Danielle shook her head. "You're very good at manipulation."

"Oh, I don't know. You've kept me checked and cornered so far." He reached up to pull something from her hair. "Twig," he said with a smile that reminded her of the balcony and his kiss, but if her knees were suddenly wobbling, she couldn't cave in. Not with her mother watching.

Having turned from those she was with, Helen Fitzsimmons looked from Gabe to her daughter in silent question.

"The garden," Danielle quickly explained, flushing from her neck up, grateful that her mother promptly turned away with an accepting smile. Danielle stepped closer to Gabe. "You're supposed to keep your hands to yourself in public."

"Just trying to be helpful." He lifted the whiskey sour he'd been carrying since leaving her earlier and gestured with it past her to the pool. "That Donald?"

Her gaze swung from him to Donald and back again. "Yes, why?"

"Just checking out the competition."

Her eyes narrowed. "If you'll recall, I told him no."

He shrugged nonchalantly. "But he didn't hear you, and with my business background I've learned it always pays to eliminate any competition."

"Eliminate..." Her eyes widened and she hurriedly looked from him to Donald. "Gabe, you won't—"

"Danielle! I was wondering where you'd gotten to tonight!"

Left with no choice but to turn and greet the wife of one of the vice-presidents, Danielle determined to keep Gabe by her side via introduction, but when she gestured to where he had been standing, unexpectedly she found him gone. Alarm immediately sent her heart lurching against her breast, but she was given no time to worry, no time to wonder as polite conversation trapped her—at least until the first splash.

The sound of water and excited chatter got everyone's attention, including hers, and when she turned to see what the commotion was about, her mouth fell open in surprise. Donald was no longer standing beside the pool—he was in it!

Movement at the water's edge caught her eye, and she watched Gabe bend with Malcolm to stretch out a helping hand to a floundering Donald. But, suddenly, it appeared Malcolm leaned too far. He went headfirst into the pool, and Donald went back under with him.

The second splash brought more people hurrying forward, but while everyone wanted to offer assistance as two heads bobbed to the surface of the pool, no one seemed in a hurry to get too close. Instead of extending arms or hands to help, an inner tube was found and tossed in, then another.

It was chaos as people jumped into her line of vision, and in the ensuing fray, Danielle lost track of Gabe. There were too many tuxedos to pick his out of the crowd, but without warning he suddenly appeared standing at her elbow.

"That deck sure is slippery."

She swung to confront him with accusing eyes. "Did you push them in?"

Gabe looked wounded. "I was standing there talking to them when your Donald dropped this."

She looked at the napkin clutched in his hand.

"We both bent to pick it up, and the next thing I knew, he was in the water." Gabe shrugged. "It happened so fast, I'm not exactly sure what happened."

Her hands settled on her hips, and he raised his hands in quick surrender.

"I tried to help him get out. Honest. So did Malcolm."

His lips twitched, and suddenly she was finding it hard to hang on to the outrage she should be feeling. Instead, incredulously, she had to fight to keep a straight face. "He slipped, too, I suppose."

"No, he reached too far," Gabe explained with an expression of total innocence. "Overbalanced."

She stared at him, caught between the need to display proper shock and the want to laugh out loud at his audacity, but rather than give in to either, she looked past him to where the two men were, dripping and disgusted, being helped toward the house. "The least you could have done was waited."

"For what?"

"Me." She turned back to face him. "I would have liked to have been the one to shove Malcolm in."

He would have laughed but was prevented from doing so when she unexpectedly shoved her drink into his hand.

"Hold this. I have to go see to my guests." But the look she gave him as she walked away said that she'd rather stay with him.

THE LIGHT on the answering machine was blinking when Gabe wandered into his home hours later. He was drunk on the scent of a certain type of perfume, and he wanted to ignore the red light because he was tired. It'd been a busy night.

A smile lingered on his lips as he thought of Donald and Malcolm landing in the drink. It wasn't something he'd planned or even intended on approaching them. More, he'd been motivated by curiosity, but Donald's arrogance had been annoying and Malcolm's introduction condescending. The urge to act had just been too strong to resist, and it had been so easy.

A nudge with an elbow, a well-placed hand. Gabe sighed. A little humiliation was good for the soul, and Donald and Malcolm had both needed a strong dose.

Stopping by the answering machine, Gabe stared at it. The urge was strong to just go to bed and listen to whatever message was waiting in the morning. But it took little enough effort to hit the Play button as he shrugged out of his jacket and unknotted the tie at his throat. Yet his euphoria evaporated rapidly when the playback of the tape began.

"Gabe, it's Sam. No matter what time it is, call me when you get in. We have to talk."

Frowning and reaching for the phone, Gabe punched out a number on the keypad and tried to get his thoughts into working order. Sam wouldn't leave that type of message unless it was urgent. The phone was picked up on the other end. "Sam, it's Gabe."

An incoherent mumble came, followed by a sharp oath. "Do you ever call anyone when the sun's up?"

Gabe grinned. "Don't blame me. You said to call as soon as I got your message."

Another murmur came from the other end of the phone line, but it definitely wasn't Sam speaking.

Gabe's grin grew. His friend was entertaining a female companion. "Anyone I know?"

"You're not the only one who likes to celebrate."

"So call me tomorrow."

"I need to *see* you tomorrow."

Gabe remembered Danielle and his promise to pick her up at ten. Together they were going to find her a place of her own, and if he was who she thought he was, he could still go. But he wasn't. So, he couldn't go. Not now. Swearing, he dragged a hand through his hair and fought the guilt.

"Bad timing?"

"No," Gabe snapped. "What's up?"

"The takeover hit a bump. A big one."

"The office tomorrow? Seven?" But Gabe immediately shook his head in denial of his own demand. "No, make it nine. You have a guest." And he didn't. He hung up and swore again.

He was tired of pretending with Danielle. Tired of the deception. He was used to open and fair dealing. But once started, the masquerade was hard to stop, especially now.

He remembered again the way Danielle had melted in his arms. He wanted her. She wanted him. It should be simple. Would be if he were just a man and she just a woman, but things were more complicated than that. As Danielle had so aptly put it, nothing in their relationship was normal.

Muttering to himself, he jerked the loosened tie from his neck. He should have said no when she'd offered him the job. Then, perhaps, they would have had a chance. They would have been dealing with each other on equal footing. She would know who he was, and he who she was. It wouldn't have been one-sided. And they could have gone forward, explored and enjoyed the chemistry and each other, but things weren't equal. Nothing was as it seemed. Or, at least, he wasn't.

Sooner or later Danielle would have to see and accept him as he really was, not who she believed him to be—whatever that was. Yet while he was sure her recognition was what he had once wanted, he wasn't as certain he wanted that anymore. Not when he couldn't predict how she'd react when she realized he was really a wolf in sheep's clothing.

Chapter Eight

"Did I get you out of bed?"

Danielle's fingers tightened on the phone as Gabe's voice rumbled in her ear and sent a shudder through her body. It was eight o'clock in the morning, and the last person she'd expected a call from was him, especially since he was supposed to be coming to the house at ten to pick her up, but she wasn't disappointed. Oblivious to the butler walking away and leaving her alone in the hall, she smiled and leaned against the table the phone sat on. "It is an unfortunate myth that wealthy people spend their mornings in bed, their days lounging around doing nothing and their nights drowning in decadence."

"Unfortunate but understandable. Everyone would love to drown in decadence."

She had to bite her lip to stop the laughter. "You *are* incorrigible."

"One of my more redeeming qualities."

"Your motorcycle makes two."

"And I thought it was my mind you were after."

"That, too."

The deep resonance of his laugh made goose bumps pop out on her flesh.

"I suppose you're calling to say you'll be stylishly late?" she suggested.

"Actually, I'm calling to say I can't make it at all."

Disappointment hit her hard. Harder than she expected. Harder than she wanted. Quickly, she assured herself it was just that she'd been looking forward to finding a place of her own. It had nothing to do with not being able to see him. It was only that she'd wished so long for independence that, faced with the possibility, she didn't want to wait any longer. But it was curious that it'd taken him to make her realize how much she'd wanted it. "I'm sorry."

"No more than I, but it can't be helped."

"Duty calls?" she asked, curious all over again. About him. About who he was rather than who he wanted her to believe him to be.

"Actually..." he began, and hesitated.

"You don't owe me an explanation," she hastily interrupted, silently cursing both her own curiosity and his stubborn refusal to satisfy it.

But he hesitated still, and his silence told her more than he was willing to put into words. He wanted to tell all but wasn't ready to. "I have some work to see to. A commitment," he finally told her.

"I'm happy to hear you believe in commitments," she responded tartly, and her effort to lighten his mood was successful. She could almost hear him grin.

"When I see something I want, I can be very committed."

She smiled herself. "I hadn't noticed."

"I'll have to try harder."

She laughed.

"But just because I can't go with you doesn't mean you shouldn't start apartment hunting. Let me give you a couple of addresses."

Grabbing the pen that was always kept with a pad of paper on the front foyer table, she quickly wrote down not only the locations for the properties but the name, address and phone number of the person she could pick up the keys from.

"I could only find one on the beach. The other two are in the canyons outside the city."

"Have you seen them? I mean, you must have when you were looking for your own place?"

Silence once more hung uncomfortably on the phone line. "I've seen them, yes. They're investment properties."

Why would a man new to the city be looking at or how would he know of investment properties unless, of course, he was investing? "Obviously, I'm either paying you too much that you can afford to invest, or you're already looking for a new job in a company of your own."

"I like working independently," he admitted, neither acknowledging nor denying her unspoken question. "But I'm finding teamwork has its rewards."

The deep timbre of his suggestion made it hard for her to concentrate on the mystery rather than the man.

"I think you'll like all the properties," he told her. "They're houses not apartments, so you'll have privacy and can decorate as you like if you decide to rent one. The canyon houses are more modern. The beach property is on the board to be developed. It's older and the owner is thinking of tearing it down to rebuild something newer, bigger, but he's not in a hurry. If you like it, it'll give him the excuse he needs to put off doing anything a little longer."

"I'll keep that in mind."

"Keep me in mind, too."

As if she could forget him. She shook her head in denial of the personal admission. "I'll try not to."

"You're a cruel woman, Danielle Fitzsimmons. A man's ego can only take so many blows."

"And here I thought you were indestructible."

He laughed. "I've been called worse."

"Tell me."

A sigh came to her over the phone. "I can't. I have to go. I've got someone waiting."

The stab of jealousy caught her by surprise and she wondered if it was another woman taking Gabe away for the day, but Danielle hastily pushed the possibility aside and the regret that, every time she appeared to be getting closer to discovering more about him, he pushed her away. "I'll see you in the office Monday."

"And you can tell me when the housewarming party is. I expect to be invited."

"Maybe I'll give you a private showing." The invitation was out before she knew it. Her thoughts were spoken before she could form the words to say. That shocked and relieved her. It also reminded her of his comment the night before about appearances strangling her. He'd been right. It felt good to be able to say what she was feeling instead of what was right and proper, and he seemed to appreciate her offer.

"That's something I could look forward to."

The phone line went dead in her hand, and she sighed as the connection with him was lost. But he'd given her a purpose. He'd given her a cause. She was going to get back the independence she'd learned to love and enjoy in college.

A quick phone call put her in touch with the person holding the keys, and within an hour she was on her way to meet him.

Randy Bailey turned out to be one of those rare individuals most people like on meeting. Danielle was no exception. Something about his easy smile, mild manner and friendly disposition just appealed and made it easy to trust him. And his personality was perfect for a Realtor. Not pushy and not too talkative, Randy didn't insist on coming along for the ride to the properties. He merely offered to accompany her, and on impulse she accepted. And it was an action she didn't regret.

Randy was familiar with the areas surrounding both the canyon and beach and provided a chatty commentary on conveniences like the nearest grocery store as well as pros and cons about each locale, but once inside each house, he left her on her own to wander, explore and inspect.

"Not what you were looking for?" Randy asked when she left the second canyon home.

"They're nice," Danielle admitted, turning with him to look back at the house she'd just left. But some part of her was saying neither was right. Not for her. "I'm sorry. I seem to be wasting your time."

"No, you're not." Randy smiled. "Besides, I've saved the best for last."

And he had. From the moment she saw the beach bungalow sitting on stilts with sand and ocean stretching out in front of it, she wanted it.

Jumping out of the car as soon as the motor was off, she enthusiastically romped ahead of him up onto a deck that overlooked the sea where gulls could be heard calling above the gentle rumble of rolling waves.

"I love it!"

He laughed and put the key in the lock. "I'm glad you like the view, but you're not going to sleep on the deck."

"Make a bet?" Laughing and lighthearted, she walked through the door he unlocked and made a quick spin of the home.

It was small and old and not as big as it could be, but it was also perfect. The place had atmosphere with its tiny kitchen, its well-worn staircase that wound up to a second floor that housed two small rooms and a bath, and a living-dining area that sat just beyond patio doors overlooking sky and sea.

"Where do I sign?" she asked Randy, rejoining him on the porch to smell the surf and salty breeze. "And can I move in today?"

Smiling, he shrugged. "The electricity is still on. Why not? As long as you have furniture?"

She grinned, and he held the key out to her before looking back at the bungalow.

"I know they're thinking of tearing this place down and putting something more modern in," Randy said. "But I wouldn't change a thing."

"Me, neither," she agreed with a sigh, and leaned back to follow his gaze. "It's exactly what I wanted to find."

BACK ON THE STREETS of San Marino a little over an hour later, Danielle was humming as she pulled into the drive leading up to the mansion. She smiled to herself as she stopped her car at the front steps. The mansion, not home. She laughed out loud. Already she wasn't thinking of her parents' house as where she belonged anymore. Yet the idea of facing her mother and father was sobering.

Skipping up the stairs to the front door, Danielle bit her lip. They weren't ones to approve of impulses or spontaneous action. Rather, thought and consideration were given before doing anything, and she had no idea how they'd feel at her sudden announcement about moving out. A frown darkened her face. But they weren't going to stop her.

Prepared for battle, she opened the door to break the news, but her parents weren't inside to hear her announcement. It was Saturday and they were at the club, and that left only the maids and butler to listen to the news. And they immediately not only volunteered to help her pack, but led a raid on the attic and basement as well.

From under dust cloths they unearthed an odd assortment of furniture. A table, a chair, a bed. An old lamp was also discovered along with a clock and dresser that hadn't yet made it to a charity's coffers. Nothing matched, but it didn't matter. Whatever could be found was brought out of the shadows and into the sunlight, and a phone call determined it could all be taken away that day.

Fortunately, in the middle of the month, getting a moving truck wasn't a problem, and in no time Danielle was directing a parade of people and objects out of the house and into the back of a van—which lumbered out the drive just as her parents were pulling in.

"Danielle, what is going on here?" her mother began, stepping out of the car to watch the truck turn onto the street, but Danielle stopped her next sentence with a hug and a laugh.

"That was my moving truck. I've found my own place."

"Your own—" her father began to object, a scowl coming to darken his face.

"Yes, I've been thinking about it for quite a while," Danielle interrupted matter-of-factly. "It's time the two of you had your freedom. You don't need me constantly underfoot anymore. And I really should be out on my own, don't you think?"

Caught unprepared and without an answer, her father could only mumble and nod an incoherent response.

"And I won't be far away. Just in Malibu." She hugged her mother again. "I did take a few things from the attic. I hope you don't mind."

"Of course not, Danielle, but this is all so sudden...."

"I'll call," she said, climbing into her car, which was packed with suitcases and boxes. "As soon as I get a phone!"

But a telephone was the least of her worries as the rest of the day was spent unpacking, setting up what little furniture she had and running to the store for food, cleaning products and miscellaneous necessities like wastepaper baskets and silverware.

Yet, when night fell and her body ached from scrubbing, lifting and arranging, she didn't head for bed but for the porch and the relaxing sound of the ocean where she leaned against the railing and thought about the day and the man who had helped make it possible.

It was odd that a stranger could motivate her to do things she'd only thought about: standing up to Malcolm, forcing her father to recognize her business savvy and moving out of the house that had once been home but had turned into more of a prison. She sighed. Maybe it wasn't Gabe so much as timing. Perhaps he'd entered her life at a time when she was ready to take action but hadn't realized it, but it was difficult not to give him credit. It was difficult not to give him thought.

He'd asked her to think about him, and she had. All day. When moving out, when moving in, when laughing at how ridiculously empty all the rooms were once the van was unloaded and she was alone—but why? What was it about him that fascinated her so?

She wasn't in love with him. But she was madly attracted to him.

She sighed. Physically he aroused. Mentally he stimulated. Still she kept holding back.

At first it had just seemed right not to acknowledge any of the electric currents sparking between them. She hadn't really known him, and her world and his had seemed too far apart. With no common ground, nothing to share, the only thing it seemed possible for them to enjoy together was satisfaction from the consummation of physical passion. But she wasn't one for casual affairs, one-night stands, or relationships that were doomed to fail—something she had seen too often with acquaintances who had picked mates with haste rather than hope of harmony.

Then later, as she and Gabe had spent time together, she'd continued to resist him and his advances because... She smiled. Because she was a coward at heart, and he had represented the unknown. She sighed. He still did.

Yet, if she was holding back, so was he. Somehow, for some reason, it seemed as if he was protecting himself, and his caution made her want to do the same. She kept putting up barriers while he kept trying to tear them down.

She breathed deeply of the sea air. What she and Gabe had was a lack of trust. Professionally, she wouldn't hesitate to turn over every dollar she had to him. He had a business acumen that, by rights, should have seen him own rather than work for a company. But personally, if he attracted, he also made her wary. Perhaps because, given the chance and despite their differences, she could lose her heart to him—a man she'd once believed owned nothing more than a motorcycle.

"I WISH I COULD have been there."

Gabe smiled at Kelly. "Yes, you would have enjoyed it. Malcolm looked very good wet." Gabe crossed his arms across his chest and studied her as he sat on the corner of her desk. She was holding the oversized glasses she usually wore that hid a face that was pretty even without makeup. "So why weren't you there? You are part of an officer's staff."

Her eyes fell from his. "I wanted to go. I really did, but I was afraid—"

"Is Danielle in?" a voice from behind them bellowed.

Watching Kelly jump and then hastily shove the glasses on her nose as if in defense, Gabe slid from the desk to face who he was suddenly sure she was afraid of. "No," he told Malcolm Reed, and let his gaze drop to run over the perfectly tailored suit the man wore. "You're dry, I see."

Malcolm's blue eyes iced over. "No thanks to you. How is it you didn't fall in when I did?"

Gabe smiled. "I didn't overextend my reach. Some people are prone to doing that—with the inevitable result."

Black and blue gazes clashed. Hurrying from the elevator and into the office, Danielle stepped out of the hallway and in between the two men with an alarmed rush. The air cracking around them was thick enough to cut, but she managed to slice through it with a forced smile. "Good morning, everybody. Sorry I'm late, but I'm not used to driving in from Malibu."

"Malibu?" Malcolm questioned, pulling his gaze from Gabe to her.

"Yes, I've rented a bungalow," she said, and slid a sideways glance to Gabe. "It came highly recommended."

Gabe smiled and stepped aside as she headed for her office door. "Did you need something, Malcolm?" she asked. But before he could answer, she turned to get a better look at him. "I see you dried off all right."

She swung away, Gabe and Kelly stifled their laughter, and Malcolm faltered before following her through the door. "I was just curious. How's the project at Malibu going? You didn't move out there to supervise, did you?"

Danielle smiled and ignored the unpleasant undertones to the conversation. "I appreciate your interest, Malcolm, but I was going to give everyone a status report at this morning's meeting." She put her purse down on her desk. "As far as moving out there, I did it because I love the ocean and my parents. We both need our independence.''

A knock came from the still-open door and Danielle looked up to find Gabe waiting and listening, his gaze black as he stared hard at Malcolm. "Grady Thompson's here.''

Again Danielle hurried to step in between the two men as Malcolm's glare narrowed in silent combat. "You'll have to excuse me, Malcolm, but Mr. Thompson's our contractor for the Malibu project. He's bringing me his bid.''

"Thompson?'' Malcolm protested, not budging from where he stood. "You didn't use who I recommended?''

Danielle put a guiding and persuasive hand on Malcolm's shoulder as she hastened him toward the door. "I'll tell you all about it at the meeting in half an hour. Gabe, please show Mr. Thompson in.''

But the contractor didn't stay long. An exchange of paper, a handshake and a promise of prompt contact, and he was out the door again, leaving Danielle alone with Gabe.

"Excited?'' he asked her.

"Thrilled,'' she agreed as she stood behind her desk reviewing the bid. "I can't believe how quickly it's gone—or how easily. Thanks to you.''

He shook his head as her eyes lifted to his. "You could have done it all yourself.''

"Maybe, but it took you to make sure I did it.''

He grinned. "Does this mean I'm getting promoted?''

"No, but I do have something else to thank you for.'' She came around the desk to stand beside him and immediately felt the heat from his body reach out to embrace her. She took a deep breath to resist the effect. And to stop herself from touching him. "The house in Malibu. I love it.''

"And you're already moved in?'' he asked, feeling the heat, too, and fighting the sudden and overpowering urge to take her in his arms. He could smell her perfume. The scent had haunted him all weekend.

"Yes, but it didn't take much effort, since most of the rooms are empty." She managed to smile even though her heart was thudding with slow, anticipatory beats. "If I have any company, I'm afraid they'll have to sit on the floor."

"I don't mind."

Her heart skipped a beat at the quiet promise. "Still looking for that private showing?"

"Still want to give it?"

She gazed up at him. He seemed relaxed, but the tension was there, sizzling between them, holding the two of them together. It was difficult to shake her head. "I'm not sure."

Disappointment collided with anger, a frown curved his mouth and his eyes darkened, but he didn't move. "Why?"

It was a simple question and she had the answer, but it was hard to give it. "Because," she said, not looking away from him, "I usually don't invite strangers into my house."

His gaze didn't leave hers. "Strangers."

"Yes." She lifted her chin slightly in unconscious challenge. "How was your weekend?"

He blinked, not surprised but unprepared for the confrontation, and slowly let go of the breath that he'd silently been holding. She'd had him worried for a moment. But it was only the weight of his true identity that was coming between them.

"You look tired," she prompted, and turned away from him to walk behind her desk again.

"It was busy," he conceded.

"Perhaps you'd like to tell me about it."

It was the perfect opportunity to throw in the towel. She didn't need him anymore. Not as an associate, not as a crutch, not as a confidant, but confession meant he'd no longer be able to remain close to her. Not during the day. But at night, if she could accept who he was. "Dani..."

"The meeting's about to start."

Kelly's pronouncement came from the open door, and Gabe cursed his timing. With Danielle, it never seemed to be quite right. He looked from her to Kelly and back again. "We better go. The lions are waiting."

She nodded and her eyes searched his, but she could find nothing. Not regret. Not hope. But it had been there. For an instant. Reluctantly, she reached for her papers. "I'm ready."

The walk down the hall was long and quiet. Unspoken words lay heavily between her and Gabe. Reaching the conference room door, she hesitated and turned to face him, but she couldn't think of anything to say.

He smiled, as if reading her scrambled thoughts, and lifted a hand to brush her cheek. "Later. We'll talk later."

The promise was enough. It calmed the anxiety, soothed her nerves and helped her stand fast when Malcolm came at her mere moments later.

Waiting until she had finished giving her report to those seated around the big conference table, he sat back and calmly started to tear it apart.

"Danielle, what do we know about this man or his work?" he demanded.

"We know only what others tell us," she admitted without hesitation. "Grady Thompson comes highly recommended. By the bank, by other contractors, but his work really speaks for itself. I toured some of the homes he's completed. They're magnificent."

She turned from Malcolm to her father.

"He's worked extensively in Malibu," she explained. "He understands the working conditions, the type of ground he'll be building on. His experience will be a major asset, and what's more, he can start work on the project immediately. He's just coming off another job and is ready to begin something new. It will mean the development of the property will be completed much sooner than we could have hoped or expected, and we'll have a quicker turnaround in capital. We can begin selling the lots as soon as the first home is finished."

Lucas Fitzsimmons nodded, approval in his eyes, but Malcolm wasn't finished with his tirade.

"You used a different bank."

"I did," Danielle admitted and was immediately aware of her father's scowl.

"Why?" Lucas Fitzsimmons demanded.

"Because they offered a better interest rate on the project account. We'll earn more on the contract proceeds while waiting to pay them out."

"But—" Malcolm began again but was unexpectedly waved to silence.

Her father drummed his fingers on the table, and Danielle held her breath along with everyone else as she waited for him to speak.

"When can the work begin?" he finally asked.

Danielle linked her fingers together and sat forward in her chair. "If we approve his bid today, Mr. Thompson can start by the end of the week."

Lucas Fitzsimmons almost smiled as he examined the bid sitting on the table before him. Approving murmurs came from around the table as others recognized his acceptance. "You've done well, Danielle. So well, in fact, that I think Malcolm should have you help him on the Henderson account."

"I . . ." Malcolm began.

"Have been having some difficulty in getting that wrapped up." Lucas Fitzsimmons smiled at his daughter.

"Perhaps Danielle can use her persuasive skills to our advantage again. As I recall, Henderson's account is one of several that have been waiting to be closed for too long."

"Of course," Malcolm agreed with a stiff nod, but Danielle barely heard. And she didn't notice his hidden scowl. Rather she saw only the wink that was sent to her by the man seated off to the side and away from the table. His conspiratorial gesture meant more to her than Malcolm's defeat. More, even, than her father's approval.

Chapter Nine

"I haven't felt this free since college," Danielle said into the phone. It was night, and she was standing on the deck with the ocean breeze fanning her face and the sound of the waves echoing around her. She couldn't remember ever being so relaxed, at ease with herself and her life. The only dark spot was Gabe. The two of them had never gotten a chance to have that talk. The events of the day had swept them away. "It's great, Linda. I wish you could see it."

The smile on her lips suddenly grew at her friend's response.

"What? You think you can come out?" Danielle laughed joyfully. "How soon?" But her attention was pulled away from the conversation when headlights cut the black of night beside the house before abruptly being shut off. She had a visitor. "Not until November?" she asked, and turned toward the corner of the bungalow and the walk leading to the door. "What?"

Danielle laughed again and temporarily forgot the headlights. "If I'd made up my mind to move out sooner, you could have scheduled your vacation earlier?"

She listened again, biting her lip.

"Why did I wait so long to get my own place? What inspired me to finally do it?" Danielle sighed. "It wasn't

what. It was who.'' And suddenly there he was. Gabe was
standing on the walk below, leaning against the house
watching her.

Linda asked another question, but Danielle didn't hear
her. She was only conscious of Gabe. Her mouth silently
formed his name, and the conversation was completely lost
when, even though she kept the phone pressed to her ear, he
pushed away to move to the stairs.

As he came up the steps toward her, she held her breath.
In a sports coat, open-necked pullover and slacks, he was
enough to make her heart stop, but before she could even
think about reaching out to touch him, her friend was calling in her ear.

''What? Yes, I'm still here,'' Danielle hastily answered
and moved away to listen while keeping an eye on Gabe.
''You want to know more about who inspired me?'' She
grinned at Gabe. ''It was a man. A tall, dark, mysterious
man who recently entered my life.''

Gabe smiled, and Linda chattered.

''His name?'' Danielle shook her head in response. ''He
says it's Gabe Tyler.''

Gabe's smile grew as he overheard the tone, if not the
words, of Linda's shocked response.

''No, it's not that I don't believe him exactly,'' Danielle
objected. ''It's just that I have so many unanswered questions about him.'' She met Gabe's steady gaze across the
deck. ''His job application gives only a post office box for
an address, and while he obviously has a lot of business
sense, he doesn't list much in the way of experience.''

Gabe watched Danielle nod emphatically at her friend's
next question.

''Yes, it's as if he's hiding something, Linda, and as a
friend and reporter, I wish you'd help me find out more
about him.''

Gabe rolled his eyes, and Danielle grinned.

"Vital statistics? Umm," Danielle murmured. "About six foot one, black hair, black eyes. He rides a motorcycle to work, but his wardrobe is out of any groupie's price range. Oh, and he did live on the east coast once, or at least I think he did because he told me that it snowed when he was a child."

Linda asked about a social security number, but Danielle barely heard her. She was concentrating on Gabe as he reclined, totally at ease, while she discussed him with a complete stranger.

"I'll try to get that to you, but listen, I have to run. Someone's just stopped by." She nodded. "Later."

Gabe cocked an eyebrow as she hung up. "Linda as in college Linda?"

"Linda as in college Linda, and she's a bloodhound when it comes to digging up a story."

Gabe swung toward the stairs. "I better go bury that skeleton, then."

Shocked, Danielle couldn't believe it when he disappeared. Alarmed, she ran after him. "Gabe!" But when she reached the end of the deck, she found him grinning up at her from the walk below.

"Have you eaten yet?" he asked.

"No."

"Good."

Before she could speak, he disappeared again but not for long. In moments he was striding back into view and jogging up the steps once more with two picnic baskets, some bags and a bright blanket in his arms. She laughed. "What are you doing?"

"Going in here," he said, stepping through the patio doors, but he stopped just inside to look around. The room was bare except for one table and one chair and a lamp. The table had papers spread out across it. He moved closer. "What's this?"

"Work."

"So's this," he said, putting the baskets and bags down and grabbing the blanket.

She watched him shake it out before setting it neatly on the floor. "What is 'this,' exactly?"

"Courtship," he responded, straightening the corners of the blanket as it lay on the floor before standing once more to meet her incredulous gaze. "The ritual by which two people of the opposite sex get to know each other better. Or, in other words, cease to be strangers."

"Really?"

"Scout's honor," he said, crossing his heart with a dramatic gesture.

"I suppose you know it's also the ritual that leads to people getting married."

He grimaced.

She smiled and crossed her arms over her breasts. "Chicken?"

"No, that's in the bag."

And it was. She could smell it, and her stomach growled in response.

"I remembered what you said about guests having to sit on the floor, so I came prepared for a picnic." He held out a hand and guided her to her knees beside him on the blanket. "We have wine, properly cooled. Glasses..." He looked at her in question as, one by one, he pulled each item from one of the baskets. "I wasn't sure you had any."

"A mismatched set," she responded with a shrug. "The good stuff comes later in the week with the rest of the furniture. Just the phone came today."

He grinned and dipped into the basket again to hand her plates and silverware and napkins as well as some side dishes of potato salad and coleslaw. "Am I missing anything?"

"I don't think so," she told him with a laugh. "But what's in the other basket?"

"A gift." He reached for it. "Normally, I would have come with roses, but not knowing if you had a vase, or a place to put them—" he gestured to the one table "—I decided on something else instead."

Danielle gasped as he opened the lid and two heads popped out of the basket. One was black with white ears, the other white with black ears. "Kittens!"

"Brother and sister," he agreed, lifting them free and into her arms. "I thought you could use the company."

Laughing as she accepted the two tiny cats that immediately began to nuzzle and purr, Danielle hugged them both in delight. "Oh, Gabe, how did you know? I was thinking of getting one."

"Now you have two."

She laughed as little noses sniffed her over as if committing her to memory. "My mother would never let me have pets, but Linda and I had a cat in college. He was a stray that we brought into our dorm room, and when we graduated, he went home with Linda. She still has him."

"Sounds like you two were close," Gabe said as one kitten escaped her grip to start to explore its new home.

"We were. Still are." Danielle let the other kitten go and laughed as Gabe unearthed a ball from the basket and sent both animals scampering across the room after it. "That's why it seemed appropriate that she be the first one I called when the phone went in."

"She's coming out?"

"Yes."

"I'd like to meet her."

"Will you still be here?"

"Do you want me to be?"

Danielle leaned toward him across the blanket, and he met her halfway for a kiss that had both their hearts beating faster.

"I think I'd like you to be," she murmured when they finally parted.

"Still making up your mind?"

"Chemistry isn't everything."

He grinned. "Maybe not, but it does have its rewards."

She arched an eyebrow at him and held out the container of food. "Chicken?"

"No, but I think you are."

His grin was hidden by the fried chicken leg he put in his mouth. Caught without a response, she bit into a drumstick of her own. But the conversation wasn't allowed to lag. Not when a black-and-white menace came from nowhere to spring with still-developing and inaccurate aim at the plate of chicken.

Gabe caught the kittens, found another ball and sent it rolling and the cats running after it. "I'm glad you like cats. I was afraid you might be a dog person."

"Are you?"

"I was. I am. All we had when I was growing up were dogs, but when I met my first cat—" Gabe shrugged. "I can't say it was love at first sight, but we got to respect each other over time." Gabe reached for his glass of wine. "I liked his independence, and he liked someplace warm to sleep at night."

"A match made in heaven."

"That's where that old tomcat is now."

Danielle smiled as Gabe bent to bump heads in friendly acquaintance with one of the kittens. "It was nice that you had a mother who let you bring animals into the house."

"She let me do just about anything," he admitted. "It was my father I didn't see eye-to-eye with."

"Tell me."

Gabe's shoulders moved again. "We fought all the time. He wanted me to be one thing, I wanted to be another, but somehow he got me into the family business. Problem was, we didn't see things the same way there, either."

"You left?"

"Not on the best of terms."

"But the two of you have made up since?"

Gabe nodded.

"I'm glad." She sighed. "It would bother me if something pulled my parents and I apart."

"Being who you are shouldn't pull you and your parents apart."

Her eyes dropped from his. "I know, but . . ."

"You prefer the slow, subtle exit to my flamboyant departure?"

"It seems less wrenching."

"Sometimes you've got to demand respect."

"Think Malcolm's going to give me any?"

Gabe shook his chicken leg at her. "That was just one victory. Don't get cocky." He put the leg aside. "And let's not talk business tonight." His hand disappeared into the basket again. "I almost forgot the atmosphere."

In minutes Danielle was sitting in candlelight with a radio softly playing.

"You know," he said, rejoining her on the blanket after plugging the radio in across the room. "Some people would say you're living like a hermit. No television, no radio, no telephone—until tonight. How many people have your number?"

"Just Linda," Danielle admitted with an unrepentant smirk.

"Are you going to give it to me?"

"Why do you want it?"

"I want to call you at midnight and breathe heavily in your ear," he told her, leaning forward.

This time she was the one to go halfway, and her eyes closed as, on his lips, she tasted chicken, wine and man. She pulled away with a sigh. "I think you're a romantic."

"You think I'm a lot of things." He grinned. "Your adjectives so far, I believe, include cocky, crazy, perverted...."

She laughed. "I have called you all of those things, haven't I?"

"Want to know how I'd describe you?"

She wrinkled her nose. "From start to finish?"

"We're not finished yet, remember?"

Her pulse leapt as his eyes glowed and the candlelight flickered. "I remember."

He reached out to take her hand in his. "When I first saw you on that deserted street, I thought you were a ghost."

She grinned. "Scared you, huh?"

"No, mesmerized."

"Tell me more," she urged, linking her fingers with his.

"I thought you were a snob."

She gasped, and he nodded.

"Yup, a blue-blooded socialite who'd lost her way, but then I realized you weren't what you appeared to be—even though you were trying very hard to be exactly what I thought you were."

She groaned and fell back on the blanket.

He grinned. "But I decided to give you a second chance."

"Why?"

"You weren't afraid of my motorcycle. And," he interrupted when she started to laugh, "you've got the best-looking legs I've ever seen."

It was hard to be embarrassed with him staring down at her. "At least I have one redeeming quality."

"Two. You like cats."

She laughed again and watched him raise her hand to his lips.

"Actually, more than two."

"What's the third?"

"You're beautiful." And she was. In the candlelight and lying back on the blanket, he thought she was the most stunning woman he'd ever met. Even with her makeup slightly smudged after a long day, even in a loose, open-collared blouse and a multicolored, crinkled lace skirt, in bare feet and with wind-tossed hair, she was the stuff of dreams. He bent down to see if she was real and found her waiting for him like a beckoning siren.

Her arms wound around him and her mouth opened under his, but she found his kiss wasn't what she expected. His kiss was never the same.

On the porch, he'd demanded. On the balcony, he'd possessed. On the blanket, he questioned, and she pressed closer in answer. But he was never able to get the message. Something attacked his ankle.

"Ouch!"

Danielle fell back in laughter and grabbed for one of the two black-and-white terrors with razor-sharp teeth that were making war on Gabe's shoelaces. "I'm so glad you brought me these little darlings."

"I should have gotten you a dog," Gabe grumbled, latching on to the other kitten. "At least we could have let him outside." He stared hard at the growing cat who was all wide eyes and innocence. "What are you going to name them, anyway? Mutt and Jeff?"

She grinned as the kitten she'd rescued chased her fingers across the floor. "No, one's a girl, remember? How about Hansel and Gretel?"

He grinned. "You like fairy tales?"

"I've always believed in Prince Charming."

He growled and leaned over to steal a kiss before handing over the other kitten to her. "Prince Charming didn't have to contend with two black-and-white troublemakers. Just seven dwarfs."

"Competition too tough?" she asked, trying to catch her breath as he stood. He always took it away whenever he touched her.

"I'm not ready to give up."

"Good."

Her smile made it difficult to keep moving toward the door. "I need to get you their food and other necessities."

"I hope that means you brought a litter box." And she quickly found he had—along with a scratch pole, two beds, a climbing tower and a load of toys. She shook her head as he ended the third trip from his car with a sigh. "I can see if you ever have children, they're going to be spoiled."

"Are we back to marriage again?" he asked.

"That's not a necessity before having kids nowadays, is it?"

"No, but it's proper."

She arched her eyebrows at him. "Gabe, you surprise me. Are you an old-fashioned sort of guy?"

"Absolutely," he agreed, and caught her arm to pull her against him and into a slow dance that followed the rhythm of the song playing on the radio. "I like old-fashioned waltzes, old-fashioned movies where the hero rides into the sunset with the girl, and old-fashioned, deep dish pizza loaded with cheese. How about tomorrow night? Pizza and a movie?"

It was difficult to think with his arms holding her close, his heart beating in time with hers and his skin burning her flesh. "What about work?"

"That's daytime. I'm talking nighttime. Care to fraternize?"

His cocky grin made her tighten her grip as he held her. "I'd love to, but..." she said, and reluctantly waved to the table and the papers scattered across it. "Malcolm's mess."

"All work and no play," Gabe objected.

"Are you saying I'm dull?" she asked, pulling back to look up at him.

"Oh, no. Anything but," he assured her hastily and pulled her close again. "Just too dedicated."

"I still need more impulsiveness."

He nodded.

"Like this?"

He was unprepared for a direct approach. The last thing he'd expected was for her to take charge, but he didn't try to fight her off when she suddenly wrapped herself around him and pressed her mouth to his. He just held on and hoped he could find a life preserver in time, but when he went under for the third time, it ceased to matter. He groaned as she pulled away. "Just how fast do you want this relationship to develop? Overnight?"

She grinned. "If you can't stand the heat..."

"Get out of the kitchen." He rested his forehead against hers. "I'm leaving," he said, but kissed her quickly before slipping away to move to the patio doors. He stopped there to look longingly back at her. "Maybe I'm not as old-fashioned as I thought I was."

The invitation was there. She almost accepted it. He'd opened up to her, given her parts of who he was and where he'd come from, but she wasn't ready yet. Even if she wanted to be. "I'll see you in the morning."

He sighed and went out the door. It was going to be a long night.

BY THE TIME Gabe got home, he was in a foul mood. The fast car ride home had done little to soothe the tension coiled in his body, and he stalked toward his answering machine praying somebody wanted him to call them. He was ready to shout at someone, but the red light wasn't blinking.

Gabe growled and paced to the bar at the side of the room. He splashed some liquor into a glass and drank. Courtship had seemed a bright option, a wonderful idea when he'd first thought of it. The perfect solution to an imperfect situation. He drank again. It still was, even though he wanted things to move more quickly. He was used to moving fast, and he wanted Danielle in his bed. Soon.

Putting the glass down with a sigh, he walked away to stand before the empty fireplace. She wasn't ready for speed. She wasn't ready for confession. Neither was he. It was beginning to grate on his nerves, the constant pretending, but with the competition heating up at the office, he was ready and wanted to stay by Danielle's side. She might not need his advice. She was smart enough to handle problems as they came up on her own, but she would need his support. Because Malcolm was going to come at her swinging. That meant he couldn't desert her. He couldn't quit. And confessing . . .

Gabe scowled and walked down the hall to his bedroom without turning on any lights.

If he told her who he really was, he wasn't sure how she'd react. Would she think he'd been patronizing her? Playing a game? He had a reputation for getting into people's lives. Not always in a popular way, and she was bound to know about that. She'd recognize who he was and what he did for a living as soon as the truth came out. How would she react? Instant hate? Or, would she give him a chance? Would he be able or allowed to explain that he hadn't infiltrated enemy ranks by using her as cover? That while his ruse had begun as a game, it'd developed into something more?

Shrugging out of his jacket and shirt, Gabe sat on the bed to pull off his shoes and socks.

When he'd first accepted the job from Danielle, it had appeared to be little more than a challenge. He had been certain he could simply go into the company, give her a boost and back out. Confessing who he was hadn't even entered into the picture. He'd figured she'd never need or have to know—unless, of course, they happened to bump into each other at some dinner club one day.

But somehow, good intentions had evolved into personal interest, and personal interest was making him worry.

Had he and Danielle met at that dinner club, their very identities would have put them at odds. They might both belong in the same class, but they came from opposite ends of that class. He didn't play social or political games. She did. Or, at least, her family did. That meant any introduction might not have gotten any further than a polite how do you do. Still, they would have had a chance. Because she was open to change, the two of them could have carried a relationship a step or two further, and from there, who knew?

But because of his subterfuge, she might not trust him. She already didn't. Not entirely. That was why he was courting her, to convince her to let him into her life and to soften the blow for when the truth finally came out. If he could somehow slowly let her get to know him as a man before she discovered who he was as a businessman, she might forgive the deception, understand it and give them a chance to go on as a man and woman interested and attracted to one another. He hoped she would. More than he wanted to examine.

Suddenly anxious, afraid of failure and alarmed at the possibility, he grabbed the phone and dialed. A call later, another line was ringing, and he beamed when Danielle said hello. "You forgot to give me your number."

She laughed, and he lay back on the bed to let the music of the sound wash over him.

"That doesn't appear to have stopped you from getting it," she told him.

"I can be very resourceful."

"I'd noticed that about you."

"What else have you noticed?"

In her own bedroom, Danielle curled up on her bed and sighed as she contemplated a response. "That you can be annoyingly determined, single-minded and argumentative."

"You forgot stubborn."

"You just like to get your way."

"Don't you?"

"Absolutely. That's why I enjoy arguing with you."

"See, we have something else in common. We're both argumentative."

She grinned. "You're also charming, persuasive and not as coldhearted, I think, as you'd like others to believe."

His eyebrows collided. "Where'd that come from?"

"Your attitude."

"That again."

She laughed at his sigh. "When you're working, you have this approach..."

"Cutthroat."

"Direct. You don't pretend."

Gabe suddenly became very serious. "And if I did?"

"I'd think you did it for a good reason."

His smile returned. "Thank you."

"You're welcome." She glanced at the clock beside her bed. "Are you home now?"

"Why?"

"I was just thinking if it took you this long to get back to your apartment or house or whatever you live in, you must live close by."

He grinned. "By freeway, you never know."

"But—"

"And I might not have called right away. What if I got home, took a shower and then decided to call wearing nothing more than a towel?"

The image was vivid. It made it difficult to think, much less speak. His black hair wet, the hard width of his chest exposed. She licked her lips. "I . . . ouch!"

Gabe jumped, pulled the phone from his ear and grinned. The kittens were proving to be great mood breakers. He put the receiver back to his ear. "Hansel?"

"Gretel."

"Those baby teeth are sharp, aren't they?"

"Don't sound so happy about it," she grumbled, but quickly received a purr and a kiss from the offender.

"I'm not happy. I just understand. I'd like to nibble on your toes, too."

When her throat abruptly closed up again, she found it impossible to answer.

"They'll probably sleep with you tonight."

But she was thinking more of him sleeping with her instead. His body next to hers. Suddenly hot, her teeth found her lower lip. "Is this the part where you breathe heavily in my ear?"

"It's not midnight yet."

"Maybe I should leave the phone off the hook."

"And miss the experience of a lifetime?"

She burst out laughing. "You are outrageous!"

"Another adjective."

"There's not enough of them to describe you."

"Is that good or bad?" he asked.

"It depends on what mood I'm in."

"How about now?"

She hesitated. "It's good."

"I'm glad. I can sleep better now."

"You couldn't sleep before?"

"Not when I was thinking of you."

Her difficulty in catching her breath had nothing to do with the little black-and-white kitten that came to curl up on her chest.

"Having the same problem?"

"I have a clear conscience."

"Sometimes it's not your conscience that keeps you up at night."

She bit her lip. "I'll keep that in mind."

"Sweet dreams."

He hung up, and she sighed and wondered how it would be possible to dream at all, or sleep, when she'd sent him away for the night.

Chapter Ten

"You look tired," Gabe observed of Danielle as she entered her office the next morning. He followed, ignoring the glare she leveled at him. "Dare I hope I was the reason?"

"I didn't have one reason," she declared, unwilling to admit he had any part in her sleepless night. "I had two."

"Ah," he said in understanding, and leaned against her desk. "Hansel and Gretel. Maybe you should have let me stay. I could have protected you from them."

Her smile was malevolent. "But who would have protected me from you?"

He grinned gleefully. "What makes you think you would have wanted protection?"

Swallowing her heart as it leapt into her throat, she narrowed her eyes. "Did I ever say you were cocky?"

"Repeatedly."

"You are."

He shrugged. "Sometimes it's hard to be humble."

"Try."

"Okay," he agreed, and shoved away from the desk. "Are we still feasting on pizza tonight?"

"After feasting on Malcolm today I could use some dessert." She sat behind her desk. "Did you go over the Henderson account?"

"Yup. You?"

She nodded with a frown. "What do you think?"

"I think we should have it wrapped up by the end of the week."

"Me, too." She grinned. "Let's get to work."

And they did. Day after day, side by side, they forged ahead on one account in expectation of being handed another, and at night they forgot it all to enjoy the sweet taste of budding romance.

If Danielle noticed Gabe kept her away from the main track, she didn't let it bother her because she didn't want anyone bothering them. When she was alone with him eating pizza or crepes or hamburgers or steak, she was happy not to have to interrupt her meal to politely greet acquaintances of hers, of her father's or of her mother's. She wanted only to concentrate on him because when he was looking into her eyes, she felt as if she was the most important person on earth.

But her joy was fragile. For, while Gabe shared himself with her, it was still with reservation. He pulled her close, but held her away. It confused her. Hurt her. But the pain was something she didn't want to look at too closely.

"You're quiet tonight."

Danielle looked up from her silent contemplation of her dessert and smiled at Gabe. It was Friday night. They were at a small, exclusive club just south of Malibu. It was close to her home. Was it close to his? "I was just thinking."

"About what?"

"You."

Gabe sat back in his chair. "I'm flattered."

"You should be."

He grinned and reached for his wineglass, but he kept his eyes on her. She looked beautiful in the muted light of the club. The strapless teal dress she wore molded her breasts and highlighted the soft skin of her shoulders and the green in her eyes, but those eyes were watchful.

He'd spent every night of the week with her, courting her with gallantry and flowers, plying her with fine food and wine, hoping that the wall between them that was born of caution could be worn down. But he'd only been partially successful. She was still holding back. Because he was.

He wasn't being totally open with her, and she sensed it and so kept her reserve in place. It was an impossible situation, tantalizing, as she remained just out of his reach, but while he wanted to end the charade, he was also fighting even harder to keep the pretense in place.

The Henderson account was finished. Danielle had forced it through over Malcolm's objections. She'd received some censure from her father due to her failure to listen to Malcolm's advice, but Lucas Fitzsimmons couldn't have been too upset because he'd taken two more accounts from Malcolm for her to work on.

The responsibility was giving her confidence, but it was also earning her enemies. Malcolm had friends. At the bank, at city hall and in the company. Gabe was braced for a setup, but Danielle seemed oblivious that Malcolm wanted to see her fall.

Danielle had a good business mind. She had a sharp instinct and was careful with detail, but she also had a soft heart. It left her vulnerable in the highly competitive and sometimes malicious world of investment, and she didn't see Malcolm Reed as a threat. Just an obstacle to be gotten around. And any effort to change her way of thinking had failed. It made Gabe afraid. For her. For him.

He couldn't protect her forever. He couldn't stay with her much longer. He had his own job to do away from her and for himself. He couldn't give it up. Wouldn't. He'd worked too long and too hard. But he didn't want to see her hurt.

Not by anyone, including himself. But how could he prevent it? He might be able to stop Malcolm, but he wouldn't be able to stop being who he was.

"Dance?"

She accepted his hand with a smile and melted into his arms when they reached the dimly lit floor. Her malleability had him drawing her closer and enjoying the heat of her body as it seared his from head to toe while she silently moved with him to the music.

"I love your perfume," he told her, breathing in deeply the scent that followed him throughout the day and into his dreams at night.

Her laugh was light and quick. "Should I buy you some?"

"No, I'll buy you more."

"Another gift?"

"I haven't done too bad so far, have I?"

She pursed her lips and considered. "Two cats, three potted plants..."

"Exotic potted plants."

She rolled her eyes. "Four bottles of wine, five silk scarves..."

"All different shades."

"And six crystal glasses."

"A matching set."

"It's like the twelve days of Christmas."

"You want some geese a-laying?"

"No!"

He laughed and twirled her in a quick circle. "I don't know. Hansel and Gretel would probably enjoy some feathered friends."

"I'll never talk to you again."

"In that case..."

His kiss stole her breath away because she wasn't ready for it. But she wasn't ready for him, either. He'd taken her by surprise, conquered her by storm. It was exciting. Terrifying. She was getting too used to him in her life. He lifted his head from hers, and she reached up to stroke his jaw. "I always thought beards would be stiff and scratchy."

He touched his whiskers, too. They were softer than he would have expected. "You like it?"

"Do you?" she asked, leaning back to study his face and trying to imagine him without it.

He shrugged and dropped his hand again to let his fingers trail down her arm. She trembled, and he pulled her closer again. "This is the first real beard I've ever grown. I'm getting used to it."

"I would think the heat would make it itch."

He moved his shoulders again, a motion she could feel through every inch of her body. "Summer's over."

"But the Santa Ana winds are still blowing. They'll be here for a while."

Gabe frowned. "Yes, they already started one fire."

"But they put it out." Yet it was still frightening. The seeming annual onset of blazes that came to mar the countryside surrounding Los Angeles whenever the dry winds began to blow. Every year the city braced for the battle, and every year the fires came to wage war. "I hope they stay away from Malibu."

Gabe grinned. "Worried about your investment?"

Her answering smile wiped all worry away. "The project's going well."

"Not even one week since the contract was signed, but the first house should be done soon. Grady Thompson isn't wasting any time." Gabe gave her a squeeze. "We should celebrate. This weekend. I could give you seven hours of fun in the sun as my next present."

"My place or yours?"

The question was casual, unexpected, and it stopped him dead. He stilled on the dance floor and was stunned to find himself suddenly afraid. "Is the courtship over?"

"Gabe! Is that you?"

The unexpected exclamation stopped Danielle from speaking and had Gabe turning to accept a hand that was shoved out to him before recognition had a chance to set in.

"Where have you been?" the man facing him asked, squeezing Gabe's fingers and pumping them enthusiastically.

Gabe shrugged in response, but his mind was whirling. He'd been recognized!

Careful about where he'd been taking Danielle, he'd steered clear of his usual haunts, but without warning and too late, his efforts were proving to be not good enough.

Conscious of Danielle standing and listening beside him, fear nearly closed his throat. After all his precautions, he couldn't believe she was going to find out about him like this. In the middle of a dark dance floor from a man he barely knew. Gabe pulled his hand back but managed a noncommittal smile. "Around."

The man laughed and glanced at Danielle. "I saw your father the other day. He looks good."

"He always does." Gabe smiled and purposely put an arm around Danielle to begin moving her away even as she seemed to stiffen in an attempt to stay. The man he knew as Steven Elliott seemed to understand.

Elliott grinned and shrugged. "Yeah, well, you stay in touch," he said with a friendly punch to Gabe's shoulder. "And let's do some business again soon. Have Sam call me."

"Tomorrow good enough?" Elliott laughed, but Gabe was already swinging away and heading for the door.

At his side, Danielle said nothing. She remained silent until they were in his car and on the road, but Gabe could almost hear her thinking. And he tried to brace himself for the questions he knew were coming.

"You didn't introduce me to your friend," she finally said, her voice flat, but the accusation was there.

"He's not a friend. I barely know him," Gabe excused himself, and glanced at her profile in the darkness of the car. "And introductions would only have gotten us dragged to his table."

"Would that have been so bad?"

"Would you have wanted to go?"

Danielle didn't answer. Not immediately. "You didn't want to introduce me. You didn't want him to know who I was."

Gabe silently damned her for her insight and cursed fate for the cruel twist. Yet it was his own vanity, his own cocksureness that had seen him trapped. He'd been so certain he could get away with the masquerade and have no one question it. He gritted his teeth. "Maybe I wanted to keep you to myself."

"I wish I could believe that." She turned in her seat to watch him. "You just didn't want me to find out any more about you. Or your father, and that man knew you both." She tried to swallow the pain and stared hard at Gabe as he kept his eyes on the road. "You do business with him. Do you own your own company?"

"Would it matter if I did?"

"I'd want to know why you're working for me."

"I like working for you." He met her gaze briefly as he steered the car around a curve. "And I told you before that I like working independently."

"A little business on the side?"

"Any objections?"

"I'm not sure." She sat straight in her seat again and crossed her arms to fend off the sudden chill that had invaded the car. "What are you hiding? What are you running away from?"

He scowled. "I'm not running away from anything. I'm helping you."

"Why?"

"Because you asked."

And she had. She couldn't deny that, but it couldn't be that simple. "And why are you staying?"

"You don't know?" he demanded, and tasted defeat's bitter bile in his throat, but she hesitated. It gave him hope. He pulled up to her house and shut off the headlights and the engine. "Don't you want me to stay? Do you want me to go?"

"I want you to be honest with me." She got out of the car and hurried toward the house.

"Honesty's always the best policy, is that it?" he asked, slamming his car door in frustration before following her.

"Not for you, obviously."

"I've never lied to you."

That stopped her. She turned from the stairs leading to the deck to look at him. "Haven't you?"

He joined her on the steps. "No."

The anger drained out of her, but confusion and distrust remained. "What about telling me that you'd just gotten to the city? How could you have just gotten to the city and know that man, know the city so well?"

"I had just gotten to the city. I'd just returned."

"From where?"

"A vacation."

"From what?"

"My life. I needed a break."

"Never a straight answer. Always evasive." She whirled away to stalk up the remaining steps to the deck. "Why don't you trust me?"

Following her once more, he watched her walk away to stare out at the sea. "It's not a matter of trust."

She spun to face him. "Then what? Why are you pretending to be something you're not?"

"How do you know that? How can you know what I am?"

"I can't because you won't tell me."

He dragged a hand through his hair. "I'm just a businessman."

"Just?"

"No, not just!" he snapped, and grabbed her. "I'm also a man who's attracted to a woman. You."

His kiss was bitter, angry, demanding, nearly cruel, but she didn't try to push him away. Instead she pulled him closer and held on tight because she didn't want to lose him, and she was afraid she was but didn't understand why.

When he let her go, they were both breathing hard. "Is that so difficult to understand?" he asked, searching her face.

"No." Reluctantly she slipped from his arms to lean back against the railing. "But if you have nothing to hide, why pretend?"

He pushed his hands into his pockets to keep them away from her. "You told me once that you believed if I pretended, that I'd have had a good reason."

She nodded, remembering. "Yes, and I still believe that."

He sighed. "But you also want to know what that reason is."

She watched him pace away.

"Maybe I'm trying to protect you."

She frowned. "From what?"

"Me."

The breath caught in her throat, and she continued to watch him. But he didn't turn around. He didn't look at her again. It was for her to go to him. And she did. Hesitantly. Anxiously. She touched his arm. "I don't understand."

He didn't move. Didn't answer.

Her fingers tightened around his jacket. "Make me understand."

Finally he turned to meet the plea in her eyes. "I wish I could."

When he abruptly turned to walk away into the night, she tried to stop him, wanted to, but the words wouldn't come. Only her hand reached out for him, but he was already gone and she was alone.

Struggling to sort out and understand why, she unlocked the house, but when she stepped inside, she barely noticed the enthusiastic greeting she got from Hansel and Gretel. Her reaction to the two kittens was automatic and instinctive. She picked them up to hug them both, but hanging on to them only reminded her of the man she'd let go.

Burying her face in soft fur, Danielle tried to blink back sudden tears, but they slipped free. Maybe he was still pretending, maybe he couldn't be completely open, but he'd been honest. He'd given her all he could.

Pain such as she'd never known crushed her chest. She didn't know why, she didn't know how it was possible, but she couldn't imagine living without him. Gabe Tyler had come into her life unexpectedly, without warning. He'd taken her by surprise, and he'd also taken her heart. She was in love with him, a man she barely knew and yet knew so well, and he'd just walked out of her life.

"SAM? IT'S GABE."

"For once you didn't get me up," Sam answered gleefully. "Early night?"

"Early night," Gabe agreed heavily.

"You don't sound too happy about it."

Gabe grunted. "If you only knew."

"Maybe I do. The name Danielle Fitzsimmons ring a bell?"

Gabe grinned wryly and flopped down into a chair with the phone. "I should know better than to tell you anything."

"Especially the name of the woman you're spending your vacation with." Sam hesitated. "Vacation over?"

"Not yet."

Sam recognized the steel in the voice. "Does she know that?"

"She knows...enough."

"Except who you are?" Sam sighed when Gabe didn't answer but knew enough not to offer any advice. "Just how did you manage to meet her, anyway? Did you take a stroll into enemy camp one night?"

"No, she took a stroll down a deserted street and found me."

Sam whistled. "I think this is a tale I'd like to hear."

So Gabe told him—briefly—about how the game had started, but Sam was used to reading between the lines.

"Your trouble is that you can never walk away from a challenge. Someone throws down a gauntlet, and you just have to pick it up."

Gabe ran a weary hand over his face. "And if I didn't, you wouldn't have a job."

"That's right. Somebody has to pick up the pieces."

Gabe didn't answer, so Sam spoke again.

"What are you going to do?"

"See it through. I'm not a quitter. I started something, and I'm going to see it finished."

Sitting at his desk on the other side of the city, Sam beat out an uneven rhythm with his fingers on the paper-littered top. "Wouldn't it be easier if you told her everything?"

"If you were her and I told you who I was, what would you think?"

"The obvious answer is she'd think you used her to get inside the company to get secrets and pick up strategies, but doesn't that mean you're selling her short?"

Gabe frowned.

"She must be pretty bright if she's where she is in her father's company. Lucas Fitzsimmons isn't the sentimental sort. If she wasn't pulling her weight, he wouldn't have her with him," Sam surmised. "And you've had a couple weeks to get to know the lady. She's certainly gotten to know you, too," he pointed out. "So, it's a judgment call. Would she believe your intentions were honorable?"

Gabe stroked his beard in silent and unconscious consideration. "At this moment. Right now, if I told her, she probably would."

"Then why aren't you doing it? Why am I hearing this doubt in your voice? Don't you want to tell her?"

Gabe sighed. "I do, but I can't."

"Excuse me for being dumb, but why not?"

"Because I smell a trap. She's being set up somehow. I can feel it, and if I'm not there, I won't be able to stop it from being sprung. And, if I tell her who I am, I'll have to quit, leave her alone."

"But how long can you stay? You've got a life, too, not to mention a company to run. You'll have to leave her on her own sooner or later."

"I know."

Sam hesitated. "Can't you just warn her?"

Gabe sighed. "She's got a blind side. She trusts people. Even co-workers. She thinks they're all part of the same team."

"That can be true...wait a minute. Is there something you're not telling me?"

"Malcolm Reed."

"That name again."

"Tell me what's happening on the BLI takeover."

Sam shook his head even though Gabe couldn't see. It was a blond head on which the hair curled in unruly disorder into an open collar and above serious brown eyes. "It's getting tight. Some of the players have dropped out."

"But not Reed."

"No, he's being pretty tenacious—and underhanded. He tried to sneak in the side door the other day."

"What happened?" Gabe asked in alarm.

"I slammed it in his face."

Gabe grinned. "Good man."

Sam shrugged off the praise. "I think this deal's going to pop within the next two weeks. The board has stopped trying to row faster to save their ship. They're seriously starting to think about abandoning it instead."

"About time."

"For some it takes a while to see the light."

Gabe grunted. "Any meetings set?"

"No, they're avoiding face-to-face negotiations."

Gabe began stroking his beard again in unconscious contemplation. "We need to get inside. Get somebody's ear."

"Got anyone in mind?"

"How about a vice president? You can invite one to lunch."

Sam considered. "It could work—as long as you're paying."

Gabe grinned. "I'm paying, and we're courting." His eyes darkened as he was reminded of Danielle. He was getting to be an expert on courtship. "Bring a gift."

"Like what, and won't it be seen as a bribe?"

"Something simple like a good bottle of wine, and take an extra one for the V.P. to pass on to his boss."

"Now that *could* be seen as a bribe."

"No, a peace offering. Tell them we want to talk, and make it clear we want to come through the *front* door."

"Understood."

"Keep me advised."

"Keep yourself out of trouble."

Gabe hung up with a smile, but a frown quickly took its place. Things were heating up, and when the meetings started, he couldn't be doing two jobs anymore. He would only be able to concentrate on one.

Shoving to his feet, he headed for his bedroom thinking of Danielle. He was going to see the game through to the end. He never did anything halfway, and he never gave up before a job was done. When he started something, he went in wholeheartedly and came out with whatever he wanted. And he wanted her.

He tossed his jacket into a chair. This time was going to be no different. He was going to get what he wanted because he was going to win. Everything. And everyone knew, even Danielle, that to the victor went the spoils.

Chapter Eleven

Danielle left the elevator and entered the main office suite with a heavy heart. It was Monday and the seemingly endless weekend was behind her, but an even longer week lay ahead.

She'd waited helplessly and hopelessly both Saturday and Sunday for Gabe to call, but he hadn't. And she hadn't been able to call him. She didn't have his number. Information didn't either, and getting the Human Resources director to go into the office files on a weekend to get her an employee's home phone number without a bona fide emergency just hadn't been an option. Gabe might not have to work with those in her father's company anymore, but she did.

Without asking Kelly, who mingled with company staff other than officers, Danielle knew the rumor mill was working against her and Gabe. The boss's daughter and her male associate. Malcolm was the only one to actually voice his opinion about the matchup, but it was an opinion that was, no doubt, shared by countless others. Danielle didn't want to give credence to anything anybody was saying by her actions. That had left her to wait and hope he'd call. But he hadn't. And now she could only wonder if she would ever see him again and if she really wanted to.

Could she trust her feelings? Did she love Gabe or only who she thought he was? Who was Gabe Tyler? What was it he was, or thought he was, protecting her from? He said himself. But that didn't seem reasonable. Or explainable. And as long as secrets continued to be held between them, how could the two of them hope to have a chance of forging a lasting relationship? And if Gabe had chosen to walk and stay away from her, did that mean he didn't really want to try? Did it matter to him how she felt?

Murmuring polite greetings to those she passed, Danielle followed the corridor toward her office and braced herself to see his empty desk. It was impossible to be prepared to find it vacant. Facing the fact that he was gone and she'd never have any answers, only questions, about what might have been left her numb.

With a hurried good-morning, she rushed past Kelly and into the sanctuary of the room with her name on the door. Alone she could hope to find solace and refuge, but inside she wasn't by herself. Somebody was at her desk. And when she entered, he turned to look up to meet her startled gaze.

"Gabe."

The word was a sigh. It hit him hard, and the hope in her eyes made it difficult to stand still. But he did. Somehow. "You're late."

More surprised by him than his accusation, she moved around him to stand behind her desk. Words bubbled in her throat, collided in her mind, but, too used to decorum and manners and control, she held back feelings to give an explanation instead. "It's a bad habit I've picked up since moving to Malibu, especially now that I have two children to look after."

He grinned, but his fingers were itching. He wanted to touch not look, and he wanted to decipher the emotions she was trying to hide behind that shield of reserve she'd quickly put in place on seeing him. "How are Hansel and Gretel?"

"They like my new furniture," she told him, her smile still in place, but she hated the polite conversation. She wasn't saying what she wanted to and didn't like talking to him as if they were strangers. Instead she wanted to dive into the undercurrents surging between them, but giving way to impulse was too new to her yet. "They like it all—and my parents. They climbed all over both on Sunday."

"Really?" His smile was quick, but she couldn't read what was in his eyes. She never could.

"Since I finally had someplace for them to sit, I invited my mother and father over for dinner," she hastily went on when he didn't say more. "I cooked."

"I'm impressed."

"Don't be. I burned everything."

"Maybe you should have tried hot dogs."

The laughter bubbled out, but her smile slowly faded as she met his steady gaze. "I didn't think you'd be here today."

"I didn't know if you'd want me to come."

She shook her head in denial. "I did. I do."

This time his smile warmed her to her toes. "Good. Because I think we deserve a second chance."

She held her breath.

"Don't you?"

She looked away from him to her briefcase. It was the only way she could hide her relief and the love she wasn't sure he would take and that she wasn't certain was real. "I think so."

"A little slower this time, maybe."

She nodded and lifted her eyes to him again. "I like slow."

"Then I'll try to be patient."

"And I'll try to be understanding."

His eyes darkened on hers. "I won't tell you everything."

"You don't have to." Her smile returned with a taunting twitch. "Yet."

He nodded acceptance of her dare. "I like a determined woman."

"I've been taking lessons from a determined man."

"Anyone I know?"

The intercom on her desk went off, and Danielle jumped in surprise, glared at it and then reached for it resentfully. "Yes?"

"Ms. Fitzsimmons," Kelly's voice answered. "Mr. Reed's—"

"Here to see you," Malcolm finished, striding through the open door and into the room. He didn't so much as look at Gabe as he approached the desk. "You know, Danielle, your new secretary seems familiar somehow. Has she worked here before?"

The urge to protect swelled up, and Danielle shrugged noncommittally before reaching for the folders Malcolm held out to her. "Would it matter if she had?"

Malcolm gestured carelessly. "Not really." He pointed to the files. "The two accounts your father wanted you to take a look at for me. I appreciate the help."

Danielle's glance flitted to Gabe, who rolled his eyes, but she accepted Malcolm's attempt to pass the turnover of accounts off as his decision with a smile. "We're a team, Malcolm. We all work for the same company and for the same board of directors."

"Perhaps you'll ask my advice this time, then?" Malcolm suggested with a studious expression. "It might go better, and quicker, if we work together."

"Of course, it's what I've wanted all along." She weighed the papers in her hand. The binders were thick. Heavy. They promised a challenge. She smiled. "I'll look them over and set up a meeting so we can go over them."

"Alone," Malcolm pressed, finally sparing Gabe a glance. "I think the two of us can work things through without any outside help."

"Absolutely," Danielle agreed with a straight face, even though Gabe's eyes narrowed.

"Later, then," Malcolm said with a wave, and was gone.

"He—"

"Is someone we have to work with," Danielle interrupted Gabe. "You could work on your diplomacy."

"I'd prefer to practice my swing."

She handed him a file. "Practice reading instead. You take one, and I take one. We'll exchange and then compare notes."

"Yes, ma'am."

But the reading took longer than expected. It was an entire day before she got through one file. The other went home that night and back to the office the next morning before she finished it. She had no time to plot strategy with Gabe because Malcolm called, anxious for the promised meeting.

She went and tried to listen with an open mind as he voiced his ideas. It was in her to trust him, but he'd deceived her once. She couldn't be sure he wouldn't do it again, but she was surprised by his candor—and by his voluntarily turning over yet another account to her without her father's prompting.

When she returned to her office after leaving Malcolm, Gabe was waiting. He rose from his desk to follow her into her office. "How'd it go?"

Danielle sat back and shook her head. "Malcolm was honest." She shrugged. "He just wasn't much help."

"Did you expect him to be?"

She bit her lip. "His approach is certainly different than mine and yours."

"Only great minds think alike."

She smothered the impulse to answer his grin with one of her own. Danielle desperately wanted to ask Gabe when they were going to spend some time together again after working hours, but she didn't. She'd agreed to go slowly. It wasn't her place to push. Unfortunately. She tapped the new folder on her desk. "He gave me a new file."

Gabe's eyebrows shot up.

"Don't look so surprised. Maybe he's turning over a new leaf."

If Gabe had any doubts, he kept them to himself. "Want me to go over it?"

"No, let's start on the other two files first."

He waved to the waiting table. "Now?"

She glanced at her watch. It was four o'clock. "It's late."

"I don't mind long hours."

Her breath hitched and her pulse jumped when his eyes fastened on hers. "Neither do I." But even though she followed him across the room to begin work, once started, she found it difficult to concentrate on the job at hand with him sitting beside her. With his jacket off and his sleeves rolled up, she could see the dark hairs curling softly along his forearms and the tan skin that covered fingers that were long and strong.

"You agree?"

"What?" she asked at the unexpected question.

"Do your figures match mine?"

"Figures?" she repeated, her eyes meeting his.

He tapped the paper lying before him with a pencil. "Figures."

"Oh, of course." She quickly dipped her head to look at her own column of numbers.

"Do you want to quit for the night?"

"No, I'm fine," she insisted, and glanced at her watch. "It's only six. But what about you? I don't want to ruin any plans you might have."

"I don't have any place to go."

His gaze fastened on her mouth, and she unconsciously licked her lips in anticipation. "I don't, either."

"Good."

When he leaned forward, she did, too, but they jumped apart on a call.

"Danielle! Are you still here?"

"My father," she murmured in apology.

Gabe smiled ruefully. "We always seem to be getting interrupted. Some day you won't be so lucky." He stood as Lucas Fitzsimmons strode into the room. "We were just calling it quits," he told the older man, and reached for the suit coat that he'd discarded earlier.

Danielle got to her feet as well and watched her father glower at Gabe before scowling at her.

"Your dedication is admirable," Lucas Fitzsimmons told her. "But don't forget you're supposed to be at the house in an hour."

"Oh, no!" she exclaimed. "I'll call Mother and tell her I'll be a little late."

"Please do," her father growled. "I'd rather she be angry at you than me." He nodded to Gabe as Danielle raced for the phone, but he didn't stay as she dialed. Instead he immediately went back out the door, leaving Danielle and Gabe alone again.

"Benefit bout?" Gabe asked as she hurriedly punched out the number.

"The auction," she agreed, and straightened to wait for the ring.

"Ah, I remember," he acknowledged, shrugging into his jacket and walking to her desk. "I'm supposed to be sold off to the highest bidder."

Her lips twitched as he stopped in front of the desk, and she barely heard the phone start to ring at her parents' house. "I think you'll bring a fair price."

"Just don't forget to rescue me," he admonished, and unexpectedly leaned toward her to press his lips to hers for a brief, if searing, kiss.

The unexpected attack stole her breath and her reason and delayed her ability to speak when the ringing stopped and someone answered. She finally managed to stammer out a hello as Gabe strolled out the door with a wink, but she was still thinking of him when she got to her car moments later. The single, perfect red rose lying on the windshield saw that she kept thinking of him, too. All night long.

DANIELLE SAT BACK from the table with a sigh. It was morning, and she and Gabe were in her office continuing where they'd left off the evening before when her father had interrupted them.

"Problem?" he asked and leaned back in his chair to study her. She was wearing a white dress today with a red blazer. The cool color clashed with the hot one, but together the shades served to set off her coloring and her personality perfectly. The cool exterior. The hot interior. He couldn't wait to unleash the passion so the ice would melt completely away.

"I'm not sure."

He watched her push some papers around.

"These accounts aren't that complicated. There's work to be done, yes, but I don't see why Malcolm didn't wrap these up a long time ago."

"Purposeful delay?"

"Why?"

"Maybe he's trying to impress your father with his work load," Gabe suggested, wondering if it was true and relieved she had sensed what he had already determined. "He's worked on both these files regularly."

"Doing something but not enough."

Gabe tapped his pencil on his tablet. "I looked over that new file he gave you before you got in this morning."

"And?"

"Same thing."

Danielle shoved her chair back from the table to sigh, and walked to the window. "I don't know what it is, but something doesn't seem right about these accounts."

"Why?" he encouraged, wanting her to find what he was beginning to suspect.

"It's almost as if..."

"Something's missing?" he provided when she grappled for a word.

"Yes! That's it exactly!"

He watched her smile immediately turn to a frown.

"But what? And why?"

"I thought we already determined Malcolm doesn't want you to succeed," Gabe reminded her.

"But we're—"

"Part of the same team? I thought we addressed that, too." Gabe stood up to walk toward her. "You're competition, Danielle, and in business, competition—"

"Has to be eliminated," she said, remembering his words from the night at the pool. Her eyes narrowed. "So what do I do?"

"If he didn't give you the entire file, you have to get what he didn't give you."

"How?"

"Who has access to Malcolm's files? Or who could gain access to Malcolm's files without raising suspicion?"

"Kelly," Danielle murmured.

"She's bound to know Malcolm's secretary, and Malcolm is out of the office this morning."

Danielle grinned, but there was no humor in her eyes. "And if we get his files, by tomorrow's meeting with the board, we might know something he doesn't want us to."

"Something, no doubt, that would end up putting egg all over your face if you didn't find out about it."

Danielle stalked to the door and found no one outside or in earshot but her secretary. "Kelly, come in here. We need you."

And Kelly answered the call, disappearing from Danielle's office only to return less than half an hour later with some folders and a sunny disposition. "It was easy. He has another temp filling in today. She didn't even go with me to see what I was taking from his desk."

Danielle took the folders but quickly shared them with Gabe, who led the way to the table. He was smiling at Kelly's successful raid, but what he read rapidly turned his smile into a frown. Slowly, he looked from the papers he was holding to Danielle who was staring at what was in her hand in disbelief. "Without this information," he told her, "you would have closed these accounts at a loss and never known it until you were sitting in front of the board."

Danielle shook her head. "He set me up."

"And would have watched you fall."

"And then shown me the door." Danielle slapped the folder shut, making Kelly jump and Gabe smile. The ice was thawing.

"What do you want us to do, boss?"

His drawl had Danielle smiling with malicious intent. "Blow him out of the water."

Gabe winked at Kelly. "Brace yourself. It's going to be a long night."

But the time was filled with energy as the three of them continued to work well after everyone else had gone home. Together they compiled data, made phone calls and plotted revenge. It was impossible to wrap up any of the accounts in a day, but it was reasonable to make projections and predict settlement dates as well as profit margins. And the bottom line was what Danielle needed.

Gabe sat back with a sigh and tossed his pencil down. It was eight o'clock. Kelly had just left for the night, and Danielle was just hanging up at her desk. "Done?"

"Done."

He grinned. "I'm glad I'll be there in the morning to see Malcolm's face."

"You don't like him much."

"You do?"

She shrugged noncommittally and watched Gabe rise to walk to her. His suit coat was off, his sleeves were rolled up and his collar was open. His tie lay loosened at his throat, and his hair was in disarray from his hand repeatedly plowing through it. But, to her, he'd never looked better, and she didn't resist when he pulled her out of her chair and into his arms. "Can I take the fifth? He is an officer in the company."

"I like loyalty."

"I'm very loyal." And she proved it by pressing herself up against him to fasten her lips on his in a draining kiss. "See?" she asked breathlessly on releasing him, and he wasn't prepared to argue.

"I hope you don't kiss anyone else like that," he observed with a sigh.

"Why?"

"Because I'd break their necks."

His growl brought her back to him again, and she had to breathe deeply to catch her breath when he let her go. Nevertheless, she kept her arms around him and her body against his. "I definitely like slow."

"We aim to please," he said, nuzzling her hair, inhaling her perfume and holding her close while she relaxed and stood pliantly in his grasp.

"The office isn't exactly the place to have a romantic rendezvous, though."

He combed his fingers through her hair, oblivious to their surroundings. "I'm adaptable."

"Helpful, too." Her gaze locked with his. "I could never have done all this without you."

He shook his head. "You knew Malcolm was up to something before I said anything."

"But what would I have done about it without you?"

He shrugged. "It doesn't matter. Whether you would have confronted him or been knocked down, you would have gotten back up again. You're a tough lady."

"Yeah?"

"Yeah," he agreed, and bent to taste her mouth again. It was delicious. Like her. Reluctantly he lifted his lips from hers. "Makes me think you don't need me here anymore."

She stiffened immediately. "Don't say that!"

"Why not? It's true."

She pulled out of his arms to step away from him. "Are you saying you're leaving now?"

He reached out to catch her and bring her back to him. "I'm saying I've done what you hired me to."

Her eyes searched his. "But..."

"I'll stick around for a while." His finger traced her cheek. "You're not going to get rid of me yet."

"But how long will I have?"

He smiled and kissed the tip of her nose. "How long would you like?"

But he wasn't talking about the office. She lifted her hands to frame his face with her hands, but the doubts and questions were in her eyes.

He caught her fingers to cup them in his and press them to his lips. "You'll have the answers soon."

She shook her head at the determined gleam in his dark eyes. "I don't know if I want to hear them. You make me afraid."

"No, it's you who makes me afraid." He kissed her fingers again. "You're going to sell me off to the highest bidder."

She had to laugh, but she also held on tight. To him. She didn't want to let him go. "You won't go on the auction block for a couple of weeks yet. You still have some time to prepare."

"So do you." He kissed her quickly and pulled away. "You have quite a view of the fires from here."

Danielle accepted the change of subject, but it was hard. She wanted to ask more, know more, but at the same time she wasn't sure it really mattered. Still holding on to his hand, she followed his gaze out the windows behind her desk to the red glow in the sky beyond the city and nodded. To the west where the canyons ran and the winds blew, smoke layered the mountains and the red reflection of flames danced across the moon high above the Earth. "The fires are bad this year."

"But not near Malibu. You're safe there."

She sighed. "And the project, too. We should go out and see Grady tomorrow."

Gabe grinned. "We'll go. After you burn Malcolm up at the morning meeting."

Chapter Twelve

Gabe watched Danielle take her place at the conference table. She was nervous. He could tell. A smile curved his lips. But no one else would notice. Not even her father. Lucas Fitzsimmons wouldn't recognize any anxiety in his daughter because he didn't know her that well. Gabe's smile grew. But he did.

He was aware of the way her gaze darted around the room, of the way her fingers were gripping her papers. He saw past the cool reserve that kept her expression neutral and her stance relaxed.

The ice was still in place, but it had started to melt. She'd become warmer inside and out since he'd first met her. The inner glow she'd been smothering with decorum was starting to show.

He wasn't ashamed of the part he'd played in breaking down her self-control. He had no fear that losing the tight-lipped composure she'd been raised to constantly exercise would leave her defenseless. To his way of thinking, he'd simply freed her of an inhibition that stopped her from being who she really was. And he was looking forward to finally being able to truly get to know the woman who'd been hiding in a shell, because the crisis lying between them was almost over.

Malcolm entered the room, and Gabe couldn't help but smile. Yes, his usefulness to Danielle in the office was just about past. Once he helped her see these last accounts she'd been given settled and having finally convinced her that Malcolm Reed was not and would never be her teammate, Gabe figured he could resign. And just in time.

A conversation with Sam the night before had alerted him to a meeting. The lunch with a BLI officer had worked. The board of directors was opening the door to negotiations. The takeover effort had been interrupting the company's already faulty production and had forced the board to recognize its inability to cope with or correct the steady deterioration of a once-thriving enterprise.

The BLI conglomerate was losing business, losing money and had no prestige. The directors were ready to bail out, and Gabe was ready to take over—once he eliminated the competition.

Gabe watched Malcolm take his seat. He was happy to let Danielle take her co-worker down a peg on the accounts she was handling, but Gabe wanted Malcolm all to himself when it came down to a war across the conference table with BLI. He was going to get a lot of pleasure out of making Malcolm Reed eat crow. The man was a coward and a cheat. He milked accounts to make himself look good, dropped those that required too much work and offered not enough profit, and made his own priorities instead of following his company's. Malcolm Reed had no loyalty. Only greed.

Gabe sat back with a smile as the conference room doors were closed. Without a doubt, he was sure that eliminating the BLI competition was going to be something that he thoroughly enjoyed.

Lucas Fitzsimmons called the meeting to order and quickly made some announcements before going around the table for updates on various business. Gabe paid little attention, waiting for Danielle's moment, but it was Malcolm who got his attention instead when her father called on him to give a status report on the takeover effort.

"It looks like the BLI project is reaching a pivotal point," Malcolm answered on being questioned, his face appropriately grave as he addressed those seated around him. "I believe we'll have a meeting shortly, and the serious negotiations we've been hoping for will begin."

"The competition?" Lucas Fitzsimmons demanded.

Malcolm shook his head. "I've tried to go around them, get to BLI first to let the company directors know of our interest, but Action Enterprises caught on."

Fitzsimmons scowled. "They're tough competitors. They've beaten us out of property before." He stared hard at Malcolm. "I don't want to lose out to them again."

"You won't. I'm ready for them," Malcolm declared firmly. Across the room Gabe smiled. He was ready, too.

"Danielle," Fitzsimmons said, turning from Malcolm to her. "You have two new accounts to report on."

"Three, actually," she agreed with a cool smile. "Malcolm and I are working on three together."

Malcolm bowed his head graciously at the recognition but gestured magnanimously. "Danielle's too modest. She's been doing all the work."

And so can take all the blame. Or so Malcolm thought. Gabe smothered his anger.

Danielle started to talk, but while Gabe listened to her, he watched Malcolm. And after a few minutes, he thought it a shame no one else was keeping an eye on Lucas Fitzsimmons's favorite vice president, too, for the expressions that flashed across Malcolm's face as Danielle went over figures, dates and projections spoke volumes.

Cocky expectation and a sublime smile turned into startled disbelief and a concerned frown. Those, in turn, changed into absolute shock and an openmouthed stare. And the performance was repeated three times. Once for each file Danielle was reporting on, because Malcolm held true to the end. He refused to have any faith in her ability to outmaneuver him one time out of three much less three times out of three.

"It will take time to wrap up the details, and the projections aren't guaranteed," Danielle concluded, her delivery cool and professional as she let her gaze flick over those seated at the table. "But I think the figures are very close to the mark."

"Excellent." Her father all but beamed. "Malcolm, I think we can finally get that backlog off your desk. With Danielle's help, we can clear your calendar so you can concentrate on BLI." He leaned forward to point at Malcolm. "Remember. I want that company to be ours. We can make a tidy profit cutting BLI up and selling the pieces off."

"Y-yes, sir," Malcolm stammered, his usual composure shattered by disbelief and his skin pale beneath his tan under the weight of defeat.

"Danielle, I want you to go to Malcolm's office and collect some more of his files," her father demanded, quickly dismissing Malcolm and focusing on her. "And I want you to give those you've been handling on a regular basis to Tony Jennings. He needs some breaking in, and you need to be free to do more important work."

"Hear, hear," one of the other officers agreed, and Danielle smiled graciously as the meeting abruptly broke up.

Smiling himself, Gabe watched her rise to accept congratulations from some of the other officers but didn't linger. He wandered instead, as she enjoyed the sweet taste of victory, toward the door to wait for her, and nearly ran into a retreating Malcolm.

"I'll go with you to your office to pick up those files," Gabe offered, effectively stopping Malcolm's hasty escape. "If you had to carry them all the way to Danielle's, something might fall out again."

Malcolm flushed. "You'll regret this, Tyler."

"Regret isn't the word I'd use to describe how I feel right now," Gabe responded with unflustered calm, pushing his hands into his pants pockets and carelessly deflecting Malcolm's glare.

Malcolm's fists clenched, his mouth thinned, but he didn't speak again. Rather he swung away to storm down the hall as Danielle reached Gabe's side.

"Was it something I said?" she asked innocently.

Gabe turned to look down at her, but he didn't have to look far. She was wearing heels again. They brought her nearly up to his height. "I don't think so."

Without a thought for those around her, she took his offered arm and moved with him out into the hall. "And what were you and Malcolm discussing? The conversation looked very intense."

"Your outfit, actually," Gabe told her with a perfectly straight face and let his gaze briefly flit over the white skirt and jacket she wore that was set off by an emerald green silk blouse that matched her eyes. A scarf tied around her neck set off the whole ensemble. "He doesn't like the ponytail, but I think it's cute."

Self-consciously Danielle put a hand to her hair that had been pulled back and tied in what she had hoped would be accepted as sleek style. "I don't think the term 'cute' has been applied to me since I was three."

"Give me time, and I'll think of plenty of other terms of endearment to describe you."

Embarrassed heat flooded her cheeks, but she was saved from comment by her father, who came up from behind to join them as they walked down the hall.

"You didn't mention the Malibu project today, Danielle," Lucas Fitzsimmons commented.

"No, because I was planning on driving out today to take a look," she answered, stopping to face him but not attempting to take her arm away from where it was hooked casually with Gabe's. And if her father noticed, he said nothing and neither did Gabe. He just smiled.

"We'll hear about it at the next meeting, then."

"Absolutely."

Her father turned to Gabe. "You've been working hard since you've come here."

"He's been a big help," Danielle quickly chimed in. "Maybe we should give him a raise."

"Indeed," Fitzsimmons agreed, and held out his hand. "Keep up the good work. It's appreciated."

"Thank you, sir," Gabe accepted, meeting the firm handclasp with one of his own. And, when the older man walked away, "How big of a raise do I get?"

Danielle turned serious eyes on him. "How big do you need?"

Gabe hesitated. The questions were back again, bubbling and standing between them. She wanted to know who he was. And he was, finally, almost in a position to tell her. "I've been patient. You have to be, too."

She bit her lip. "I'm trying."

"And I'm going to get those files from Malcolm before anything gets pulled out of them."

She nodded understanding and swallowed her questions to let him slip away. "I'll have Kelly meet you in the file room."

But Kelly was already there when Gabe arrived. She was in the corner with Malcolm, who was towering over her as he cornered her against a wall.

"You took the files, didn't you? My secretary said you came looking for some files. You knew I was gone and used that excuse to get into my office and take those folders from my desk like the little thief you are," Malcolm accused, shaking her as he held her by the arms. "And all the time pretending to be some mousy little thing in your stupid disguise."

Kelly squealed as he grabbed her oversized glasses and smashed them underfoot.

"Did you really think you'd fool me for long?" He dragged her toward him, his grip fierce, his head dipping and his intent clear.

"Let her go."

Malcolm froze.

"I said, let her go."

The words were cool, sharp and demanding. Each one was pronounced with perfect precision. Malcolm couldn't miss their meaning or ignore the threat that lay beneath them. Slowly he straightened, released Kelly and turned to face Gabe. "Get out of here, Tyler."

But Gabe didn't move. "If I go, she's coming with me."

Malcolm sneered. "You're only an employee here, Tyler. I'm an officer. You can be fired for insubordination."

"And you can be sued for sexual harassment," Gabe shot back, his stance set and his gaze bitter black. "I believe that's why Kelly's wearing the disguise. To discourage your unwanted attentions."

"What makes you think they're unwanted?"

The smile made Gabe cringe in repulsion, but he was given no chance to respond or react.

With an angry cry, Kelly suddenly shoved into Malcolm. The unexpected force of her push knocked him aside and gave her the room she needed to squeeze past him and the filing cabinets surrounding them to get to Gabe's side.

Gabe caught her when she reached him. "Are you all right?"

She nodded emphatically but kept her eyes on Malcolm. "I'm fine now that I have a witness."

Malcolm made an unfathomable sound and took a step forward, and Gabe immediately put himself in front of Kelly, his fingers clenching into fists.

"Stay away from her, Reed, unless you want to eat your teeth for lunch."

"Don't threaten me, Tyler!"

"It's no threat. It's a promise," Gabe retorted hotly. "You touch her again, you'll answer to me. You try to set Danielle up again, you'll answer to me. And just so you know, the only reason Kelly went to your office to get those files was because Danielle asked her to go."

Disbelief clouded Malcolm's face.

"That's right, Reed," Gabe warned. "Danielle isn't as dumb as you'd like her to be, and she's proving it to the board. You better start working harder, or she's going to have your job."

Malcolm growled again. Gabe wouldn't have touched him if he'd stayed still. But Malcolm moved. He lunged forward. And, without the slightest hesitation, Gabe swung.

His knuckles connected solidly with Malcolm's jaw.

The power of the blow lifted Malcolm off his feet. It sent him reeling backward and into the metal filing cabinets behind him. The drawers reverberated loudly at the collision and clanged again when Malcolm bounced from one drawer into another.

Malcolm tried to regain his balance but, staggering not only from the blow but from the loss of equilibrium, he tripped over his own feet, flailed madly for a handhold and collapsed on the floor.

He'd barely fallen when the noise brought people running. Secretaries and file clerks mostly, they came to see what had happened. Danielle was among them. Searching for Kelly to send her to join Gabe, she was in time to see Malcolm hit the carpet and stood, stunned and speechless with the other latecomers, to watch him wipe blood from his mouth.

"Malcolm, what...?" But the rage and satisfaction she saw in Gabe's angry glare when she looked to him stopped her. She didn't have to ask. She knew what was going on, and when she saw a disheveled Kelly standing beside Gabe, she knew how the fight had started. "Kelly, are you all right?"

The strength of Kelly's smile surprised her, and Kelly turned her grin on Malcolm as he lay on the floor staring up at her. "Fine. In fact, I've never been better." She swung away to face Gabe. "Thank you."

He shrugged carelessly, but his eyes were shining as they met hers. "My pleasure."

With a final victorious look at a fallen Malcolm, Kelly whirled away to march past the other bystanders, and Danielle stepped aside to get out of her way.

Clearing her throat as Gabe shook his hand and assured himself that at least *he* wasn't bleeding, she looked from him to Malcolm, who was struggling to rise again. "I think you better go."

"Why? Afraid we'll go another round?" Gabe asked with a malicious grin that told her he was more than ready, willing and able.

"No, afraid I'll have to pick up the pieces." She gave him a shove toward the door and motioned to one of the young file clerks. It was time for damage control. "Give Mr. Reed a hand. He's had an accident."

"Yes, he sure has," Gabe agreed, and stopped at the door to watch Danielle take charge and to wink at one of the secretaries. "He slipped off the ladder."

Danielle's gaze flew to his at the comment, too well aware that no ladder was in sight.

Gabe didn't care about technicalities as he went out the door because he knew Malcolm had slipped, all right. Straight off the ladder of success.

"I STILL CAN'T BELIEVE you hit him," Danielle said hours later as she climbed with Gabe around the Malibu site. Their suit coats were off, left behind in her car and on his motorcycle. The hot Santa Ana breeze was whipping sand around them.

"He deserved it."

"Kelly would agree."

Gabe smiled. "I suppose I'll see her dressed as Kelly not Karen tomorrow?"

"I suppose," Danielle admitted, and turned a leery eye on him. "Just remember that you're already spoken for."

"Afraid of a little competition?"

"Not after learning how to throw a right hook."

Gabe laughed and put an arm around her as they stopped on a hilltop to look down the beach at the construction. The skeletons of several houses could be seen from where they stood, along with cement trucks, stacks of lumber and dozens of pieces of equipment and men. The whine and call of machinery and workers could be heard above the cry of sea gull and ocean, but it was a happy sound. "Exciting, isn't it? To know you're making something grow."

She nodded without looking away from the various scenes of organized chaos. "Incredible. I think I like dealing in real estate."

He moved his shoulders in uncertain agreement. "Investment can be the same. You put money into something and watch it expand, become more than what it was."

"We usually don't hang on to any investment that long." She sighed and turned away from the building and the workmen to the endless ocean beyond both. "We always seem to sell everything after putting a minimum amount of development into it."

"Sounds like you don't follow your father's philosophy to conquer and then divide."

She lifted a hand to brush the hair from her face. The wind that seemed to be hot one minute and cool the next as it shifted direction from land to beach had loosened it from its ponytail, but she didn't care. "I don't. I think, beyond the original purchase price, sometimes we should spend more money to get a good return back, but my father doesn't believe in putting more into an investment than is absolutely necessary. Just enough to improve and sell. Never enough to expand and grow."

Gabe nodded thoughtfully even though she wasn't watching him. "Maybe you can change his way of thinking."

She snorted in unladylike disbelief. "Ever try telling the sun not to come up in the morning?"

"I would if I was in bed with you."

Her heart stopped. But just for a moment. Adrenaline kicked it into rhythm again. "That wouldn't stop the sun from rising."

"Maybe not, but it would sure make me hope it wouldn't."

Slowly she turned to face him, her mind suddenly and ir-revocably made up. "We'd still have to go to work in the morning."

He held his breath and met her green gaze with a casual shrug. "We could play hooky."

His suggestion had her arching an eyebrow. "The day after we've been given a pile of new accounts?"

"There's always tomorrow."

She smiled as he moved closer. "I might let you convince me, even though the gossip will be merciless."

"Appearances."

"They can strangle you."

"And giving in to impulses can set you free." He pulled her into his arms, and time was lost. He was lost. In her.

She pulled away slightly, leaving her lips a whisper length from his. "Your place or mine?"

"Still want to see where I live?"

She closed her eyes as his mouth covered hers again. "Only if you'd prefer to not spend the night wrestling with Hansel and Gretel."

"Maybe I can show them a trick or two."

Her gaze locked with his again. "I'd prefer you show me."

Letting out a whoop, he spun her in a circle. "Oh, what Donald's missing."

She laughed when he set her down, and pushed away. "We have company."

"So what."

She swatted at him when he tried to catch her again and stepped back to greet Grady Thompson. "Grady, we came to have another look."

The big man nodded, politely refraining from comment-ing on the intimate exchange he'd witnessed. "We're cook-ing along."

"Literally," Gabe observed, and wiped sweat from his brow with his shirtsleeve.

Grady grunted agreement. The T-shirt he had on was caked with sand and sweat. "The Santa Anas are making it hot, but we're watching them."

Danielle followed his gaze to the horizon and Los Angeles where smoke and flame could be seen dancing in the hills that stood high above the skyscrapers. "The fires have stayed to the south so far."

"She's a worrier," Gabe observed aloud, and Grady grinned appreciatively.

"I worry myself when those winds blow. I don't want them touching my buildings." He gestured to the nearest structure that was lacking walls but had the beams and staircases laid. "It's a bit cooler today with the wind coming off the ocean once in a while. How about I give you a tour?"

"I'd love to," Danielle agreed, her eyes lighting up, but Gabe shook his head.

"You go," he told her. "I'm going to take the bike back to town. I'll meet you in a couple hours."

"I'll warn Hansel and Gretel to expect you."

He laughed at her smirk and Grady Thompson frowned, but Gabe could have cared less about what the big man thought. He had a seduction to plan, and he was going to do it in grand style.

Yet if his mood was bright when he left, it was a black ride into the city, as he had to detour around roads blocked by fire crews and flame. Without a doubt, Gabe knew it was going to be a bad year for the Los Angeles basin.

Years of drought had left dried vegetation and dead trees for kindling. Any new growth that had come from winter and spring rain had long since been scorched away by the heat of summer and was now being baked by the Santa

Anas—winds that came from the weather systems that blew in from the Mojave Desert.

He'd seen the pattern before. A simple spark in these conditions could start a blaze that would take out hundreds of acres. Already the new year's siege had taken nearly twenty thousand acres, countless homes and two lives. And while the season was drawing to a close, it wasn't over yet.

Feeling as if he'd just driven through a furnace, Gabe jumped in the shower on reaching his home and cooled off, but he didn't remain under the water long. He left the bathroom for the bedroom, where he changed into a white polo shirt and slacks. It wasn't elegant attire, but he didn't figure what he was wearing was going to change things much, so chose to go casual rather than formal.

In no time he was out on the road again, driving his car this time and stopping at a florist and a liquor store before swinging past a restaurant where he knew he could get the best in carryout. But he was already thinking past dinner to dessert.

Whistling a nameless tune and turning the air-conditioning in the car on high, he returned to the streets leading from the city and zigzagged his way through rush hour traffic under a sky that was eerily lit by nature's display of earth, wind and fire. It was a trip that took longer than normal under the conditions at hand, but patience was easy to come by when he knew what—and who—was waiting for him.

Yet the idea of culmination brought a vague sense of uneasiness as well as elation. He'd waited for Danielle a long time. Playing a knight on a motorcycle, a hero on the business battlefield and a suitor in candlelight, he'd wooed and charmed in an attempt to win her over, but he was almost nervous by the time her Malibu house came into view. If he hadn't known better, he would have sworn his palms were sweating, but he put that possibility down to the heat wait-ing for him when he stepped out of the car.

Skipping up the walk and onto the deck with his hands full of flowers, champagne and food, he knocked, but no one came to answer. And when he looked inside, Hansel and Gretel were the only ones he could see. Danielle wasn't in sight.

Staring through the glass, he watched Hansel and Gretel pat the panes, listened to their muffled cries and wondered if Danielle was in the shower. Or if perhaps she hadn't yet come home.

He scanned the living room, searching for some sign of her return. He couldn't believe she was still at the site with Grady Thompson. But then again he could. Victory could be sweet, and it was her first win. But then he saw the scarf.

Tossed on a chair leading to the steps and the upstairs bedrooms, it was the same green one she'd had on at the office during the day. His concern deepened and was made worse by the ominous wind. Rushing down the shoreline, the breeze carried the smell of smoke.

Following the scent, he turned on the deck and felt his heart stop when he saw the flames. A wall of fire was com-ing down toward Malibu, and Grady Thompson's building site was right in its path.

"Danielle."

The word was a whisper, a plea, and Gabe suddenly knew what had happened. She'd come home, started to get ready and then seen the flames. Without thinking, she'd gone in the car to get a closer look, probably to reassure herself that the beams laid to form new homes weren't in any danger.

Without further thought, Gabe dropped the champagne, the food and the roses and started to run. He had to get **to** her before the fire did.

Chapter Thirteen

The heat was scorching. The smoke blinding. And Danielle was surrounded by both.

Coughing as a blast of wind clogged her lungs with ash and burned her eyes with flying debris, she held up her hands to fight off a merciless foe and struggled to see where she was going.

The only chance she had was to get back to the car. The only way she could escape was to return to the road the fire was threatening to jump. But it was getting impossible to see, difficult to breathe.

Ducking behind a pile of lumber, she tried to gather her wits and think. It had been a stupid idea to come back to the building site, but she hadn't been able to help herself.

Gasping, she caught a mouthful of fresh air carried to her by an ocean breeze and turned to stare at the beams and girders standing behind her like silent sentinels as smoke swirled around them. She'd finished touring one of the nearly completed structures only a short time ago with Grady Thompson. It had been an hour or so before quitting time when the tour had finished, but she had headed for her car and home rather than the office with only a vague twinge of guilt. She'd worked hard over the past couple weeks. She figured she deserved an hour or two of unscheduled downtime, especially considering the night that lay ahead.

Already planning the evening with Gabe, she'd hurried back to the bungalow to shower, change and prepare for a night of promise. She'd ignored the nerves, the butterflies and doubts as she'd slipped into a cool cotton jumpsuit and pushed aside the questions about who he was. Who they were separately didn't have to come between who they were together. Finally ready and waiting for him to arrive, she'd strolled out onto the deck. That's when she'd seen the fire.

Uncertain at first if it was real, she'd stood holding her breath and praying the brief flare of light had come only from her imagination, but the fire had flickered once more.

Appearing up the coast, it'd been far away from the bungalow, miles from her small section of ocean shore, but had glowed exactly where it could do the most damage. At the Malibu construction site.

Unable to believe that the beauty of the land Grady Thompson was so carefully developing was about to be blackened by the fury of Mother Nature, worried that he and his crew were unaware of the danger and still working, she'd hurried to the phone to call for help. But no one had been able to come. Not right away.

The fires had units scattered across the counties surrounding L.A., and equipment was scarce. No guarantee could be given for speed, so she'd hung up and run for her car.

Speeding up the coast highway, oblivious to the retreating traffic and any personal danger, she'd raced to reach the construction site, praying she was wrong and that the fire was nowhere near where she thought it was. But on the way to rescue and to perhaps find reassurance, she'd gotten trapped instead.

Danielle gasped as the wind abruptly shifted from off the ocean to the land and back again and threw sand in her face. The wildfire was making the breeze crazy. Erratically it changed direction.

Trying to catch some of the sea air, she took a deep breath and felt flame scorch her lungs and tears squeeze from her eyes. She smothered a cry of startled pain and cursed her stupidity again. She should never have gotten out of the car once she'd arrived at the site and seen that Grady and his people were all gone. After determining that the fire was actually close, really near enough to consume the work done so far, she should have turned around and gone back to the bungalow. But she'd wanted to see if the flames had jumped the road.

Grady had decided to do the beachfront property first. The land on the other side of the coastal highway would wait until last for completion. That meant if the fire stayed on the other side of the two-lane route, the site would be saved, and that blind hope had seen her get out of the car to try to look around the property on foot.

Rather than risking being cut off if the flames managed to leap over the cement, she'd thought it better to leave the car on the highway and complete the investigation on foot. That was her second mistake.

Coughing as haze swirled around her, she left the pile of lumber behind and tried again to get to where she'd parked the car. But she couldn't see it. She couldn't see anything. Not until the breeze whipping back and forth across the seashore suddenly ripped the smoke from the sky.

But the clearing didn't last. It came and went very quickly. Yet it lingered long enough for Danielle to lift her head and see her car. It was sitting where she'd left it. It was waiting on the road that could see her escape.

Eagerly she took a step forward, preparing to run, but before she could go any farther, the hill behind the vehicle abruptly exploded into flames.

She threw her arms up in front of her face in self-defense, a startled cry tearing from her throat. The fire seemed to have ignited out of thin air, but in reality a piece of floating ash had started it. And more ash erupted into the sky as the dry scrub lining the ground on the hill just beyond her car burst into a wall of crackling fury.

The intensity of the sudden heat and light drove her back. She stumbled backward even as the firestorm roared toward her. But in that instant, she knew she was going to die.

GABE SLAMMED ON the brakes. The highway was behind him. He was on a dirt path instead, rocking the hell out of his shocks, but he hadn't been given a choice. He'd been forced to leave the road. Not by the flame and ash that was littering the sky, but by a red pickup truck that had come roaring out of the smoke straight at him.

The only way to escape collision had been to dive onto one of the makeshift tracks Grady Thompson and his crew had made with their equipment.

Gabe again cursed the insanity of the fleeing driver. They both could have been killed by the trucker's panic, but the dirt track was proving better than the highway. It ran closer to the water and was farther away from the haze. That meant he could see more.

Jumping from the car and leaving it to stand deserted by the spreading beams of a growing home, Gabe struggled against the heat and the wind and ran toward the spot where he thought he'd seen Danielle's car. He had to get to her. He had to get her out of the site and back into the city. But first, he had to find her.

Charging up a sandy hill, he squinted against ash and whirling sand, ignored the blistering heat and the danger of flickering flame approaching ahead and stopped when the breeze abruptly cleared the air.

For a fleeting moment he could see everything. The car, the road, the hill, the land, but it was all forgotten when directly ahead, a fireball ignited and burst with a shower of sparks across the sky.

He ducked at the sight, swore when he realized he'd never reach the car in time if Danielle was inside, and yelled when he saw her off to his left. But she couldn't hear him. Not above the scream of the firestorm's howling gale or the roar of combusting grass, twigs and dying trees.

He started to run again. She was feet away, frozen in terror at the sight of impending death. He grabbed her, and she screamed, her paralysis broken.

"Gabe!"

But he didn't try to answer the fear in her eyes. He just grabbed her hand and pulled. "Come on!"

If she heard him, he couldn't tell, but she followed and he dragged her along as he swung back toward his car and the sea, back toward the hollow structures that it seemed, now, would never become homes.

As they went, he could hear and feel the blast and roar of the flames following behind them. The heat licked at their heels, scorched their skin and scalded their lips, but the wind off the Pacific as they drew nearer seemed to be growing. He ran into it, taking her with him, but the salty breeze abruptly surged up to hit them with a blast of air that seemed an attempt to try to push them back. But Gabe wasn't going to go. He held on to Danielle as they stumbled to a halt by his car.

She immediately grabbed the doorhandle, ready to jump in, but he stopped her.

"No, we'll never be able to drive back!" he called over the howling wind scorching the coast. "We'll have to head for the beach!"

She hesitated, unwilling to believe him when all she wanted to do was escape. He grasped her hand once more, and pulled her into a run again. They didn't stop until the water was lapping at their feet.

Gasping for breath and standing together, with the surf circling their ankles, they watched the wall of flame come toward them.

It was a terrifying sight, awing, but even as they retreated farther, stepping into knee-deep water, the raging inferno seemed to shudder, stop and unexpectedly—miraculously—burn out as suddenly as it'd begun.

In disbelief Gabe watched flames lick the ground in search of fresh fuel as the ocean breeze pushed the fire back on itself, but the dry brush was used up. The grass that had once grown beneath the questing tendrils of red and orange was already burned. No fodder existed for fresh fire and further destruction.

"It's stopping."

Danielle's whisper was incredulous, but Gabe realized it was true. The flames were either disappearing in a cloud of smoke or reappearing on new ground where ash landed and found new roots. But, regardless, the storm was moving away from them. It was moving back from the shore. He put an arm around her and held her close as the inferno began to race inland from the sea, away from them and the water, and leaving the construction site untouched.

On a sob, she turned into him, burying her face against his chest. He trembled, too, as he caught her to him. It was incredible, unbelievable that they'd been saved, that the emerging buildings hadn't been demolished, but wildfires had no direction, no intelligence. They went only where they could burn and where the wind blew them.

No one could explain why one house was left standing on a street where every other home was burned to the ground, or why one hillside lay consumed while those around it remained untouched. Logic and sound reasoning didn't apply when destruction was driven by a mindless force.

Taking her with him, Gabe turned to splash back to dry sand, and he caught her as shock dissolved into a flood of tears. Collapsing to their knees together on the beach, he put both arms around her in stunned relief. Death had come very near. Its smoky aftermath still lingered in the air.

Lifting her chin in his hand, he stared down into her soot-lined face and terrified eyes and was overwhelmed by a wave of emotion. She'd been spared. He'd gotten to her in time. He kissed her once. Hard. And then turned with her to watch the sky that stayed lit even when the sun disappeared behind the horizon.

"I WAS SO STUPID," Danielle muttered, stumbling up the steps of the bungalow with Gabe a countless number of minutes, perhaps hours, later. The air on the shore had finally cleared of smoke, but the stench of it was in her clothes and the danger it represented on her mind.

"You weren't stupid. You were concerned about the men and went to warn them," Gabe objected as he followed her. He was too relieved to be alive and to have her with him to place blame.

"I could have gotten us both killed!"

"You couldn't have known the fire would turn like that."

"I should have," she said, and stopped abruptly when she saw the shattered champagne bottle and wilted roses lying on the weathered wood where he'd obviously dropped them. "Oh, Gabe."

Taking his arm from around her shoulders, he let her go to watch her kneel by the gifts he'd brought in expectation of enjoying a perfect evening, then turned to open the patio doors to greet Hansel and Gretel. Scooping the kittens up, he stepped inside feeling weary, dirty and very hungry. "Forget the flowers. Bring the food."

With a regretful sigh, she did. She brought the discarded bags that still held the lingering smells of fish and fries along with the rapidly deteriorating roses. "It's cold."

"So? I'm starving." He brought the kittens up to eye level. "Quite a night, guys," he told them as the two mewed plaintively and wiggled to escape. Thank God the worst was over, for them and for him and Danielle. Using the car phone on the way back to her bungalow, he'd called in the fire at the site and advised the authorities of Danielle's deserted car by the road. In turn, he'd been assured the fire was headed out of Malibu. It was safe to be where they were.

"They'll never know," Danielle said, smiling as she watched him set Hansel and Gretel down.

"I'm glad," Gabe said, and grimaced. "Rescuing them would have been a bit more tricky than you. I don't think they would have willingly gone into the ocean."

Too tired to laugh, she sent him a wry smile and headed for the kitchen, and he followed. But rather than stopping with her by the sink, he moved on to the refrigerator.

"Got anything to drink?" he asked, opening the door.

"No champagne."

"A beer will do."

She wrinkled her nose. "How about wine?"

"I'm not fussy." And he wasn't. He grabbed the first bottle he saw—soda, not liquor—twisted the cap off, put it to his lips and drank. It tasted wonderful. Cold, wet and soothing. He came up for air with a sigh and found Danielle watching him with a lopsided grin.

"What would my mother say?" she asked.

"Who cares?" he returned, and held the bottle out to her. Her face was streaked with sand, dirt and tears. Her clothes were soiled and wrinkled and ruined. "You look like hell."

"Thank you," she said, accepting the bottle and his kiss.

"And you taste like ash."

She arched an eyebrow at him. "You know just how to make a woman feel beautiful and desirable."

He grinned but didn't say anything. He just watched as she drank much the same as he had, with a thirst that had no end. He felt as if he'd been baked dry. He opened the refrigerator again. "I don't suppose I look too great myself."

She finished the last swallow on a heartfelt sigh and turned to watch him open a new bottle. The white polo shirt he had on was smudged with smoke, ash and sand. His pants were much the same. "You look almost as good as you did the first time I saw you."

He nearly choked on the soda.

"I'm going upstairs to take a shower."

The declaration came before he could answer her smirking crack and wiped any words of retort right out of his mind. Swallowing a mouthful of Coke, he recovered in time to see her saunter to the steps, hips swaying enticingly in her stained jumpsuit. "Can I watch?"

She paused and leaned on the railing. "You can join me."

He didn't need a second invitation, but he did need another drink. Tipping his head back, he nearly drained the second bottle before following her to the staircase, but he didn't get far. He stopped a few steps up to retrieve her discarded jumpsuit.

A grin slowly stretched its way across his mouth, and he started walking again. When he found her bra at the top of the stairs, he heard the water turn on. When he found the silk panties, he put aside the soda bottle he'd been carrying along and took off his own shirt. By the time he reached the bathroom, steam was beginning to fill the air, and he was naked.

The frosted doors of the shower showed a silhouette. The detail was smothered by the panes, but the body inside was sleek and slender and covered by skin that appeared smooth to the touch. He reached for the door and stepped in beside her.

The wave of cool air that came inside with him told her that she was no longer alone. With her head under the spewing shower head, she didn't have to wait long for his touch. His fingers slid across her abdomen in a warm caress. "You're slow," she accused, turning to face him as he drew her close and smiling as water ran over her face and hair.

"I thought you liked slow."

She lifted her hands to circle his neck. "Show me."

He growled a response that was lost against her lips and under the power of the shower he turned them both into, but the water didn't distract or detract from the way she felt in his arms. It enticed, as did the way her skin slipped hotly across his.

Yet passion wasn't quick to explode. The fire and the fear had taken their toll. Interest was high but energy was low, and satisfaction was waiting. He was willing to take his time, and so was she.

Moving with him in and against the water, she let the spray wash over her as she got used to the strength of his hands and accustomed to the feel of his skin. His flesh was slick and surprisingly soft against hers, but the muscle beneath was hard and rippled as she followed streams of water down his hair-roughened chest.

Shy but sure, with slow strokes, teasing touches and gentle caresses, she explored with him as the moisture and steam rejuvenated bodies scorched by horrific heat and nearly wilted by a raging storm. She tipped her head back as he nuzzled her neck and reached for the shampoo.

The lotion was thick and sudsy. It consumed her hair before being transferred to his. She giggled as she used it to scrub his beard, and he enjoyed her humor and led her into the rinse cycle.

Using his fingers to comb through the thick, wet strands of black on her head, he tasted both her and the shampoo with a kiss.

Its scent, if not its flavor, was one he recognized. The fragrance always blended with the perfume she wore. He picked up the soap to see if its texture and smell were also part of the mystique that was hers, but she didn't let him keep the bar to himself.

Lathering up, too, she tried her own version of massage, but he proved to be the expert. Soon it was difficult to concentrate on what she wanted to do to him because of the explosions of sensation he was arousing in her.

Sliding off and against him, she quickly forgot the fire on the hill as he ignited a blaze of his own within her, but the water they were standing in swiftly reminded them that they weren't on solid ground.

Gabe slipped, she squealed and the bar of soap went flying from his hands.

Laughing and clinging to him, she let him dip her under the shower but shuddered when he nuzzled her neck with his wet beard.

"I think we need to move someplace drier," he murmured in her ear, but even after shutting off the taps and stepping out of the bath, it was a while before he got her to the door.

Towels had to be played with first. Hair had to be wrung out and combed, but he didn't mind the delay when the excuse gave him a chance to examine her from the top of her head to the soles of her feet.

"Which way?" he asked, backing her out into the hall. She was wearing a towel toga-style and he had one wrapped around his waist. Both were slipping.

Holding him off as her fingers linked with his, she nodded to a black-and-white streak that shot across the corridor. "Just follow Hansel. He sleeps with me every night."

"Until now," Gabe promised, and stooped to sweep her up into his arms and throw her over his shoulder.

She squealed at his unexpected charge and held on tight as he took off running with a battle cry for the bedroom door.

It was a strategic move that startled both felines from their resting places in the middle of the bed. The two kittens headed for cover at his wail and were racing down the stairs to safer territory by the time he stopped briefly at the foot of the bed to unleash his cargo.

Danielle wasn't sure who hit the sheets first. Her or him. But it ceased to matter when she found herself quickly in his arms again. "You're crazy!"

"There's that adjective again." He caught her lips with his. "Are we going to try perverted, too?"

She caught his head between her hands. His hair was still wet and he smelled of shampoo and soap, but she hardly noticed for the gleam in his eyes. "Maybe."

"Maybe? Sounds promising." He pulled her gently to him again, but this time his kiss was slow and draining and ended on a mutual sigh. "I see you have the sheets turned down. Expecting someone?"

She smiled and traced his mouth with her finger. "Only you."

"Good," he declared and caught her hand in his, but looking into her eyes, he suddenly remembered them dark

with fear and her face smudged with ash. He almost hadn't
seen her bed tonight. He'd almost lost the chance to ever
hold her again. "Very good," he told her and rolled with her
across the bed as a wave of emotion too intense for him to
stop and analyze washed over him. And she felt it, too. The
power of feelings too long denied, and she held on to him as
the towels were stripped away.

Slowly the heat built again and the fire that had been ignited in the shower flared to life once more. It flickered over
them both with taunting tongues of flame, urging them on
as hearts pounded, breath became ragged and spirits soared.

Gaining in strength, the inferno threatened to consume
them both, but while equal in power to the wildfire that had
rioted across the countryside, no destruction came in this
blaze's wake. Rather the flare of passion burned harm-
lessly but totally until consummation washed the heat away.

Collapsing together on a cry, the smoky wonder of aftermath lay with and surrounded them as, tangled together,
they remained unmoving until pulses slowed and they found
sleep in each other's arms.

"IS IT TIME TO GET UP YET?"

Danielle hung up the phone and turned to answer the
groggy rumble that had come from within the pillow beside
her. Gabe's face was buried in it. The back of his dark head
was all she could see of him, that and the hard length of his
body that was stretched out on his stomach beside hers.

Easing down, she kissed one muscled shoulder and traced
the firm lines of his back. "Not unless you want to. I just
called my father to tell him about the fire."

Gabe moved and managed to fasten one open eye on her.

"I told him we were nearly caught in the blaze up there,
and that you rescued me."

"Was he suitably impressed?" Gabe asked, unable to suppress the tremor that slid through him as her lips touched the base of his neck.

"Umm," she murmured, enjoying the taste of him once again. She'd enjoyed his flavor twice during the night. "I told him that I just had to reward you with the day off."

Gabe grinned. "And what about you?"

"He thought I should take the day off, too."

"What a wonderful idea."

Danielle squealed as he abruptly and expertly flipped to pin her beneath him. "I thought you'd like it."

"I believe I was the one who thought of it." He lowered his mouth to hers and stayed there until it was necessary to come up for air. "You know," he told her, leaning back on one elbow to look down at her, "we never got to eat last night."

She rolled her eyes.

"What? I'm hungry."

She sighed. "Here I am wantonly offering you my body, and all you can think of is food?"

He grinned. "I can have dessert first." He bent down to her once more, and she responded back, surrounding him with her embrace, enticing him with her smile and driving him mad as she squirmed beneath him.

But the lovemaking was playful this time, light and breezy. Yet it was no less satisfying. In fact, it left him wanting more, but his stomach was grumbling and Danielle laughed when she heard the roar. "Go eat. I'm going to go shower."

"Won't you be lonely?" he asked, watching her go and enjoying the view.

"You can always join me," she said, walking out the door, but as much as he wanted to, Gabe decided it was energy he needed at the moment.

Grabbing a discarded towel from the floor, he wrapped it around his waist and wandered toward the steps, past the litter of clothing still lying in the hall, hesitating only briefly by the bathroom door.

Hansel and Gretel met him on the stairs, nearly tripping him as they wound in and out of his legs and plagued him with woeful cries until he picked them both up. It was the wrong thing to do. For, once they had his attention, the two young cats weren't about to give it up.

Danielle found the three of them sitting on the dining room floor. Or, rather, Gabe was sitting and the kittens were running after any and every toy that was put into motion. "I thought you were hungry."

Gabe turned to look up at her. She was leaning against the wall leading to the kitchen, wrapped in a silk kimono that draped her body with revealing detail. His pulse skipped a beat. "I was. I am. But they were bored." He tossed another ball across the room and rose. "Where'd you leave the food?"

"On the sink," she told him, and stopped as soon as she entered the kitchen. "Oh-oh."

Right behind her, he followed her gaze. The bag containing the fish and fries was still where she'd left it. But it had a hole in it, and the fish was gone. "They ate the fish!"

Danielle wrinkled her nose and approached the tattered bag. "At least they left the fries."

He grimaced and reached for the refrigerator. "One egg or two?"

"Are you going to cook?" she asked in eager surprise.

"Unless you can promise me that you won't burn my eggs."

"You cook," she hastily agreed. "I'll set the table."

But they didn't eat there. Instead they ate and lounged on the couch together while watching the kittens play.

"They are good company," she told him when her stomach was full and she was lying against him. She couldn't remember feeling so relaxed or complete.

"So am I."

She laughed. "I'm glad, because we're going to have to spend the day together."

"What a shame."

"And maybe even the weekend."

"Whatever will we do?" he wondered aloud.

"I don't know. Got any ideas?"

He turned her into his arms. "One or two."

"Show me."

"Gladly," he said, abruptly standing and hoisting her up against his chest. "But I'd rather do it upstairs."

Laughter followed them up the steps and into the bedroom, and the joy they found in each other was explored again as outside the sun shone and sea gulls circled across the sky.

Chapter Fourteen

"Good morning, Kelly," Danielle greeted brightly on Monday morning. She'd risen early to beat the traffic and because Gabe had already been out of bed. He'd had to leave to go home and get a change of clothes—not that they'd worried much about what they wore over the weekend.

"You're early," Kelly responded from where she was reading the morning paper at her desk.

"So are you, and you look like you, too."

Kelly grinned. The frumpy clothes were gone, and the sleek secretary was back. The suit she had on wasn't anything out of the ordinary. It was just normal business wear, but it fit, rather than draped, her slender form. Kelly touched a hand to her carefully styled hair that swung loose around her shoulders. "It feels good to be me again."

Danielle looked up and down the hall. "You haven't had any more visits from Malcolm, have you?"

"No," Kelly said with a barely suppressed smile. "But he left the office early on Thursday, just like you and Gabe. Rumor is he went to get his teeth checked."

Danielle smothered a grin. "And Friday?"

"Stayed in his office all day." Kelly's mouth twitched, too. "He had a fat lip. But what about your Friday? Your father stopped by to say you were taking the day off because of the fires.''

Danielle sighed. ''We came close to losing the construction site out at Malibu.'' She grimaced. ''My car got scorched.''

''Oh, no.''

Danielle shook her head, remembering going with Gabe on Sunday to pick it up. That was the only time they'd left the bungalow. The rest of the weekend they'd spent inside. Alone. Together. ''I'll need a new paint job, but otherwise it seems okay.''

''Thank goodness. Gabe was with you?''

Danielle felt her heart jump just at the mention of his name, but it was hard to regret the feeling. More, she enjoyed it. ''To take cover, we dove into the ocean together.'' She nodded toward his empty desk. ''He should be in any minute.'' Her mouth curved into a smile. ''You can reintroduce yourself.''

But Gabe was late. He had some calls to make. The first one was to Sam. The second to the arson division of the fire department.

When he'd gone with Danielle to retrieve her car from the construction site, they'd met some inspectors. The team had been investigating the Malibu blaze that had seemingly come out of nowhere, and had been hoping to discover why it had started. And they'd been successful. The cause was arson. A person or persons unknown had purposely lit a match for no understandable reason and set the countryside on fire.

Gabe's mouth thinned as he maneuvered through traffic and headed for the parking ramp. He'd hoped by this morning some clue might have been found to lead the arson squad to whoever was responsible for torching the beachfront, but not enough evidence had been recovered to point definitively to any individual. All the inspectors had to go on were the discarded remains of a fire-blackened gas can—the type that could be bought in any store anywhere—and Gabe's description of the red pickup truck that had come flying out of the smoke.

Guiding his motorcycle into the parking structure and roaring up the levels to stop by Danielle's car, Gabe frowned. The truck might not have been involved with the fire. The driver could just have come along at the wrong time and floored his vehicle to get through the smoke and out of harm's way, but for some reason Gabe didn't think so.

Parking the bike, he stopped to walk around Danielle's car one more time. It wasn't bad. The paint was blistered on one side from the heat, but otherwise, the damage was minimal. A body shop would be able to redo the paint, and once that was accomplished, no one would ever know how close she'd come to the fire. Or to dying.

Cold fury exploded again as Gabe thought once more of the arson. She could have been killed because some maniac had had the urge to play with a box of matches, and that maniac might never get caught. Probably wouldn't.

Shrugging into the suit coat he'd thrown over the back of the bike and shoving aside his black thoughts, Gabe straightened his tie and headed for the elevator. Danielle was waiting, and the idea of seeing her again had his steps quickening. But a flash of red caught his eye.

Stopping, he turned and found himself staring at a red pickup truck. It wasn't the big variety farmers used. It was the sporting type owned by city dwellers and suburbanites, and it was identical to the truck that had come roaring out of the smoke and driven him off the road.

Frowning and knowing the odds were long that in a city the size of Los Angeles he could find the one red truck that had been in Malibu at the moment the fire started, Gabe nevertheless went to look the vehicle over.

The body was in good condition. The truck had seen some wear, but the owner obviously took care of it. The dents were few, the tires were in good shape and no rust could be seen.

Gabe circled to the open back. Nothing was stored there. It and the cab were empty of cargo, but the truck's bed did have some dirt in it. Dirt and ash.

Reaching for and picking up a fragile piece of blackened debris that immediately crumbled in his hand, Gabe frowned and wondered. With all the fires surrounding the city, how many trucks driving into L.A. were actually carrying ash?

Grabbing a pen from his pocket, he returned to the windshield to jot down the vehicle identification number and to the bumper to copy down the license plate. It was a long shot, but he was going to check.

Abruptly turning and heading for the stairs, in no time he was striding into the office and past Kelly's desk.

"Hey, beautiful."

She stopped typing and looked over her computer monitor at him. "Watch it. I know this guy who has a fabulous right hook."

Gabe stopped at his desk and shot her a grin before grabbing the phone. "I want to know about the guy with the sore jaw."

"I already told the boss about him. He had to go see the dentist." Kelly smirked. "He left right after you hit him and never came back that day." Her grin grew. "He hid in his office all day Friday, too." She pointed to Danielle's door. "By the way, she's waiting to see you."

His finger hesitated as he dialed his number, and his gaze strayed toward Danielle's office. He wanted to see her, too.

Hopefully behind locked doors, but the phone started to ring in his ear and was quickly answered. Gabe was forced to give the person he called his attention. "Sam? Gabe. Do me a favor. I need to know who owns a red pickup truck." He rattled off the make, model and license and VIN numbers. "I'll call you in an hour for any result."

Hanging up, he swung toward the office door and Danielle, but Kelly stopped him.

"Gabe, I'm sorry, but I couldn't help but overhear. You want to know about a red pickup?"

He nodded. "It's parked down in the garage."

"And the license plate is HERE I AM?"

Gabe reluctantly turned away from Danielle's door to walk to Kelly's desk. "You know who owns it?"

"Who doesn't?" she said with a shrug. "It's Malcolm Reed's."

Shock hit Gabe hard.

"He made a big deal in the office about buying it and an even bigger deal when he got the license plates." She grimaced. "He claimed it was his personal advertisement for any interested women."

But Gabe barely heard her. His mind was whirling with possibilities and disbelief. Competitive, yes. Obnoxious, yes. But a murderer? An arsonist? But the fire had started in Malibu. Precisely on the land being developed by Grady Thompson.

Gabe didn't want to believe it. Business could be deadly in the figurative sense of the word. Executives were often cutthroat in their dealings, merciless in their attempts to get ahead, but few would stoop to literally trying to burn out an opponent.

"Gabe, are you all right?" Kelly asked, rising as his jaw clenched and Danielle appeared in the office door, drawn by his voice.

"Is Malcolm in?" Gabe demanded, answering her question with one of his own, but he was already turning toward the hall.

"I think so, but..."

He didn't hear her, and he didn't see Danielle. The only person he cared about at the moment was Malcolm Reed.

Watching Gabe go, Danielle felt a tendril of fear. She'd seen him angry before. She recognized the posture, the look, the walk. "No, not again." She ran after him, but she was too late. Ahead of her, he brushed past Malcolm's fluttering secretary and threw open the office door.

"Malcolm, I want to talk to you."

Behind his desk, Malcolm stood up. In front of it, Lucas Fitzsimmons rose as well, his face darkening with a ferocious scowl. "I'm busy, Tyler," Malcolm snapped, and then smiled with malevolent delight as he gestured to Danielle's father. "In case you hadn't noticed."

"I noticed," Gabe answered, but didn't stop moving. He strode up to the desk and past Lucas Fitzsimmons. "Where were you Thursday afternoon?"

"Where...?" Malcolm glared at him and then looked to his boss. "This is ridiculous!"

"Answer the question!" Gabe demanded, and abruptly leaned across the desk to catch Malcolm by the shirtfront. "You own a red pickup truck that has ash in the back bed. How is that possible?"

Malcolm's mouth worked.

"You work in L.A., you live in a condo in L.A. How would ash get in the back of your truck?"

Malcolm jerked free with a growl. "I also camp out. Ask anyone. Who knows how long the ash has been in there?" he demanded, but his face was red and his eyes were nervous.

"Thursday," Gabe prompted, moving around the desk.

Malcolm hastily retreated around the other end as Gabe advanced. "The dentist. I was at the dentist. I can prove it."

"When? And for how long?"

"I don't remember," Malcolm blustered, trying to keep some distance between himself and Gabe.

"The hell you don't," Gabe growled. "You left the office right after I decked you, and that was before lunch. Why didn't you come back?"

"What's it to you?" Malcolm returned, and suddenly stopped to hold his ground. He stiffened as Gabe came to a halt in front of him. "You have no right to question me."

"I have every right when I have reason to believe you're the one who set the fire that almost killed Danielle." To his right Lucas Fitzsimmons gasped, and to his left Danielle did, too, but Gabe barely heard their intake of breath. He was watching Malcolm lick his lips and glance uneasily toward the door. "Tell me where you were Thursday, Malcolm, and tell me you have witnesses, because the fire marshal is going to want to talk to each and every one of them after he comes out to take prints of the tires on your truck."

Malcolm bolted, but he wasn't fast enough.

Gabe grabbed and whirled him around, but Malcolm swung first. His fist connected with Gabe's stomach, and not six feet away, Danielle heard the air rush out of his lungs. But the blow didn't seem to affect him. Gabe swung a right jab, and Malcolm's head snapped back from the contact.

A chair turned over as Malcolm staggered into it, and Lucas Fitzsimmons scrambled to get out of the way.

Gabe followed Malcolm after the chair, already cocking his fist for another hit, but Malcolm wasn't standing still. And he wasn't unable to fight back. He was part of the health scene. He went to the spa. He worked out. He lifted weights, and when he blocked Gabe's punch to land one of his own, lights flashed in Gabe's head.

Danielle smothered a scream as Malcolm landed two solid blows in a row and Gabe tripped backward, but her father held her back when she took an alarmed step forward. He held her beside him at the door and watched Gabe recover enough to charge.

Careening straight into Malcolm's midriff, he carried them both back onto the desk. The lamp perched on the end flew off, as did papers, books, a coffee cup and a pile of folders. But he didn't hear the crash of glass breaking. He only felt his knuckles collide again and again into Malcolm's abdomen.

Caught at a disadvantage, pinned against the mahogany he usually wrote on, Malcolm flailed wildly for something to grab as more papers fluttered to the floor. But the only thing he could get hold of was Gabe. Latching on to Gabe's shirtfront, he pushed back and tried to stand up straight. It was a strategic error. Sitting up on the desk's edge gave Gabe a clear shot.

An uppercut to the jaw lifted Malcolm up and over the desk and sent him sprawling on the floor behind it.

Gabe immediately started to follow, but Danielle rushed up to grab him from behind. "Stop! Gabe, stop it! That's enough. You've beaten him. You've won."

Swaying on his feet, his breath ragged, his ears ringing and with the taste of blood in his mouth, Gabe obeyed more because she threw her arms around him than because he had won or didn't want to go on. "Call the police."

"They're already on their way," Lucas Fitzsimmons announced from the door where he'd ordered another employee outside Malcolm's office to make the call. But he didn't stay there. He walked across the room to stare coldly down at his fallen vice president. "Malcolm, you're fired."

With his hair mussed, his tie askew and his face beaten and bruised, Malcolm fell back on the carpet with a groan from where he was trying to sit up, but Danielle was more concerned with Gabe than the man he'd defeated. There was blood on his jaw, and his cheekbone was already swelling from where another blow had landed.

"Come on," she urged, trying to get him to the door, but Gabe wouldn't go. He refused to leave until the police came, he gave a statement and Malcolm was taken away.

"YOU STUBBORN IDIOT," Danielle told him an hour later as he lay on the couch in Malcolm's trashed office. Around them chairs lay tossed on their sides, papers were scattered across the floor and a broken glass lay shattered on the rug. "We'll never get the swelling down now."

Gabe wasn't inclined to argue. He simply held the cold cloth with ice cubes in it against his throbbing face. His teeth hurt, his lip stung and his ribs ached, but all in all, he felt pretty good. "I bet I look better than Malcolm."

"What a ridiculous thing to say!" she admonished, pacing back and forth beside the couch, twisting her fingers together in agitation and remembering how each blow Gabe had taken had seemed to bruise her, too. But when she abruptly stopped to look down at him, she had to laugh. He looked pathetic with one eye half swollen shut, a bloody lip and a rapidly coloring cheekbone. She strongly suspected he was going to end up with a black eye. "I bet he does, too."

Gabe held out a hand to her.

She took it and fell to her knees beside him. "My hero," she said, lifting a hand to brush the hair back from his face. "I suppose it would have been too simple to just call the police and let them question Malcolm?"

"This was personal," Gabe objected, taking the ice from his eye to press it to his split lip instead. "Besides, I liked punching him."

She shook her head. "I just can't believe he did it, that he'd want to hurt me so badly that he actually tried to burn the Malibu project down."

"He probably didn't give it much thought. After you got him in the boardroom and I nailed him in the file room, he just wanted to strike out. The Malibu project was the only place that was both vulnerable and accessible, and through it, he figured that he could hurt us."

"But we have insurance."

Gabe moved his shoulders. "I told you that he wasn't thinking. Just reacting."

"And so were you." She took the ice from him to dab at his cheekbone. His eye looked awful. And painful. She bit her lip. "Mr. Tyler, I've definitely seen you look better."

"You won't be able to tell in the dark."

He tried to smile but winced at the effort, and she leaned over to kiss his forehead. "I think you better take it easy for a while. In fact, I think you should go home and get some rest."

"I did have a very busy weekend."

Her gaze narrowed on him and the twinkle in his eye. "Don't be funny."

"I'm being perfectly serious. You wore me out."

Her smile was anything but regretful. "Did I?"

"Absolutely." He lifted his head to meet her lips. The kiss was brief and it stung, but it was sweet agony. He leaned back against the couch again with a satisfied sigh. "Are you going to come and nurse me back to health if I go home to bed?"

"Only if you give me your address."

He tried to grin again and regretted it instantly. "That was mean."

"You deserved it. You were being cocky." She caught a motion at the door out of the corner of her eye and turned to see Kelly enter.

"I'm sorry to interrupt."

Danielle shook her head and stood. "You're not interrupting anything except sympathy for our hero."

"More, more," Gabe groaned with alarming realism.

Kelly reacted with immediate concern. "Is he . . . ?"

"Fine," Danielle assured her dryly, and pinned Gabe with a warning gaze. "Did you need me?"

"Your father does," Kelly answered. "He wants to see you in his office right away."

Danielle sighed and shook her head at Gabe. "Duty calls. You be a good boy for Kelly, and maybe she'll get you some more ice."

Gabe groaned again and closed his eyes, opening them almost immediately to see Danielle slip out the door. He sighed and pulled the ice bag away to finger his swollen lip. "Being a hero is more painful than I thought it'd be."

"That's because you're not living in Hollywood. The punches you and he were throwing were real," Kelly said sympathetically. "Can I get you anything?"

"A new face, maybe?"

She grinned. "I don't think so. The one you've got is so handsome."

He choked on his own laughter as bruised ribs raged in protest. "Don't make me laugh. Please don't make me laugh."

WHEN DANIELLE RETURNED a short while later, Gabe was sitting on the couch rather than lying on it, and he was watching Kelly try to pick up the myriad papers and folders that had been knocked on the floor during the fight. His head and body still ached, but lying still wasn't the answer. He was only going to get stiff. He looked up as Danielle entered, and even with only one good eye, he could tell something had happened. Something good. She was literally glowing.

Her eyes were shining, her face was animated and the energy she was feeling was just busting to get out, but as usual, she suppressed it to come to sit beside him with demure control. "How do you feel?"

"I'll feel a lot better when you tell me whatever it is you're trying not to say."

She laughed immediately and reached out to brush his cheek, conscious of Kelly watching but uncaring of any reaction her secretary might have at a display of intimacy. "I have good news."

Gabe sat back as she jumped off the couch to pace the floor and explain.

"With Malcolm gone, there's going to be a lot of work to do."

Kelly looked from her boss to the files scattered across the floor. "Oh, boy."

Danielle laughed at Kelly's forlorn expression. "Yes, some late nights, but you get a raise."

Kelly's eyes lit up, and she watched Danielle turn to look at Gabe.

"And you get a raise."

"And you?" he asked. "What do you get?"

"BLI!"

If he'd been flattened with another punch, Gabe couldn't have been more stunned. Whatever he'd been expecting her to say, it hadn't been that. Not BLI.

When he'd gone after Malcolm, he hadn't stopped to consider the possibility that someone would have to take

Malcolm's place on the BLI bid. His only thought had been for justice, but if he'd won the battle, it appeared Malcolm was going to even the score. For, as Gabe watched Danielle and Kelly chatter in excitement, he realized what he'd feared most had happened.

"I'll need your help, of course," Danielle said, spinning back to him, oblivious to his expression or his reaction to her news. "It's a big file and my father wants to work with me on getting ready, but isn't it great? Aren't you proud of me?"

"Of course," he murmured, putting the ice bag aside and trying to figure out how he could tell her that he couldn't do it. He couldn't work with her. Not on this. Morally, ethically, it wasn't right. He knew more about BLI already than she could possibly learn in the time before the first meeting that was set for the end of the week.

"Kelly, you'll have to find the file, and I'll have to read everything on it. I've got to be prepared by Friday."

"I'm on my way," Kelly said, dropping the papers in her hand and heading for the door.

Danielle quickly moved to sit by Gabe, but excitement was blinding her to everything but the moment. "This is what I've been working for. I can't believe it! We'll have to start right away...."

He reached out to take her hand. "Danielle, I can't."

Suddenly focusing on him, on his face, on the scraped knuckles of the fingers holding hers, she sobered. "Oh, Gabe, I'm sorry." She reached out to comb his hair back from his forehead. "Of course you can't. Not now. Why don't you go home and get some rest?"

"Danielle..." he began, but she interrupted him.

"Or you can go to my place. I'll give you the key, and I can meet you there later." She jumped up. "I don't want you to worry about me or BLI or anything else. Just get some sleep."

He let her pull him to his feet.

"Are you sure you can drive your bike? Do you want to take my car? Or I can have someone drive you?"

"I'll be fine," he assured her, but her concern was killing him. She was worried about him when he was about to crucify her across the negotiation table. He pulled her into his arms. Baptism by fire. She was going to get initiated into the business world at its most ruthless time—when too much was at stake for him to back off and be a nice guy. But how could he tell her? Brace her?

"Are you sure?" she asked, looking up at him and recognizing pain in his eyes but mistaking its cause. "Maybe I should go with you. You don't look very well."

"No," he assured her, cupping her cheek in his hand. "No, you have work to do. We'll talk tonight."

"Tonight," she agreed, and kissed his hand.

But it was hard for him to let her go. And it was nearly impossible to comprehend how what he'd hoped to avoid at all costs had come to pass. He was going to face Danielle as the enemy. His worst nightmare had begun.

Following her toward the door, he stopped to look back at Malcolm's demolished office and felt defeat drag at his shoulders. How was he ever going to be able to make her understand?

Chapter Fifteen

"What happened to you?"

Gabe glanced up from his desk as he sat in the chair behind it. It felt good to be back. Back where he belonged, in his own office. But part of him was already missing Danielle, missing their working together and knowing she was no longer just a few steps or a call away.

Sam came closer, cocking his head as he examined his friend's battered face. "Did Danielle Fitzsimmons find out who you really are and sic her father on you?"

Gabe's gaze narrowed ominously on his business partner. "Get me the BLI file."

"Yes, sir." But Sam's retreat was brief. He was back in no time with a stack of folders, and if he remained curious about how Gabe's face had been demolished, he knew enough to keep his questions to himself. Experience had taught him to recognize when Gabe wanted to talk and when he didn't, and he didn't now. Not about Danielle Fitzsimmons, at any rate. Instead he wanted answers on BLI, and Sam gave them to him as he moved with Gabe to the corner table to pore over figures, calculations and possibilities.

And Gabe welcomed the distraction as well as his friend's silence. He wanted to bury himself in the work because he couldn't talk about Danielle or about the situation he'd boxed himself into. Not yet. Not until he tried to sort it all out for himself first.

He was already dizzy from trying to discover just the right way to tell her the truth. Only he was no closer to finding an easy way to make her understand and accept who he was and how he'd come to be with her than when he'd first realized he was going to have the problem of explaining. That was why he needed a break. For a little while, he had to fill his mind with something else besides her and defining a method to help her see who he was, why he had gotten involved with her and that BLI was one account she would never win.

Yet, ignored, the problem of confession didn't go away. It remained with him through the hours as he worked beside Sam, lingering steadfastly in the back of his mind, and so constantly served to remind him that if he was going to keep Danielle with him—and he desperately wanted to—he had to find a way to soften the revelation of his true identity and to make her see that a harmless ruse had turned into something more complex and complicated than he ever could have anticipated or imagined.

When he began the drive to her bungalow that night, he was still struggling to find the right words to tell her what he had to say. Unfortunately, the hours of reprieve and work hadn't helped. Clearing his mind even for a little while hadn't enabled him to come up with a simple solution. He continued to search for an easy way to give her what she wanted and needed to know about himself and his work, but pulling to a stop beside the house, the hard way was the only one that appeared to exist.

Straight out and direct. It was how he usually dealt with any crisis that developed, and it remained for him to use the same approach with her.

The trouble was that Danielle was more than a crisis, more than a problem he wanted to fix, and as soon as she opened the patio doors to let him inside, he swept her into his arms to try to convince her how much more.

"Feeling better, I see," she teased when he finally lifted his lips from hers but kept her trapped against him. She reached up to touch his cut lip. "Does it hurt?"

"Not if you kiss it and make it better."

She squealed as he abruptly swung her off the floor and against his chest and headed with her toward the stairs, but she didn't protest. She simply circled her arms around his neck and fixed him with an inquiring look. "Just how much better do you want me to make it?"

He grinned as he hit the first step. "As good as it can be."

If his lovemaking was tinged with a desperation he didn't want to give a name to, she didn't seem to notice. She merely accepted his embrace with an openness that allowed her to give more than take, and it left him frustrated when they collapsed to lie together.

Sensing his distress but not certain of its source, she snuggled against him to offer what comfort she could and to enjoy the heat of his skin next to hers. She suspected it was the mystery of who he was that was worrying him, but any questions she had about his past, his present or his future didn't seem to matter when they were together. She closed her eyes and listened to the rhythm of his heartbeat beneath her ear. The feeling of safety and completeness he gave her was overwhelming, and she sighed and let the wave of love she felt for the man he was, even with the unknown still lying between them, wash over her. The answers would come when he was ready to share them with her.

She opened her eyes again to prop her chin on his shoulder. "You look tired. Didn't you get any sleep today?"

"I thought I'd sleep tonight."

She saw his teeth flash in the darkness of his beard and the shadows of the room, and she smiled, too. "What makes you think I'll let you get any?"

"Promises. Threats." He rolled to pin her beneath him. "Do we have to go to work in the morning?"

She circled his neck and linked her fingers behind his head. "Of course. We have a very important investment to work on."

The joy in him died, and he rolled away to drop back down beside her.

"It's really exciting, Gabe, this BLI takeover. And scary, too," she told him, laughing at what she thought was mock disappointment, and leaned on her elbow as she lay against him. "I've only been able to get through part of the file, but it's complicated. More so than anything else I've ever done."

He didn't answer, but she knew he was listening. He always did when she was worried or excited or happy. It meant he cared for her, too, even if his feelings weren't as strong as hers were.

"I've done straight purchases, buyouts, but never a takeover," she went on. "There's so much to think about and consider. I'm really going to need your help."

"Danielle," he interrupted, lifting a hand to frame her face with his hand. "We have to talk about this."

"I know," she interrupted. "And this isn't exactly the time, but I'm so nervous. My father really wants this to go through." She covered Gabe's fingers with her own. "He's counting on me, and I'm counting on you."

Gabe moved against her, an objection on his lips. She couldn't count on him. Not this time. He couldn't support her on this project. "Dani..."

"We can do this together. I know it."

The hope was there. The need to do well, to prove herself worthy. She was putting it all in his hands, but he couldn't accept it.

"I need you, Gabe."

The terrified plea was his undoing and he cursed himself for his weakness. He couldn't refuse her. He couldn't abandon her. Not when she was asking for his help.

Damning himself, his vanity, his cocky belief that he could wheel and deal and always win, he pushed her back on the bed with a growl. "We'll do it. Somehow."

But it was hard. For him. For her as they worked together day and night on the file. She tried to grasp all the subtleties, the possibilities, but BLI wasn't a simple transaction. A takeover was never easy, and this was one of the worst he'd seen. It involved more than one company, thousands of employees, endless complications, and she didn't know half of them. Malcolm hadn't done very good research, and she was only working with half the facts.

Gabe bit his tongue a million times as she worked and struggled. He could tell her much, but it wasn't information he could or should share. She would learn nothing if it was given to her, but she did well on her own. She even found some leads for more data without his assistance, but he knew it wasn't enough. She'd never win. And even though she was going to try, he couldn't let her.

WHEN THURSDAY AFTERNOON finally came, Gabe went into Danielle's office at quitting time to find her behind her desk shuffling papers into piles and folders. Outside Kelly was locking up before going home. Danielle would be expecting to leave, too. With him.

"Ready?" she asked as he came in. She was taking the papers from her desk and putting them into her already bulging briefcase and looking beautiful as always, even if nerves and excitement were already beginning to show. He had to stuff his hands in his pockets to keep himself from crossing the room to touch her, to offer reassurance or to try to talk her out of even attempting to make a bid at the meeting scheduled for the next morning.

"No."

She looked up in surprise.

"I'm not coming home with you tonight. And I won't be there with you in the morning."

"Gabe..."

"Final lesson, Dani. You've got to do this by yourself."

Stunned by the unexpected declaration, all too clearly she recognized his direct gaze, his tense stance and the grim set to his jaw. He meant what he said. It would do no good to argue with him, but that didn't stop her from wanting to or prevent her stomach from sinking in trepidation. Something else was wrong. Swallowing, she looked away briefly to snap her case shut. "This isn't about BLI, is it?"

"No. It's about me and who I am."

Slowly, struggling to remain calm in the face of the unknown, she moved around the desk to walk toward him. "And who you are won't let you stay with me any longer?"

"Not here. Not as your associate."

She stopped before him, her expression calm, but she was trembling. She linked her fingers together in front of her so that he wouldn't see. "You're quitting?"

"Effective today."

Nodding, she searched his face. The bruises were fading. His lip was already healed. But she was more concerned with his eyes. She couldn't read what was behind them and, at this moment more than at any other since she'd known him, she wished she could. "New job?"

"An old one I have to finish."

"I see," she murmured, but she didn't. She didn't understand his sudden withdrawal and there was more she wanted to know, but she didn't think he'd tell her. He was still holding her at arm's length. She accepted the pain and clenched her fingers more tightly together to stop from reaching out to touch him, to pull him back when he was trying to pull away. "Does your leaving here mean I won't see you again at all?"

"Only if you don't want to," he told her, lifting a hand to brush her cheek with tender fingers and wishing he could take away the doubt and the fear she was trying to hide behind the cool composure she was draping herself in again.

Her hand covered his. "Do you think I'd willingly let a man who makes such a fantastic omelet go?"

A smile broke through the darkness of his beard, and he brought her to him to wrap his arms around her. "You like my cooking, do you?"

She nodded and held on tight, keeping her head down to stop him from seeing the tears of relief in her eyes. He wasn't leaving her permanently. "I'd starve without it." Blinking back the moisture, she tipped her head back to look up at him. "You can't come over tonight? We don't have to work...."

But he shook his head and took his arms from around her. "We both have work to do."

She nodded and stepped back, determined to let him have the room he seemed to need, but the fear of finality lingered near. He wasn't saying goodbye, yet she couldn't shake the feeling of finality behind his announced departure, and her worry shone in her eyes. Gabe had to push his hands in his pockets to stop himself from crushing her to him.

"We'll talk tomorrow."

"Tomorrow," she agreed, and smiled acceptance, her composure secure behind a practiced face, but she hated the pretense more than she ever had before. She wanted to show her feelings, to tell him she didn't want him to go—not now or ever—but uncertain of how he'd react if she tried to share them with him, she remained silent.

He turned away and, crossing her arms in front of her, she watched him go, but it was the hardest thing she'd ever had to do. And out of sight wasn't out of mind.

She thought and worried and wondered about him through the night. His sudden resignation was frightening, his withdrawal terrifying, but she kept reminding herself as she tried in vain to again review the BLI papers that if he had left her office, he hadn't left her. He'd promised they'd talk again. She held on to that and to the confidence he'd promoted in her as the sun dawned and the time for the showdown came.

Without Gabe, she brought Kelly to the negotiation with her, and as a team, they stepped off the elevator and moved toward the lion's den where not only the BLI board members were waiting in a conference room set on the tenth floor of the waning company's building but her competition, as well.

Action Enterprises was a firm experienced at negotiation, takeover and investment, and its strategy was always simple. Win. But Danielle wasn't prepared to let them taste victory this time. She was going to prove Action Enterprises could be beaten.

Stepping into the conference room, carrying her briefcase and her poise with equal calm, she glanced around the room where men and women were gathered and was quickly greeted by one of the BLI officers, who introduced himself and the other BLI board members before presenting her to someone outside BLI's employ.

"Sam Cody of Action Enterprises," the BLI president, Thomas Waterton, said and motioned for a tall, blond man to come forward. "He's part of your competition."

Danielle nodded and extended her hand to receive a firm shake and to meet intelligent brown eyes. Sam Cody was younger than she'd expected. She'd thought Action Enterprises would have a more weathered leader. "Part?" she asked, cocking an inquisitive eyebrow at Sam.

"Half."

She recognized the voice before she saw the man, and her smile was instantaneous. But when she turned to greet him, the face she confronted wasn't the one she knew. Gabe's beard was gone. Shaved off. It left his jaw clean, but his eyes were the same. Deep and dark and unreadable. Glancing quickly from him to Sam Cody, she shook her head. "I don't understand."

"I'm Sam's partner," he told her, reaching out to take her hand. "Francis Gabriel Tyler III, but my friends call me Gabe."

The information and the betrayal hit with incredible force. He wasn't at the meeting for or because of her. He'd come for himself and his own company. Struggling to comprehend and to conquer disbelief that rapidly changed to anger and hurt, she managed to smile as she shook hands with him as the stranger he was. "Francis Tyler of Boston?"

"My father," Gabe acknowledged, his eyes not leaving her face.

"I've heard of him. And of you," she said, turning to Sam.

Gabe remembered the nightclub, too, and the man who had ruined the evening and driven Danielle from his arms. At least for a night. "But not of me."

His fingers were warm, but she felt cold. She pulled her hand from his. "I thought we met once, but I was wrong," she declared, and had the satisfaction of seeing him blink. At least she'd learned one lesson from him. Never let emotions get in the way of business. She turned from him to the BLI president. "Shall we begin?"

"By all means," Tom Waterton agreed, and motioned to the table, but he frowned at Gabe. "Did you have an accident? I see your face is bruised. A door, perhaps?"

"Actually," Gabe said with a winning if sheepish grin, "it was a competitor."

Laughter erupted but wasn't long lasting. It died as everyone moved to take their places at the table, and Danielle found herself sitting across from Gabe. It was a position she would have preferred to avoid. The wood separating them seemed to emphasize the split between them. Emotion clogged her throat, but control cleared it when Waterton turned to her to begin the proceedings with her presentation.

It was one of the most difficult things Danielle had ever had to do, but feelings were put aside as she began the fight for BLI. And it was a long battle.

The coffeepots set out along the table were emptied and filled again. The neat pads of paper provided to write on were filled with notes, and the tabletop disappeared beneath a layer of white as handouts and financial statements were exchanged. But an hour into the struggle, the first tendrils of defeat began winding their way around Danielle's heart.

Statistics and data she wasn't familiar with were being brought into the open. She was forced to guess at answers she should have known before the questions were asked, and she silently damned Malcolm for her shortcomings.

He hadn't looked at the whole picture, and she should have been prepared for his lack of diligence in his research. She'd stumbled on some facts he hadn't put in his report. She should have realized there would be more....

"I think I've heard enough," Waterton finally announced two hours later, dragging a hand through his already ruffled hair. "I'm ready to make a decision."

Two of his officers immediately leaned closer to whisper in his ear, but he waved them away and looked to Danielle.

"Your offer is fair. More than fair, but I know Lucas Fitzsimmons," Waterton told her. "He's a good man, and he'll see that I walk away with a settlement that will insure I personally don't go through bankruptcy. But there's more than me to consider here. There's my employees, the ones who have worked for BLI for years. I can't forget them, and I can't ignore the fact that Lucas won't take them into account when he starts breaking BLI up, as I'm sure he will."

Danielle opened her mouth to object, to deny the truth of his statement, but she couldn't. Her father would think of nothing but profit, not of those who would end up on the unemployment line if BLI became his. "We'll do all we can for your people," she offered in compromise.

"I believe you would," Waterton assured her, but turned to Gabe. "Yet, I have your guarantee that no one will lose a paycheck because of me."

"There will be reorganization, changes," Gabe assured him soberly. "But we'll put it in writing that no one you employ will be out of work because of the takeover."

"That said," Waterton declared, standing and extending his hand to Gabe, "I accept Action Enterprises' bid."

Gabe stood and accepted the handshake with a firm grip. "We'll do right by your people."

But Danielle barely heard him. She only saw him. The consummate professional. The cool business executive. The stranger she'd fallen in love with.

GABE SAW DANIELLE slip out the door, but he wasn't about to let her go. Not before they'd talked. Not before he'd had a chance to explain.

Leaving Sam to take charge of the final details, Gabe hurried after and caught her in the hall. "Dani."

She swung to face him, and Kelly quickly jumped out of the way. "Don't call me that!"

She was trembling. He could see it. He could also see the tears she was trying to hide. Motioning to a room that appeared empty, he stepped toward the door. "Let's talk."

She stiffened, and for a moment he was afraid she'd refuse. But finally the rigid control snapped and she preceded him inside, but the door was barely closed before she turned on him.

"Why?"

"Why what?"

"Don't play coy, Gabe, it doesn't become you," she snapped, and slammed her briefcase down on a table. "Why did you do it? Why the deception?"

He shrugged helplessly. "You asked for my help, and I gave it."

"I asked you if you needed a job," she accused, and crossed her arms to confront him. "You lied to me."

"I never lied."

"You didn't tell the truth!"

"You didn't ask for it. You assumed, and I gave you what you wanted. An associate."

She gestured wildly. "Why bother? You have your own company to run. You didn't have to pretend to be some penniless drifter."

"I never pretended to be anything that you didn't perceive me to be." He shook his head when she would have spoken again. "When I first met you, you intrigued me. So did the situation. It was a challenge."

Her mouth dropped open in surprise. "A challenge? Is that what I was? A poor little rich girl who needed your help, and you, the big, bored, powerful business executive had to see if you could give it?" She glared at him. "Was it fun? Did it amuse you to play me for a fool?"

He gritted his teeth. "It wasn't like that."

"Then how was it?"

Gabe shoved his hands into his pockets and moved away from her to look out the window at the city. "When I took the job you offered, I admit, it was just a game."

"A game?" she repeated in stunned disbelief.

His jaw worked. "I said *was*."

"*Was*," she repeated, unwilling and unable to see reason. "What was, was my faith in you. I trusted you, and you set me up! You used me to get what you wanted. Information on BLI."

"You're wrong," he denied.

"I don't think so." She swung for the door, and he lurched across the room to grab her.

"Please listen to me!"

She tried to twist free, but he held on tight.

"I tried to warn you," Gabe said, and dragged a hand through his hair. "I told you to be sure to check out your competition."

"I did!"

"You checked on Action Enterprises," he protested with an adamant wave of his hand. "The company, not the people you'd be going head-to-head with."

She lifted a cool eyebrow, pain blinding her to any explanation. "Is this a free lesson?"

"You already paid for it. In there." He jerked his thumb toward the wall separating them from the conference room.

She stared at him. "You could have saved me the humiliation."

"Why? You wanted to play in the big leagues. That's what you told me when I first met you," he said. 'You wanted to earn respect. I let you. I stopped being your crutch."

"You were more than that."

The blow came low and hard, and he took it that way. "I tried to tell you the truth."

"You should have tried harder." She shook her head, refusing to let the tears burning her eyes to fall, and paced away from him. "I was so blind, so naive. I can't really blame you for the deception, can I? I let you use me because I wanted to believe in something. In you." She swung back to stare at him. "The bungalow in Malibu that was conveniently available. Yours?"

He nodded. "Yes."

"And the property in the canyons, too?"

"Investments."

"So you're my landlord?"

His jaw worked. "You can stay as long as you want."

"Thank you, but I think I'd rather not." She reached for her briefcase but stopped. Keeping her eyes off him, she gave in to the pain and shook her head. "Why did you have to play make-believe? At the start, why couldn't you just have been who you really are?"

"An enemy? It's how your father sees me," Gabe retorted, wanting to go to her but knowing she wouldn't accept the gesture. Her back was stiff with rejection. "It's how you would have seen me, too. If you'd known who I really was, you never would have invited me into your house that first night. You would never have wanted to see me again."

"How can you be so sure?" she demanded. "How can you know that? I can't, and I won't because you never gave me the choice."

"No," he agreed. "No, I didn't. But I'm giving you one now. I'm asking you to give us a second chance."

It was tempting. With him looking into her eyes, it was tempting, but she shook her head. "How can I? You tricked me. You deceived me. I thought I could trust you. I thought..." She bit her lip. "I thought I was in love with you."

The declaration stunned him. It wasn't what he'd expected, but it was what he'd hoped. He realized that as she swung away, but he recovered too late to stop her. He moved, but with her cool reserve and inhibitions thrown aside, she did what he'd thought to teach her to do all along. She slammed the door shut with a decisive bang.

Bitterly his lips twisted. It was ironic that she'd accomplished the last act and concluded the final lesson by closing it in his face.

DANIELLE STARED at the phone as it started to ring. She didn't want to answer it. She didn't want to talk to anyone. At least, not until the answering machine clicked on, and she realized it was a friend.

Hastily she grabbed the receiver. "Linda?"

"Danielle? How are you?"

"I've been better."

"Oh-oh, I know that tone. Bad day?"

Tears burned Danielle's eyes. "You couldn't possibly imagine."

"Well, maybe I have something to cheer you up."

"Anything."

"You remember you told me about that tall, dark, handsome guy that was so mysterious? You said his name was Gabe Tyler, or at least you thought it was."

"Yes," Danielle agreed, trying to find some reason, to understand what he'd done, to reconcile who he was with who she'd thought he was, and to determine if any of it mattered. "I remember."

"Could he be Francis Gabe Tyler?"

Danielle frowned. How could Linda possibly know who Gabe really was when she'd only just found out herself? "Why do you ask?"

"Francis Gabriel Tyler lives here in Boston, or rather Francis Gabriel Tyler II does. He has a son who lives in California, and according to this picture I just ran across when researching an article for the paper, he's tall and dark."

Danielle could almost hear her friend frown.

"But he doesn't have a beard. At least, he didn't then."

"He doesn't now, either. He shaved it off," Danielle said, sitting up straighter. "Tell me more."

"This is the guy?"

"Yes, and I want more." She needed it desperately. She had to understand.

"The article's old, almost ten years old, but it says that the son started out working with his father."

"But?"

"There was a big split. That's why the article got written."

Danielle heard paper rustle from the other end of the line.

"This was written in the business section and ran because anything Francis Tyler does is big news. He's a mover and shaker out here."

"Just like his son," Danielle murmured.

"Excuse me?"

Danielle abruptly stood up. "Linda, how'd you like some company for the weekend?"

"What? You're flying out?" came the enthusiastic response.

"Yes, I am." Danielle's eyes glinted. Gabe had told her to know the competition, which meant before he'd even met her, he'd known all about her. She was going to do the same. By looking into the past, maybe she'd find some answers for the future. "Can you put me and my two kids up?"

"Kids?"

"Hansel and Gretel. They're kittens."

Linda howled with laughter. "That old tomcat of ours is sure going to be surprised to see you!"

Chapter Sixteen

Gabe adjusted the cuff of his sleeve beneath his tuxedo and prepared for his moment on stage, but he was barely aware of the other men standing around him, waiting their turn in the spotlight and for the chance to be "purchased" for the night. He was thinking of Danielle.

He'd left her alone for as long as he could. One whole day. Then he'd gone to see her when she'd stubbornly refused to answer the phone, but when he'd arrived at the bungalow, it'd been empty. Not even Hansel and Gretel had been in sight to greet him.

That she'd run away didn't seem likely. Danielle didn't run away from opposition, but she was at least avoiding him. He'd tried all week to leave messages for her with a frosty-toned Kelly, but none of his calls had been returned. His only option had been to go over to the office to confront her, but he didn't relish a public scene or a right hook from Danielle's obviously dedicated secretary.

His hero status had definitely been diminished in Kelly's eyes. But betrayal was a good way to alienate people—whether he'd actually done anything wrong or not.

Gritting his teeth against the helpless anger, he refused to give in to the guilt. He *hadn't* done anything wrong. Not intentionally. He'd met Danielle by accident, gotten to know her out of curiosity and fallen in love with her despite himself.

One thing he'd never imagined himself as was married. Not with a business to run that took up most of his time, but on meeting Danielle, he'd discovered he could make time for other things. He would again once he got her alone and convinced her to hear him out.

Whether she wanted to or not, she was going to hear him out, from beginning to end. He was going to start with when he met her and make her listen and understand why and how things had gotten so out of control. Emotions weren't something he was well equipped to deal with. He should have known that and refused her invitation on its being offered, but she'd intrigued him. She still did. And he wasn't going to give her up willingly.

The woman in charge behind stage motioned him forward, and Gabe stepped toward the curtain and what he saw as his final chance to reach Danielle. He already knew her mother was in the audience, and Helen Fitzsimmons would have insisted her daughter be present, as well. Unless Danielle had learned to slam the door on her parents, too.

Abruptly the curtain opened, and Gabe strode out. He didn't listen to the announcer or the numbers being called out. He ignored them all and zeroed in on Helen Fitzsimmons and those seated at the table around her, but he was disappointed to find Danielle wasn't among them.

Scanning the audience, he tried to see through the bright lights illuminating the stage as he trod diligently up and down the runway, but he couldn't find her. Cursing himself and fate, he stopped and heard a bid for three thousand dollars.

Surprised, amused and a bit embarrassed, he tried to see the caller but was stopped when the bidding erupted into a furious crescendo of counteroffers.

Unable to help but smile as women screamed and laughed at one another, he shoved his hands in his pockets, struck an arrogant if appealing pose, and tried to enjoy the moment, but it was a hollow experience without the woman who'd allowed him to be there. And it would be an empty night when the evening ended and she remained somewhere other than at his side.

"Five thousand," someone called.

"Five thousand one hundred," came another voice, and the announcer all but purred.

"Ladies, ladies, we can do better for this glorious male."

Gabe turned to look in surprise at the woman behind the microphone, who was old enough to be his mother, but she wasn't embarrassed by her declaration even if he was, and the audience loved his consternation. The bidding rose.

"Seven thousand!"

"Eight!"

A hushed murmur fell as two finalists seemed prepared to duke it out, but without warning a third voice called out of the shadows.

"Twenty thousand dollars."

Gasps erupted, but Gabe grinned, humiliation forgotten. His rescue had just arrived.

"Do I hear any other bids?" the announcer all but shouted, beside herself with ecstasy at the upward turn of events.

No one answered.

"Then he's going, going, gone to the highest bidder!"

Gabe followed the applause off the ramp and into the audience even though he was supposed to go backstage to be claimed. He wasn't willing to wait for Danielle to come to him. He was going to find her, and he didn't have to go far. She was standing under the exit light. "Danielle . . ."

But when he reached for her, she backed away.

He clenched his teeth but refused to give up. He followed her into the hall where he tried to touch her again, but she held up her finger in warning.

"Hands off."

Frustrated but determined, Gabe let his arms drop to his sides even as she crossed hers in front of her and leveled him with a deep green glare.

"I kept my word. I rescued you."

"I wasn't concerned with rescue. I was only concerned with finding you."

Her breath caught as she looked at him, but she managed not to let him know it.

He watched her chin rise and prepared for battle. "Dani, we have to talk. I went to see you last weekend—"

"But I wasn't there," she concluded. "I was in Boston."

His eyebrows shot up in surprise until he remembered her college roommate. "Linda."

"Partly," Danielle agreed. "Mostly I went to meet your father and to find out about you."

His jaw dropped, and he tried to speak but suddenly found himself with nothing to say.

"Someone told me that I should know my competition. When I realized my competition had already done their research on me, I did mine on them."

Impressed and amused, Gabe smothered a smile and shook his head as he studied her. The expression was haughty as was the posture, but she was wearing the black dress. The same one she'd had on when he'd first seen her on a deserted street. His hopes rose. "Find out anything interesting?"

"I know why you had a fight with your father and left to form your own company."

"My father's like yours. He prefers to invest and sell fast, but I didn't want to do that. I wanted to invest and build."

"Like BLI."

"Like BLI," he agreed.

Danielle paced away, walking around him. "Okay, I can understand that. I can even applaud your motivations, but you must have known we were after BLI at the same time you were."

"I did."

"But you still came to work for me."

"Not because of BLI," he denied firmly, and captured her gaze with his. "Because of you."

"But you researched me before you met me."

He shrugged, watching her as she circled him again. "No. I didn't know anything about you until the day after I met you."

"Did that influence your decision to come work for me?"

"No, because there wasn't anything to read." He cocked his head at her. "You keep a very low profile."

"Like you."

He shrugged again. "I'm not like my father."

"Neither am I." She stopped before him to search his eyes. "You hurt me."

"I didn't mean to." He gestured futilely. "It started so simply. It was like a dare."

"And you couldn't resist?"

He shook his head. "Sam says no."

"He's a good friend?"

"Like Linda."

Her eyes dropped from his, but he wasn't willing to let her go.

"When I accepted your job, I didn't think I'd be working with you long. After what happened with my father." Gabe watched her gaze lift to him again, and he moved his shoulders helplessly in explanation. "I don't know. I just thought I'd come give you a shove in the right direction, quit and then disappear. But once I touched you, I was lost. And when I realized I'd fallen in love with you, there was no way I could just walk away and not look back.''

Her eyes warmed under his, and he quickly looked away.

"I was wrong not to tell you the truth. When I started, I didn't think I'd ever have to. Then, when I wanted to, Malcolm got in the way." Gabe's mouth thinned. "He was setting you up. I knew it, but I couldn't make you see it."

"I finally did," she said softly. "But too late. The fire came and the fight, and I trapped you when you were trying to break free."

His gaze locked with hers. "I tried to tell you that night."

"I know." She opened her arms, and in an instant he was in them, hugging her, twirling her and holding her close.

"I missed you."

She pulled back to gaze up into his eyes. "I missed you, too." She let him go to lift a hand to trace his clean-shaven jaw. "You look different without a beard."

"I'll grow it back," he assured her. "Just for you."

She wrinkled her nose as she held his face in her hands and shook her head. "No, you'll do as you are, but I do have one small problem."

He grinned. "What's that?"

"I'm broke. I just cleaned out my bank account for you, and I don't have a job."

His eyebrows arched in amazement. "You quit?"

"I had to. I couldn't get along with the boss."

"Different philosophies?"

She nodded.

"No problem. We'll find you a new job where the pay is better."

"Kelly needs a job, too."

Gabe grinned. "I like loyalty."

"So do I, and I want to reward it. Any suggestions?"

"I think I know a place that has a vacancy for an up-and-coming executive, and she'll need a good secretary."

"When do we start?"

"Right now." Pressing his mouth to hers again, he held her close but soon became conscious of too many watching eyes as people wandered in and out of the hall. Reluctantly he released her to gesture to the dress she had on. "You wear this for me?"

She did a simple turn in front of him. "I remembered you liked it."

"I liked what was inside it."

She grabbed his tuxedo. "I like what's inside this, too."

He grinned. "Then let's go get naked."

"Okay, the bike's outside."

"No, I brought my car."

She grinned. "But I brought my bike."

He followed her out into the parking lot, a frown lining his forehead. "You have a motorcycle?"

"I told you that I wanted one." And she led him to a smaller version of his with lots of chrome and plenty of sass and held out the keys. "But you better drive. I'm not too good on the turns yet."

"Yeah? Well, I'm a good teacher."

He swung onto the bike, and she hastily followed, put her arms around him and leaned close to whisper in his ear. "I can't wait for the lessons to begin."

The sound of the starting engine drowned out his laughter, but the happy sound followed them as they roared off into the night together.

UNLOCK THE DOOR TO GREAT ROMANCE
AT BRIDE'S BAY RESORT

Join Harlequin's new across-the-lines series, set
in an exclusive hotel on an island off the coast of
South Carolina.

Seven of your favorite authors will bring you exciting stories
about fascinating heroes and heroines discovering love at
Bride's Bay Resort.

Look for these fabulous stories coming to a store near you
beginning in January 1996.

Harlequin American Romance #613 in January
Matchmaking Baby by Cathy Gillen Thacker

Harlequin Presents #1794 in February
Indiscretions by Robyn Donald

Harlequin Intrigue #362 in March
Love and Lies by Dawn Stewardson

Harlequin Romance #3404 in April
Make Believe Engagement by Day Leclaire

Harlequin Temptation #588 in May
Stranger in the Night by Roseanne Williams

Harlequin Superromance #695 in June
Married to a Stranger by Connie Bennett

Harlequin Historicals #324 in July
Dulcie's Gift by Ruth Langan

Visit Bride's Bay Resort each month wherever
Harlequin books are sold.

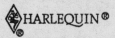

BBAYG

Bestselling authors

ELAINE COFFMAN
RUTH LANGAN
and
MARY McBRIDE

Together in one fabulous collection!

OUTLAW
Brides

Available in June wherever Harlequin
books are sold.

HARLEQUIN ®

OUTB

HARLEQUIN®

AMERICAN ◆ ROMANCE®

®

He's at home in denim; she's bathed in diamonds...
Her tastes run to peanut butter; his to pâté...
They're bound to be together

for
Richer,
for
Poorer

We're delighted to bring you more of the kinds of stories
you love in FOR RICHER, FOR POORER—where lovers
are drawn by passion...but separated by price!

Next month, look for:

#640 BLUE-JEANED PRINCE

By Vivian Leiber

Don't miss any of the
FOR RICHER, FOR POORER
books—only from American Romance!

Look us up on-line at: http://www.romance.net

FRFP-2

HARLEQUIN®

A M E R I C A N ◆ R O M A N C E®

A NEW STAR COMES OUT TO SHINE....

American Romance continues to search
the heavens for the best new talent...
the best new stories.

Join us next month when a new star
appears in the American Romance
constellation:

Liz Ireland
#639 HEAVEN-SENT HUSBAND
July 1996

Ellen couldn't believe her former husband
placed a personal ad for her—her *dead*
former husband! Well, at least that
explained the strange men showering
her with calls and gifts, including
Simon Miller. Ellen was attracted to
Simon—but how was a girl supposed to
start a relationship when her dead
husband kept lurking over her shoulder?

RISING STAR

Be sure to Catch a "Rising Star"!

American Romance is about to ask that most important question:

Where were you when the lights went out?

When a torrid heat wave sparks a five-state blackout on the Fourth of July, three women get caught in unusual places with three men whose sexiness alone could light up a room! What these women do in the dark, they sure wouldn't do with the lights on!

Don't miss any of the excitement in:

#637 NINE MONTHS LATER...
By Mary Anne Wilson
July 1996

#641 DO YOU TAKE THIS MAN...
By Linda Randall Wisdom
August 1996

#645 DEAR LONELY IN L.A....
By Jacqueline Diamond
September 1996

Don't be in the dark—read
WHERE WERE YOU WHEN THE LIGHTS WENT OUT?—
only from American Romance!

HARLEQUIN®

Don't miss these Harlequin favorites by some of our most
distinguished authors!
And now, you can receive a discount by ordering two or more titles!

HT #25645	THREE GROOMS AND A WIFE by JoAnn Ross	$3.25 U.S./$3.75 CAN.	☐
HT #25648	JESSIE'S LAWMAN by Kristine Rolofson	$3.25 U.S./$3.75 CAN.	☐
HP #11725	THE WRONG KIND OF WIFE by Roberta Leigh	$3.25 U.S./$3.75 CAN.	☐
HP #11755	TIGER EYES by Robyn Donald	$3.25 U.S./$3.75 CAN.	☐
HR #03362	THE BABY BUSINESS by Rebecca Winters	$2.99 U.S./$3.50 CAN.	☐
HR #03375	THE BABY CAPER by Emma Goldrick	$2.99 U.S./$3.50 CAN.	☐
HS #70638	THE SECRET YEARS by Margot Dalton	$3.75 U.S./$4.25 CAN.	☐
HS #70655	PEACEKEEPER by Marisa Carroll	$3.75 U.S./$4.25 CAN.	☐
HI #22280	MIDNIGHT RIDER by Laura Pender	$2.99 U.S./$3.50 CAN.	☐
HI #22235	BEAUTY VS THE BEAST by M.J. Rogers	$3.50 U.S./$3.99 CAN.	☐
HAR #16531	TEDDY BEAR HEIR by Elda Minger	$3.50 U.S./$3.99 CAN.	☐
HAR #16596	COUNTERFEIT HUSBAND by Linda Randall Wisdom	$3.50 U.S./$3.99 CAN.	☐
HH #28795	PIECES OF SKY by Marianne Willman	$3.99 U.S./$4.50 CAN.	☐
HH #28855	SWEET SURRENDER by Julie Tetel	$4.50 U.S./$4.99 CAN.	☐

(limited quantities available on certain titles)

	AMOUNT	$
DEDUCT:	**10% DISCOUNT FOR 2+ BOOKS**	$
ADD:	**POSTAGE & HANDLING**	$
	($1.00 for one book, 50¢ for each additional)	
	APPLICABLE TAXES**	$_____
	TOTAL PAYABLE	$_____
	(check or money order—please do not send cash)	

To order, complete this form and send it, along with a check or money order for the
total above, payable to Harlequin Books, to: **In the U.S.:** 3010 Walden Avenue,
P.O. Box 9047, Buffalo, NY 14269-9047; **In Canada:** P.O. Box 613, Fort Erie, Ontario,
L2A 5X3.

Name: _____

Address: _____ City: _____

State/Prov.: _____ Zip/Postal Code: _____

**New York residents remit applicable sales taxes.
  Canadian residents remit applicable GST and provincial taxes.

HBACK-AJ3